Carol Stream Public Library
616 Hiawatha Drive
Carol Stream, Illinois   60188

Screenscam

Screenscam

Michael Bowen

Poisoned Pen Press

Poisoned Pen Press
6962 E. First Ave. Ste 103
Scottsdale, AZ 85251
www.poisonedpenpress.com
info@poisonedpenpress.com

Printed in the United States of America

For MJB, with deep affection

Chapter 1

On the twentieth day of June in the thirty-first year of his life, Rep Pennyworth thought for a fleeting instant that he saw his mother walking up Commerce Street in downtown Indianapolis. This had happened previously, but not for several years and never before on a day when he'd done something illegal, unethical, and dumb.

To be fair, he couldn't remember anything he'd ever done before that was all three. So technically, you couldn't rule out coincidence.

The rare intrusions of unpleasantness into Rep's well-ordered adult life tended to involve his partners. This one was no exception. It had begun eight days earlier, around the polished teak desk of Chip Arundel and before the hooded gray eyes of Steve Finneman. Arundel was introducing Rep to a client named Charlotte Buchanan.

When Arundel described his legal specialty, which was often, he said he was "in M and A," articulating the initials as if he'd just gargled with testosterone. After saying this to Buchanan, Arundel had told her that Rep was "one of the firm's top intellectual property lawyers," the way you might introduce a Miss America hopeful as one of the prettiest girls in Wichita. Rep wondered wistfully whether his niche would sound more impressive if it were identified with initials. *"I'm in IP?" Maybe not,* Rep thought.

"Ms. Buchanan is here because she wrote a book," Finneman rumbled at that point to Rep.

The prudent response to an obvious lie by your firm's senior partner is a polite smile, and Rep produced one. Writing a book wouldn't have gotten John Updike or Saul Bellow into Arundel's office, unless they were undertaking a merger or acquisition along the way. Ms. Buchanan was there, as Rep knew before he laid eyes on her, because her father was the chief executive officer of Tavistock, Ltd., an Indiana company that was often in a merging or acquiring mood.

"I'm afraid I don't know the book," Rep said. "What's the title?"

"*And Done to Others' Harm*," Buchanan said, handing him a slim, hardbound volume with a muddy brown dust jacket. "It's a mystery/romance. And here's *In Contemplation of Death*, the movie that ripped it off."

Rep's belly dropped as he accepted the videocassette. His fond hope that Arundel and Finneman had summoned him here for some kind of harmless busywork, like marking up a form contract from a vanity publisher, evaporated. The Problem was apparently plagiarism.

"Saint Philomena Press," Rep commented placidly as he checked the copyright page. "Excellent house. First-rate reputation." He had always been intrigued at the notion of naming a publishing company after the fourth-century martyr who'd become the patron saint of dentists because her heroic faith had survived the brutal extraction of all her teeth by Diocletian's torturers.

"You know mysteries?" Buchanan asked.

"Not terribly well. But my wife, Melissa, reads about a mystery a week and shares her views very freely. She's completing her Ph.D. at Reed College, where she works in the library and teaches a mini-term course in creative writing every year."

"I know, I've thought of taking it. Maybe she's one of the one thousand eight hundred thirteen people who read *And Done to Others' Harm*."

Rep refrained from chuckling at this comment, whose risibility he correctly surmised to be unintended. He instead gave alert and ostentatious attention to Buchanan, waiting for her to continue.

You assume that children of the rich will be good looking—that those favored by fortune will be favored also by nature, and if they aren't fortune will help nature along. Charlotte Buchanan belied this assumption. In her mid- to late twenties, she was neither homely nor fat, but she was big. Five-eight, anyway, with broad shoulders and not much in the way of taper below them. Her expensively coiffed, fine-spun hair and her lustrous, pearl gray jacket and skirt outfit seemed to emphasize bulk instead of suggesting elegance. Her face might have been pretty, but it seemed set in a permanently sour expression combining cynical resignation with self-pity.

"*Others' Harm* was published in nineteen ninety-seven," Buchanan said. "*In Contemplation of Death* was released in early ninety-nine."

"Who was your agent?" Rep asked.

"Julia Deltrediche, New York."

Rep had pulled a Mont Blanc from his upper right-hand vest pocket and was now industriously scribbling notes on a legal pad.

"Did she shop it to any paperback houses?"

"She claimed she did, but said there wasn't any interest because the hardcover sales were so low."

"Did she send it to any studios or film agents?"

"She told me she had a subcontractor named Bernie Mixler pushing it hard on the coast," Buchanan said. "Not hard enough, apparently."

"Reviews?"

"None, except the *Press* in Valley Grove, where Tavistock has a chemical plant. Not even *P-W* or *Kirkus*. That's how much effort Saint Philomena put into it."

"That does seem pretty toothless," Rep said without thinking. He noted with anxious relief that neither Buchanan nor Arundel seemed to have caught his allusion. "National distribution?"

"Yes. Bookstores from coast to coast returned copies." Rep made a brisk, final notation on his pad and paused, leaning back in the mate's chair where Arundel had parked him. Arundel drummed the eraser-end of a pencil on the Moroccan leather frame of his desk blotter. Finneman kept a look of placid expectation on his weathered, age-mottled face. Rep gathered that he still had the floor.

"There are two issues right up top," he said in standard-issue deskside manner.

"Access and similarity, I know," Buchanan said impatiently. "We have to show that Point West Productions had access to my story, and that the movie is similar enough to the book to create a legitimate inference of direct borrowing."

She pulled a sheaf of photocopied pages from the thin attaché case balanced on her knees and flourished them briefly. Rep saw with dismay that they looked like caselaw headnotes from the *West Digest*. This meant that Buchanan had already consulted another lawyer who didn't like her case, which was an unpleasant thought; or that she was the type of client who did amateur legal research herself, which was a thought too horrible to contemplate.

"Right," Rep continued gamely. "Publication and general distribution probably give us a leg up on access, at least if the movie followed a normal development and production schedule. So let's talk about similarity."

Buchanan foraged once more in the attaché case, emerging this time with a black vinyl three-ring binder. Plastic-tabbed dividers studded the open side. Flicking the binder open to the third or fourth section, she tendered it to Rep, who laid it on the corner of Arundel's desk and with seeping despair began to read:

Similarities and Identicalities Between
And Done to Others' Harm and
In Contemplation of Death

Others' Harm	*Death*
The climactic confrontation between the protagonist and the villain takes place on the upper floor of a large country house, at night.	The climactic confrontation takes place on the top floor of an office building, at night.
A suspect is identified by DNA analysis of ejaculate on a woman's slip.	A suspect is identified by DNA analysis of ejaculate on a woman's pantyhose.
A key clue is the misspelling of "you're" as "your" in a ransom note.	A key clue is the misspelling of "you're" as "your" in a threatening letter.
The protagonist graduated from a Seven Sisters school with a Ph.D. in philology.	The protagonist graduated from an Ivy League school with a Ph.D. in semiotics.
The protagonist smokes cigarettes—an unusual habit among contemporary women under 30 with advanced degrees.	The protagonist smokes cigarettes—ditto.
The plot revolves around threatened exposure of fraud in a government-subsidized research program at a university on the West Coast.	The plot revolves around threatened exposure of fraud in a government-sponsored research program at a California foundation.
The protagonist develops a romantic relationship with one of the suspects.	The protagonist develops a romantic relationship with one of the suspects.

Rep stifled a sigh as he finished scanning the first page. Whoever wrote *The Thomas Crown Affair* had a better claim against Buchanan so far than Buchanan did against the producer of *In Contemplation of Death*. He turned the page and began running down parallel columns of what Buchanan took to be similar dialogue, mostly from the "if you know what's good for you you'll listen to reason" school of action-adventure writing.

Halfway down this second page, his pulse quickened. His heart began to race. He kept his face carefully frozen, but felt fire on the backs of his ears. He read:

Page 118: "Percy came out of the bathroom, still sodden and holding a wicked-looking quirt. 'Honestly, Luv,' he said incredulously, 'a riding crop?'

Minute 53: Harry tumbles out of bed and his hand lands on something under the headboard. He comes up holding a riding crop. Harry: "The English vice?"

'Why not?' Ariane said languidly as she reached for the Silk Cut pack on the bedside table. 'All my vices are English.'"

Glencora: "Well that'd figure, wouldn't it, luv?"

"Well," Rep managed, almost stammering, "this is quite helpful, but it's going to take some detailed study. Can you leave these materials with me?"

"That's why I brought them," Buchanan snapped. "I have to go to Tavistock's Fond du Lac, Wisconsin facility for the rest of this week, but I'll stop by Monday for an interim report. Happy hunting and take no prisoners."

"We never do," Finneman assured her complacently. "The best defense is a good offense."

The line was lame and shopworn, but it was better than anything Rep could've come up with just then.

Chapter 2

"Identifying a perp from DNA in a semen stain on a woman's clothes," Melissa Seton Pennyworth murmured dubiously at seven-thirty that evening as she studied Buchanan's comparison columns. "Now where could anyone making a movie in the late nineties possibly have gotten that idea except by reading Charlotte Buchanan's story?"

"Even if they hadn't seen Jane Fonda and Donald Sutherland in *Klute*," Rep sighed, "which came out before Ms. Buchanan was born and used the same basic gimmick long before anyone heard of Bill Clinton's concupiscence or Monica Lewinski's blue dress. When did you start saying things like 'perp,' by the way?"

"It's a word you're required to use when you talk about mysteries even though you'd never use it in real life," Melissa said. "Like 'sleuth.'"

"Scratch the DNA point," Rep concluded, returning to their main topic. "Do you think maybe she's onto something with cigarettes? *In Contemplation of Death* isn't a noir film from the forties, after all, and smoking is a lot rarer than it used to be."

"Rarer in the real world, yes," Melissa agreed. "But in the surreal universe of mystery fiction it's almost a cliché for lazy writers because having someone smoke is an easy characterization shortcut. I tell my students to come up with some other self-destructive behavior for their existentially reckless characters, like driving without a seatbelt or drinking whole milk."

"How about 'your' and 'you're'?"

"Afraid not," Melissa said. "Lawrence Sanders used the same clue as a throwaway in one of his *McNally* stories, and some writer I can't remember used it even before that in a mystery called *Fielder's Choice* or something."

"In other words, Ms. Buchanan is dangerously close to having nothing but plot similarity to rely on," Rep said. "And if I remember your lecture notes correctly there are only seven basic mystery plots anyway."

"Right," Melissa said. "Pride, Anger, Avarice, Lust, Envy, Sloth, and Gluttony. Every mystery plot is a variation on one of the deadly sins."

"Well, six of them, maybe. I mean, gluttony?"

"Don't forget *Silence of the Lambs*."

"So with a lot more than seven mysteries being published every year," Rep said, "a certain amount of plot overlap is mathematically inevitable."

"It looks like Charlotte Buchanan doesn't have much of a case," Melissa said.

"Thank God," Rep said fervently. Loosening his white-polka-dots-on-green bow tie, he shivered with relief. "Snappy little nine-page memo and I'm out of this thing. What a nightmare this could have been."

"Wait a minute," Melissa said. "Don't you want your client to have a case?"

"Good heavens no. If she had a case I might have to pursue it."

"Isn't that what you do?"

"Not if I can help it. Pursuing a claim involves consorting with litigators—who have a nasty habit of blaming the intellectual property lawyer involved whenever they lose a copyright case. Plus there's at least a fifty-fifty chance we'll draw a judge who'll make some kind of Joan Collins-type crack in one of his opinions."

"Ouch," Melissa said, wincing. "What was the gist of the ruling? *Pay the lady, Random House, you knew she couldn't write when you signed the contract.* Nasty. But maybe you'll just settle for lots of money."

"Most non-corporate plaintiffs have to be dragged kicking and screaming into a sensible settlement, and two weeks after they cash the check they start telling everyone they got shafted because their lawyer was a spineless crook who couldn't negotiate his way out of a wet paper bag. And winning wouldn't be much better, even if the judge behaves himself."

"I don't understand," Melissa said, as puzzlement replaced the mischievous glint that ordinarily brightened her green-flecked brown eyes.

"If we win," Rep said, "which we won't, but for the sake of argument let's pretend. Start over. If we win, Charlotte Buchanan will take the lawyers out to dinner and be very happy for about three days. Then she'll notice that after you take off the legal fees and court costs and expert witness fees, she doesn't really have all that much money to show for everything she's been through. And she'll realize that now she's burned her bridges, and no producer or publisher in the country is ever going to look at a manuscript with her name on it again, because she's officially bad news and they don't want to be sued for plagiarism. All of which isn't the worst part. The worst part is that, somewhere in her fevered imagination, it's all going to somehow be my fault."

"So are you just going to blow her claim off without analyzing it in detail?"

"Of course not," Rep said. "That would be unprofessional. I'm going to analyze her claim in excruciating and expensive detail. Or, rather, we are. Then I'm going to blow it off."

"Got it," Melissa said. "Okay, you start with the book. I'll start with the movie."

⊛ ⊛ ⊛

Even as he settled into the leather chair in the den and dutifully opened *And Done to Others' Harm*, Rep's right hand twitched toward his computer. The mere prospect sent a little electric thrill running through him. Boot up, then a couple of mouse clicks and few keystrokes and he'd be immersed once again in a breath-catching, pulse-quickening fantasy that Charlotte Buchanan's prose had no chance of matching.

More than fantasy, really. Communion with a number-less throng of fellow spirits sharing in the anonymous vastness of cyberspace Rep's rich sexual interest in grown men being spanked by women. (He always called it an "inter-est" when he thought about it, not "fetish" or "kink" or "specialty." "Interest" was a neutral, non-judgmental term that you could use just as well if the subject were, say, bass fishing or rugby.) It wasn't the sexual excitement per se so much as the knowledge that he wasn't alone; that all these others shared his perverse taste and thrilled to its explora-tion, just as he did; that he wasn't a freak.

Tonight, though, after enjoying a few delicious seconds of tantalizing temptation, Rep sternly willed the twitches to stop. He left the computer off. He turned his undivided attention to the book.

If Arundel, say, had known about Rep's exotic taste, he would have considered it about the only facet of Rep's personality that was remotely interesting. In one sense, he would have been right.

Rep had figured out sometime in third or fourth grade that he was never going to be tall or athletic. He'd topped out at five-seven. The only high school letter he'd earned still nestled in its clear plastic wrapper somewhere in his aunt's basement because it was in chess and the real jocks at Chesterton Public High School would have beaten him silly if he'd been insane enough to wear it. He had defaulted into the life of the mind, aiming for college as an irksome pit-stop on the way to law school.

The most useful course he'd taken in law school, by far, had been Antitrust. Not because he would ever practice in the area, but because he found his personal philosophy crystallized by a single casual comment from the professor who taught it. Monopolists didn't bother to maximize profits the way economists said they should, the tweedy gentleman had explained, because stratospheric earnings weren't what they really wanted: "The real reward of monopoly power isn't excess profits but a quiet life."

Epiphany! That, Rep decided, then and there on that sleepy Friday afternoon in Ann Arbor, Michigan, was also the true reward of analytic intelligence. From that moment he'd lived by this creed. Let the Arundels of the world bill over two thousand hours a year for half-a-million bucks; Rep would bill sixteen hundred for less than half that much, giving him eight more hours a week to enjoy Melissa's playful eyes and gentle banter. Arundel and his peers could revel in macho fields like corporate transactions and litigation; Rep would find a serene niche in trademark and copyright, thank you very much. In law school Rep had been happy to let future trial lawyers take Introduction to Advocacy; Rep's fancy had fallen to an imaginary class that would have been called Introduction to Adequacy.

The only exception to this rule was Rep's pursuit of his special sexual interest, and that was what was intriguing about it. In no other sphere did he even consider putting security, comfort, and reassuring routine at risk for the sake of excitement. True enough, the risk introduced into his life by occasional visits to naughty magazine shops and postings to spanking sites on the net seemed pathetically minuscule. The remarkable thing, though, was that he allowed it any entrée at all into an existence that was otherwise sedulously arranged to avoid the unpleasant and the extraordinary.

And so, tucking his glasses into the breast pocket of his shirt, brushing his wispy, light brown hair off his forehead, he plunged dutifully into *And Done to Others' Harm*.

Like many people who "don't read" mysteries, Rep actually read three or four a year. He paged through them on airplanes or during vacations, expecting them to divert him without making much of an impression, and then not consciously remembering much about them after he'd flicked past the final page.

Either despite or because of this background, Rep found himself entirely unprepared for the sheer awfulness of *And Done to Others' Harm*. After the epigraph, which disclosed that the title came from T. S. Eliot, things went downhill in a hurry. The writing itself (leaving aside the solecisms you'd expect from someone who thinks "identicality" is a word) wasn't bad, just pedestrian. There were even lines, like the one about "all my vices are English," that were pretty good— good enough that Rep couldn't help wondering where Buchanan had found them. And the plot and characters seemed serviceable, although rather familiar and without a spark of anything special about them.

The real problem was deeper. As Rep slogged through page after dreary page, he gradually realized what it was. Instead of either passion or any notion that reading and writing this stuff might be fun, Buchanan wrote with a kind of desperate, labored urgency, a driving, compulsive need to get words on paper. As Oscar Wilde (Rep thought) had said about Henry James (he was pretty sure), Buchanan created prose as if writing were a painful duty—as if she'd desperately needed to write not this story but a story, any story. Reading *And Done to Others' Harm* was like watching a defensive tackle dance ballet: it's never pretty, and even when he brings off a *pas de deux* he looks grotesque rather than elegant.

Somewhere around page one-forty-three Rep looked up gratefully as he heard Melissa glide into the room. Her eyes didn't seem completely glazed over, so the movie couldn't be as bad as the book. When she spoke, in fact, Rep warily sensed an undercurrent of excitement in her voice.

"Does the main character in Charlotte Buchanan's story have a down-to-earth, very practical sidekick/girlfriend who serves as a cheap vehicle for exposition every five or six chapters?" she asked.

"Yes, as a matter of fact," Rep said, consulting a half-page of notes. "Named Victoria. She mentions her boyfriend's name once, and it isn't Albert. I was disappointed."

"You won't be surprised to learn that *In Contemplation of Death* features a character meeting that description as well."

"You're right, I'm not surprised. I think the Mystery Writers of America may have a by-law or something specifically requiring a character like that in every mystery/romance with a female protagonist."

"Well," Melissa said, "that character in the movie is named Carolyn. But about an hour into the thing, one of the other characters slips and calls her Vicki instead. Apparently no one caught the continuity mistake."

Rep closed *In Contemplation of Death* without marking his place and set it down next to the computer.

"Vicki," he said.

"Right."

"Short for Victoria."

"Yes."

"Bloody hell," Rep muttered, although he seldom used off-color language in Melissa's presence. "I'm going to have to write a longer memorandum."

Chapter 3

Rep made a relatively rare weekend appearance at the office that Saturday morning, but not because Charlotte Buchanan's plagiarism claim challenged his moderate work habits. He had actually finished his claim-assessment memo early Friday afternoon, although he had waited until 4:30 to send copies to Finneman and Arundel in order to minimize the risk that either of them would have read the thing by Saturday morning.

Even so, he hid out in the library when he came in instead of burying himself in his own office. He passed his time paging idly through the *Journal of the Patent Office Society*, which was the only law review he knew of that included jokes.

In principle the library ploy should have worked and in practice it did fine for awhile. After an hour or so, however, Rep found it prudent to journey to the men's room. It was there that, by sheer bad luck, Arundel fell on him.

"Good morning," he boomed in serendipitous triumph. "By the way, on Saturdays we have free donuts in the fourteenth floor lounge."

"I had one with vanilla frosting," Rep said mildly.

"I thought you might have forgotten in the time since you were last here on a Saturday. Anyway, I have your memo."

"And you brought it in here with you, I see. I suppose that could be taken two different ways."

"Thirteen pages," Arundel said as he appraisingly snapped a fingernail against the document. "A real *magnum opus*— explaining, no doubt, that Ms. Buchanan's claim is a crock. When you chat with her on Monday, just remember who she is and let her down gently, can you?"

Before responding Rep ostentatiously checked for legs under stall doors. (Firm policy forbade discussion of confidential client affairs in venues where unwelcome ears might be listening.) He knew that this implicit rebuke would irritate Arundel, and Rep took occupational pleasures where he found them.

"Actually," he said after his reconnaissance, "when you get a chance to read the memo, you'll find that her claim isn't necessarily a crock. There's a non-trivial chance that Point West Productions actually did steal our client's story. The memo goes on, of course, to explain why this would be extremely hard to prove, and why our client would find the attempt distasteful and success only marginally more profitable than failure." He punctuated this summary by zipping up on the last syllable.

"I'll read your analysis with interest," Arundel said, "even though you've spoiled the suspense. But if Charlotte Buchanan is anything like her old man, she won't be particularly impressed with pessimistic palaver about litigation difficulties. If there's a colorably legitimate claim there, someone's going to get paid to try proving it, however futile that might be—and the someone might as well be us."

"When I say hard to prove I'm not just talking about the rules of evidence," Rep said as he soaped his hands under running tap water. "The movie business has its own rules. One thing the memo doesn't spell out, for example, is the delicate matter of where Point West's money comes from."

"And where's that?"

"I don't know. But about ten percent of the financing for Hollywood pictures in general comes from the traditional mob. Another five percent or so comes from drug lords south of the border. If we come up with a case that's really good enough to scare Point West's money men, we might wish we hadn't."

"I see," Arundel said soberly. Macho M&A jocks weren't supposed to get muscular inside information like this from intellectual property lightweights. "Well, maybe you can talk Ms. Buchanan out of chasing her broken dream, but I'll be betting the other way. I'll have Mary Jane Masterson come see you so you can get her started on the grunt work—just in case."

"Isn't she the second-year associate who complained that it was sex discrimination for partners to keep using metaphors like 'put it on the numbers' that come from male-dominated sports?"

"Yeah," Arundel admitted, "but that was just because she thought she was about to get fired, which she wasn't, though she probably should've been. She was building a file in case she had to gin up a wrongful termination claim."

"Am I supposed to find that reassuring?"

"Yes. See, she's already shot the sex discrimination arrow at somebody else. Besides, who'd believe you use sports metaphors? So even if her job insecurity resurfaces she can't bellyache about you unless she can work herself into some protected class other than women. What's she going to do—turn herself black?"

"I'll look forward to your comments on the memo," Rep said. "My personal opinion is that I hit it right across the seams."

⊞ ⊞ ⊞

"The only difference between Oklahoma and Afghanistan is that Rodgers and Hammerstein never wrote a musical about Afghanistan," Louise Krieg was telling Melissa rather dreamily in Krieg's faculty office about the time Rep and

Arundel walked out of the sixteenth-floor men's room at their firm. "My only tenure-track offers were from Oklahoma State and Reed University here in Indianapolis, so that's why I'm in Indiana. Want a hit?"

"Why not?" Melissa said. She accepted the deftly rolled joint from Krieg, sucked marijuana smoke into her lungs, held it for a five-count, then expelled it and handed the weed back.

"Does Reppert know you smoke marijuana?" Krieg asked.

"Yeah. I don't rub his nose in it, but he knows."

"But he doesn't want to share it with you."

"Not a Rep kind of thing," Melissa said. "Not that he's judgmental about my little naughty habit. He knows when I say I'm coming to see you on a Saturday that after we finish talking about my dissertation on Dorothy L. Sayers and your deconstructionist theory that Lord Peter Wimsey was really gay, we're going to take some tokes. He always claims he has to go to the office anyway, so I won't feel guilty about leaving him alone."

"Well, that's not *too* anal, I guess."

"I think it's kind of sweet, actually."

"Of course," Krieg added hastily. "I mean, I know Reppert is truly wonderful, once you get to know him." (Melissa recognized this as a faint-praise dismissal of someone Krieg regarded as a stiff in a suit.) "I have to admit, though, there are times when I really wonder how you two got together in the first place. You're almost from different planets."

"We met when he was still in law school and I was working off a student-aid grant by putting in twelve hours a week with the library's tech support department at Michigan. He was helping one of the professors develop a PowerPoint presentation, and it was turning into a very frustrating project."

"That certainly sounds promising," Krieg said with high-pitched irony behind a fragrant cloud.

"So on the seventeenth or eighteenth revision of the screens, I tried to lighten things up a little. I smiled winsomely at him and sort of half-sang, '*Four weeks, you rehearse and rehearse.*' And he came back instantly with, '*Three weeks, and it couldn't be worse.*'"

"Everyone has seen *Kiss Me, Kate*, though. And that's from the opening number."

"That occurred to me," Melissa said. "I even tested that theory a bit. I kind of chanted, '*And so I became, as befitted my delicate birth*—'. And he warbled right back at me, '*— the most casual bride of the murdering scum of the earth.*' No telling what key he was in, but he got the lyric right."

"That's impressive," Krieg admitted. "There are a lot of people who've never seen *Pippin*."

"Technically, that was from *Man of La Mancha*," Melissa said. "Anyway, I clinched it. As long as we'd taken the game that far, I tried, '*This is a guy that is gonna go further than anyone ever susPECTed.*' He answered, '*Yesterday morning I wrote him a note that I'm sorry he wasn't eLECTed.*' And there are a *whole* lot of people who've never even heard of *Fiorello*, much less seen it."

"Your point. So because Reppert had an encyclopedic knowledge of American musical comedy you figured he was good in bed?"

"No, I figured he was gay. Which happened to appeal to me right then: a male friend I could go out with and talk to intelligently about things that didn't include Michigan's chances of beating Wisconsin, but who wouldn't be fishing a greasy condom out of his wallet as we walked back to my room."

"You mean this entire romance was a misunderstanding?"

"You could say that," Melissa agreed. (The joint had gone back and forth a couple more times by now, and while Melissa wasn't baked she had reached that mellow stage where you agree about anything except the existence of God.) "On our first date I found out that he was totally fascinated by me. And on our fourth date I found out he wasn't gay."

The little *ping* in the back of her head scarcely registered with her at the moment, but it signaled that Melissa would reproach herself for that crack tomorrow morning. That would sharpen her usual pot hangover—a vague feeling of sheepish disgust at succumbing once again to this juvenile habit she should have gotten past years ago. She didn't think smoking marijuana was morally wrong, the way using heroin would've been. And she didn't think it was unspeakably stupid, like smoking cigarettes. It was just so, so—inappropriate. For her.

It was fine for Krieg, Melissa thought. The campus area apartment where Krieg entertained casual lovers of both sexes smelled of brown rice and incense. Hundreds of paperbacks and hardcovers in three languages filled blocks-and-boards bookcases along its walls. Krieg wrote articles about things like deconstructing the vagina, taught gender-and classes ("Gender and the Male Honor Construct in Victorian Literature" was the current term's offering), and in her spare time she got large checks from corporations for giving weekend seminars on diversity adaptation strategies. For Krieg marijuana was an integral part of a lifestyle as authentically bohemian as you could get in Indianapolis.

Melissa, though, didn't eat brown rice unless gravy from her roast beef slopped onto Uncle Ben's Converted. For her pot was a kind of nostalgic denial, like middle-aged CPAs dressing in tie-dyed t-shirts and cargo pants to go hear the Grateful Dead. For a few hours once every five or six weeks, she could pretend she wasn't thirty-two with a house and a mortgage, looking into a church to join when she and Rep finally had kids, married to a partner (a very *junior* partner, admittedly) in an establishment law firm where casual Fridays mean you don't wear a vest, a little ticked despite herself about how much they paid in taxes. She could halfway kid herself that she was really still a student at heart, twenty in her soul, with an untamed spirit and a universe of possibilities before her.

"Is Reppert working on something with Tavistock, by the way?" Krieg asked. "I was over there yesterday afternoon planning a seminar I'm doing for them and I thought I heard his name mentioned."

"Is Tavistock really worrying about diversity adaptation?" Melissa asked, in order to evade Krieg's question. Melissa was feeling pretty good, but she wasn't mellow enough to let slip any professional confidences that Rep shared with her.

"A little different angle," Krieg explained. "Three years ago they decided to outsource their whole video presentation and AV department. 'We're in the chemical business, not the film business.' That kind of brilliant executive thinking. They had me in to facilitate adaptation-to-change strategies. It was the latest thing for forward-looking corporate thinkers. Now they've decided to bring some of the audiovisual stuff back in-house."

"So they need some more adaptation-to-change facilitation, except in the opposite direction?" Melissa asked.

"Bingo."

"And they say women are slaves to fashion."

"Hey, don't turn your nose up at it," Krieg admonished Melissa. "It keeps me in primo grass."

⌗ ⌗ ⌗

"Do you need a legal pad?" Rep asked Mary Jane Masterson about forty-five minutes later.

"No," she answered, flourishing her own. "I came here prepared to practice law."

"Good. Then here's a list of the three writers who got script credits for *In Contemplation of Death*. Copy it down. What I need you to find out is who their agents are and what other projects they've worked on in the last five years. Also whether they've been sued for plagiarism or had a Guild arbitration on any issue."

"No RICO research?" Masterson asked.

"Uh, no," Rep said, somewhat flustered by the off-the-wall query. "This is a copyright case. We're a long way from worrying about claims under the Racketeer Influenced Corrupt Organizations Act."

"It's just that Chip Arundel is very knowledgeable in this area," Masterson said. "He told me that about fifteen percent of movie financing comes from the mafia, and another ten percent from the Medellin cartel. He thought RICO might be one area you'd have me working on "

"Facts first," Rep said, "theories later."

"Uh *huh*," Masterson said. "I *see*. Look, who's walking point on this claim?"

"Um, I am, I guess," Rep said.

"I mean who's the partner in charge of the file?"

"Me again," Rep said. "Otherwise I wouldn't be walking point, would I?"

"I mean—" Masterson paused in apparent perplexity. She dropped her right hand to the legal pad on her knees and gazed at Rep's framed eleven-by-fourteen photograph of Melissa.

"Okay," she said then. "I know that you're technically a partner—"

"Thank you," Rep said.

"But is Arundel really just staff and you're line on this? I mean, if you're actually the senior line officer for this claim, then no offense but this whole thing is a shit detail that isn't going to get anyone's ticket punched except the wrong way."

"How could anyone possibly take offense at that?" Rep asked. "It would be like claiming that overuse of military jargon is sex discrimination because war is a male-dominated activity."

"So you're really telling me to ignore Chip Arundel's suggestion and follow your instructions on this case?"

"By one o'clock on Monday afternoon," Rep said apologetically, "I need agents, projects, and claims. If you have any spare time between now and then, please feel free to research a RICO memorandum to impress Mr. Arundel."

Masterson stood up slowly. Raising her arms, she joined her palms just above her forehead and inclined her head and shoulders slightly.

"I bow to the Buddha nature in you," she said solemnly. "To everything that is true and good in you and in all living creatures."

"Uh, thanks," Rep said. "But I thought you were a libertarian atheist materialist, platinum member of the Ayn Rand Book Club and that kind of thing."

"Though the void contains nothing, it is defined by everything and everything therefore exists in relation to it."

"I guess that would follow," Rep said.

Masterson was four steps out of his office before the light bulb came on.

"Minority religion," Rep muttered to himself. "Protected class. She figures that taking orders from me means she's about to be fired."

Chapter 4

Rep waited until the thirty-sixth minute of his forty-one minute office conference with Charlotte Buchanan on Monday morning to mention the risk that even a favorable court decision on her claim might include nasty and hurtful comments. He did this as tactfully as possible.

"When kids are twelve, they think sarcasm is worldly. Most of us outgrow this. Those who don't become judges. Plagiarism cases bring out their worst instincts."

With this low-key finesse he approached the climax to his let-her-down-gently interview. Avoiding legalese, he had laid out the pros and cons of suing Point West Productions. He had conveyed the implicit message that he was salivating at the prospect of ripping Point West's lungs out, but felt constrained by a professional sense of Sober Responsibility to ensure that Buchanan had No Illusions. (This is known in the trade as Making the Client Say No.)

"This is a case that *could* be won," he said now. "It could also be lost, and the road to any victory will be long, hard, expensive, and uncertain. The only sure thing is this: If you do give us the green light, at some point along the way you'll say to yourself, 'If I had it all to do over again, I wouldn't do it.'"

"So what do you recommend?" Buchanan asked innocently.

"Tough question," Rep said with a well-practiced rueful grin. "If it were my money, I don't know if I'd have the wisdom to walk away from a claim that's morally right and might be legally viable. But I hope I would, because if I did the odds are that twenty-four months from now I'd be richer and happier."

"I see. Well I have some issues with that." She paused for two or three seconds—long enough for Rep to acquire the first inkling that he was no longer in control of the conversation. "This isn't my money, *this is my life.*"

Buchanan didn't yell these words or sob them or spit them. She spoke them with a steely, quiet intensity that seemed to hit Rep with physical force. Her eyes gleamed with the kind of zealous glow Rep associated with street preachers.

"When you have a rich daddy people assume that his money and influence explain your own achievements, from making the girls' volleyball team in high school forward," Buchanan said then with the same tautly leashed fervor. "I'm not doing a poor-little-rich-girl number on you. Rich is good, and on balance I'll skip the credit and take the trust fund. The worst part, though, is that you don't really know yourself. Did I really get into Brown on my boards and my grades, or did I get in the same way the Eurotrash did? Did I make my quota the very first quarter I was on the road for Tavistock because I know how to sell chemicals, or did my dad make some phone calls and give me a creampuff client list?"

"I see," Rep said, trying to suggest some interest in the esoteric problems of millionaire self-esteem.

"Well," Buchanan said, "*And Done to Others' Harm* is one thing I know dad had nothing to do with. Underwriters return his calls before lunch, but there's not a single string he can pull in the publishing business. I can put that book on my tombstone: 'She was a spoiled rich girl and her marriage to a fifth-round NFL draft pick fell apart after eight months. But by God she wrote a story that one thousand eight hundred thirteen people read.' When someone steals that from me I'm not going to walk away based on a cool, calm, carefully calibrated cost-benefit analysis."

Gift for alliteration, Rep thought, then immediately regretted the flippancy. What he'd just heard was neither a tantrum nor an act. He recognized that. At the same time, though, he wondered what Buchanan expected him to say. *You want a second opinion? Okay, you're an idiot*—that definitely wouldn't qualify as letting her down gently. He asked himself the question any lawyer has to ask in this situation: Whom do I have to sleep with to get off of this case?

"Perhaps you'd be more comfortable if an attorney in whom you have more confidence examined this issue," Rep said.

When Buchanan responded by reaching into her purse, Rep figured she was taking him up on his suggestion. If she wasn't going after cigarettes—and Rep would've bet the house that she didn't smoke—the most plausible guess was a cell phone so that she could call daddy and have him bounce Rep off the case. Behind his contact lenses a tiny, mental Rep punched his fist in the air and yelled "YES!"

A moment later, though, Rep's heart started racing and his gut clinched. What Buchanan pulled out of her purse was neither a cell phone nor a cigarette case. It was a hairbrush.

Not one of those dinky, longish, plastic hairbrushes, either. An old-fashioned hairbrush. Oversized. Oval. With what looked like a very sturdy wooden back. *Cripes*, he thought, *does she know? How COULD she know?*

"Fortnum and Mason," she said, flourishing the brush in the midst of brisk, no-nonsense strokes through her hair. "Picked it up in London a month ago. I don't usually handle personal grooming in other people's offices, but my shrink says it's a key stress reflex for me."

She knows, Rep thought. Fortnum and Mason hairbrushes from London won consistently high praise from spanking enthusiasts on the net.

The conclusion left him hollow bellied and jelly-legged. It wasn't just the risk of acute embarrassment from having colleagues and clients learn about his special little interest, though that was plenty. It wasn't even the thought of Melissa enduring arch remarks about it, though that shredded his gut like five-alarm chili.

The subtle blackmail implicit in Buchanan's gesture threatened the very core of the life-strategy Rep had started working out on that magical day in Antitrust class. Arundel and his peers thought they were winning, but they weren't because *Rep wasn't playing*. Rep met their mega paychecks and corner offices not with gnashing teeth but with politely superior indifference because *what mattered to them didn't matter to him*. He didn't care what they thought of him; they were his partners, not his heroes.

But this was something that couldn't possibly not matter to him. They would all know from primal male instinct that it had to matter. They'd have the chink in his armor, the gap in his defenses, the area of vulnerability. And they'd exploit it. The mere thought of how they'd exploit it dried his tongue and iced his viscera.

This is my life, Rep wanted to shout. But he didn't think that would help, somehow.

"As I was saying," he managed, "if you'd rather—"

"I don't *want* another lawyer," Buchanan said. "I want you." (*Why?* Rep thought with astonishment.) "But I want you for real and not for show."

"Ms. Buchanan, if you feel that I have approached this problem with less thoroughness than it warrants, then the necessary course—"

"Skip it," she instructed him. "If my father walked into this law firm with a bet-your-company patent claim or hostile takeover bid pinned to his fanny, you wouldn't treat it like you were handicapping the third race at Aqueduct. You'd say this is war, we're pulling out all the stops, we're taking our stand here, we're going to the wall, no retreat and no surrender."

"Okay," Rep said.

"That's what I want to see before anyone talks to me about blowing my claim off. I'm the victim here. I want some passion. I want some emotional commitment. I want a little *enthusiasm.*"

I don't do passion, Rep thought insistently as he tried to banish an uncomfortable mental image of a fifth-round NFL draft pick getting this pep talk in bed. *Enthusiasm is for litigators.*

Rep instinctively reverted to a reserved calm that he couldn't have made any more subdued without losing consciousness. Those passionless logical processes in his cerebral cortex that Buchanan had just slighted whirred and clicked and in one-point-three seconds spat out the correct fall-back position: Call The Client's Bluff.

"Telling a lawyer that money is no object and he should vet a claim to his heart's content can be expensive," he said as he glanced at his watch and his calendar. "Tell you what. I'm leaving for New York at three-fifteen this afternoon because I have a client meeting there first thing tomorrow morning. I'll be back in Indianapolis by four tomorrow afternoon. Can you get in touch with your agent, your editor, your publicist, and your West Coast contact by then and tell them to expect calls from me?"

"Be careful what you ask for," Buchanan said with a smile that didn't do a thing for Rep. "You might get it. Where are you staying in Manhattan tonight?"

"Hilton Midtown."

"Tavistock's Gulfstream is supposed to drop me on Long Island around two because my coast contact is visiting Manhattan and I want to talk to him. I can have you across a table from him and my agent by seven-thirty tonight. I'll send a driver for you at seven."

Rep viewed optimism not as a rational attitude but as a psychological defense of last resort. It was something you fell back on when no hope lay in any other direction. He resorted to it now.

Maybe she doesn't know after all, he thought. *Maybe it was just some kind of grotesque coincidence. Or maybe it was projection or displacement or one of those Freudian things. When you got right down to it, really, how could she possibly know? After all, she hadn't said that the hairbrush was brand spanking new, had she?*

Chapter 5

She knows all right, Rep thought as he slid out of the Chrysler Imperial that had taken him and Buchanan to 101 East 2nd Street in lower Manhattan.

The restaurant called itself La Nouvelle Justine. Anyone who had passed too lightly over the Marquis de Sade's *oeuvre* to pick up the allusion would have gotten an even heavier-handed clue from the drawing of the nearly naked woman on the marquee. She was on her knees, bent over at the waist, with her hands tied behind her back.

Inside, the waiters would have looked pretty much like waiters anywhere if they'd been wearing shirts. A tall and less than slender hostess nodded unsmilingly at Buchanan's murmured introduction, then brusquely beckoned one of the *decamisado* waitstaff. Before Rep could absorb much more ambience, a voice that reminded him of air brakes blared through the dimly lit interior.

"What's the matter, Charlotte, you couldn't get reservations at Paddles or The Loft?"

Buchanan led Rep in the voice's direction. The source turned out to be a woman in her fifties with abundant, graying hair and the general manner of a hippie who had impulsively dressed like an investment banker and was waiting for everyone to get the joke. She shared a table with a pudgy man who looked about ten years younger.

"We're from the unjaded Midwest, where decadence is still exciting," Buchanan said as they approached. "This is Reppert Pennyworth, my lawyer. Mr. Pennyworth, I have produced, as promised, Julia Deltrediche, my agent, and Bernie Mixler, who tried to peddle *And Done to Others' Harm* on the coast."

Rep smiled, shook hands, sat down, parked his laptop case under his chair, and opened the menu that the pouty waiter handed to him. The left side offered a predictable selection of salads, chops, and seafood. Under a heading misspelled "Special Fares" the right side proposed an array of more exotic choices at $20 each. These included "Dinner Served as Infant's Fare in the Highchair," "Foot Worship," "Public Humiliation," and "Spanking."

Rep ordered steak and salad. As soon as the waiter left, he shoehorned a miniature legal pad onto one corner of the table and turned an all-business expression toward Deltrediche.

"Where did you shop the manuscript before you sent it to Saint Philomena?" he asked.

"No befores, all at the same time," Deltrediche said dismissively. "Saint Phils, SMP, Dutton, NAL, Mysterious Press, HarperCollins, Scribner, Back Door. I don't believe in exclusive submissions."

"When did you send the manuscripts out?"

"Seventeen months before publication. Got a quick hit and ran with it."

Rep tore a page from mini-pad and slid it across the table to Deltrediche along with a ballpoint.

"Please write down the names of the editors or readers you submitted it to at each place—"

"Any property I'm willing to represent, I don't send it to some reader making sixteen thousand a year three months out of Smith. Senior editor and up. They know my name and they look at what I give them. That's why writers come to me."

"And well they should, I'm sure," Rep sighed. "Please write down their names, and next to each one the name of his or her Hollywood contacts."

"You think if these people had Hollywood contacts they'd be working in print?" Deltrediche snorted. "That's why I have Bernie."

"Well, yes, I do think they have Hollywood contacts, actually," Rep said. "I think they each have one or two people on the coast that they call confidentially when they stumble across something that looks like it might be really big or offbeat enough to be interesting out there. I think these people on the coast cultivate your senior editors for exactly that reason, so they're not behind the curve when everyone else in town goes after this year's version of *The Joy Luck Club* or *The Bridges of Madison County.*"

"Savvy schtick from flyover country," Deltrediche said with the hint of a nod and a we-only-kid-the-guys-we-love nudge. "*Entertainment Weekly* must be offering hayseed discounts again."

"If you would please just—"

"I'm writing, I'm writing."

"I thought publication established access all by itself," Mixler said.

Tell you what, Rep thought, *you hustle books and I'll practice law.*

"It does," Rep said, "depending on timing. We know when *In Contemplation of Death* was released, but we don't know when the first script was done. More important, we don't want just the bare minimum evidence we need to squeak past a summary judgment motion. We want a verdict in our favor. So I need to take Charlotte Buchanan's story in every permutation it had and trace it through every twisted highway and byway it followed until it turns up beside the word processor of a writer doing script revisions for *In Contemplation of Death* during principal photography. Which is where you come in."

"Oh?" Mixler responded, gazing bemusedly through chocolate brown eyes under heroically bristling eyebrows.

A deafening glass and metal crash eight feet away intervened before Rep could respond. They all looked up to see a waiter with his hands clapped theatrically to his cheeks as he stared in hammy dismay at a tray he'd just dropped. The hostess stalked over to him.

"Clumsy fool!" she shouted melodramatically, evoking a cringing whimper. Then she bent him over an empty table and administered the kind of spanking you'd expect (with the genders reversed) in a high school production of *Kiss Me, Kate*. The waiter howled in unconvincing agony quite disproportionate to the severity of the two-dozen open-handed smacks that peppered the seat of his leather trousers.

"A few more turns of the lathe before that one gets his Equity card," Deltrediche commented, shaking her head.

Rep was grateful for her assessment, because it gave him time to get his breathing back under control. The performance might have been pure camp, but it had sent his pulse rate soaring and his loins twitching all the same. It was one thing to see it on videos. Live and eight feet away was, as a Charlotte Buchanan character might say, something very else. Doing what he could to suggest blasé indifference, he turned his attention back to Mixler.

"Did you start pitching the story on the coast before publication?" Rep asked.

"Sure. First thing I did when Saint Phil's said yes was make twenty-five copies of the manuscript."

"You charged me for fifty copies," Buchanan said.

"Musta been fifty, then."

"Any left?"

"Long gone."

"Whom did you send them to?" Rep asked.

"Everyone."

"You'll probably need more than one page then," Rep said patiently, tearing out several leaves from his pad and sliding them across the table. "I'll need everyone's name, and the name of everyone's agent. Also, a copy of the short written treatment you used. Who wrote the treatment, by the way?"

"I did."

"Good. And the name and agent of anyone you sent the treatment to who didn't also get the manuscript."

"Tall order."

"Before you start filling that order, though, tell me about Aaron Eastman."

"Producer of *In Contemplation of Death*," Mixler shrugged. "Point West is his personal vehicle, no question. Let's see, what else? Had a nine-figure epic several years ago that was supposed to be Oscar-bait and only drew one nomination, for Best Song in a Movie Made by White Guys About China or something. That's about it."

"Did you pitch *And Done to Others' Harm* to him?"

"If I had I would've had the brains to mention it before," Mixler said irritably. "Apparently you didn't hear me just now. Around the time I was pushing *Done*, Eastman's last big wrap was a movie that cost a hundred-million plus before they bought the first newspaper ad. I would've been lucky to pitch Charlotte's story to Eastman's third assistant go-fer."

"Did you ever pitch anything to him?" Rep pressed.

"'Ever' is a long time. Let's see, must've, I guess. Years ago I think he gave me five minutes to tout a biopic on Rosa Luxemburg. She was a commie, but we would've soft-pedaled that part and gone with the costume drama visual stuff: arrested by the czar's police while she was in bed with her lover; got laid more often than a Clinton intern; always carried a gun because half the comrades wanted to kill her over her politics and the other half wanted to nail her for her love life; goes on trial for sedition in Germany the day World War I starts; tries to overthrow the German government after the war, captured in bloody street fighting, then assassinated by the *Freikorps*. Plus you've got all kinds of colorful history in the background—the Dreyfus Affair in France, Paris in the *belle époque*, troops breaking strikes, duels every fifteen minutes, bolsheviks behaving badly, guys getting assassinated in cafes, brawls and riots every time you turn around, the whole thing."

"I don't remember seeing the movie, so the pitch must not have gone well," Rep prompted.

"He gave me my five minutes," Mixler said. "Then he leaned back in his chair and said, 'Do you think we can get Jennifer Aniston for Rosa?'"

"From *Friends?*" Deltrediche demanded in astonishment.

"Right. That was how he said no."

"So he's a jerk," Rep said. "Is he a thief?"

"Not that I know of. No more than anyone else in Hollywood."

The waiter appeared with their food.

"Now you can start writing," Rep said.

"Between bites," Mixler said.

Forty-five minutes later, as the waiter cleared post-dinner coffee and Deltrediche and Mixler took their leave, Rep gathered the potentially precious scraps of yellow paper they had given him and began studying them. Something about the way Buchanan scraped her chair when they were finally alone told him that she was about to speak. He looked up.

"Would you like the hostess to give you a spanking?" she asked, her voice a trifle huskier than usual. "I'll ask her, if you want me to. You won't have to say a word. Open hand or paddle. Out here in public, if that's what floats your boat, or behind that beaded curtain by the hostess desk."

"Uh, no, thanks, actually."

"Don't bother telling me the idea doesn't turn you on. I know it does."

It turned him on all right. In fifteen years of technicolor fantasies Rep had been over the knees of pop icons from Meg Ryan to Sean Young to Cameron Diaz to Julia Roberts.

"I don't think your offer calls for comment one way or the other," he said with as much dignity as he could muster.

"Suit yourself," Buchanan said, shrugging. "It doesn't bother me one way or the other. I just thought you might be curious about how the real thing matches up with your fantasies."

Curious doesn't come close, Rep thought.

"I'm curious about party drugs like Ecstasy," Rep said, "but I've never done any."

"Why not?"

"I draw lines."

"Where?" Buchanan asked.

"This side of cheating. Fantasizing is on one side. Actually engaging in a sex act with someone other than my wife would be on the other." Rep managed to keep his voice calm and clinical. He deliberately chose stilted, bloodless, lawyerly words.

"A lot of people might say that that's a pretty fine distinction."

"Whenever you draw a line you'll have cases close to the line on each side, and they won't be very different," Rep shrugged. "But you still have to draw the line."

"You're coming off as super high-minded, talking like that. But even though you put your fantasies on the okay side of the line, I'll bet you hide them from your wife."

"That isn't really any of your business, is it?"

He didn't *hide* it from Melissa, actually. "Hide" wasn't quite the right word. He knew from early and clumsy overtures that she didn't share his fascination, that she could never be more than a mildly disgusted good sport about spanking. So he didn't bring it up at all anymore. But he didn't call that hiding it, as if he were conducting some kind of backstreet affair. He treated his esoteric interest the same way Melissa treated her taste for marijuana.

"You're right," Buchanan said in response to his rebuke. "It isn't any of my business. I'm sorry."

What you should be sorry about is blackmail, not clumsy questions, Rep thought.

"No offense," Rep said.

"I'm not trying to blackmail you," Buchanan said then, "I'm just taking out motivational insurance. I've told you what this claim means to me. I don't want you just mailing it in."

"Did tonight look to you like mailing it in?" Rep asked.

"You were energetic and well prepared," Buchanan said. "But tell me something: What did we really accomplish?"

It would have been child's play to stall her, and he was tempted to do exactly that. Instead, almost impulsively, he took a full-sized page of legal paper out of his inside coat pocket, unfolded it, and spread it on the table between them. On a line two spaces below the center of the page he had printed three names:

JAMES CRONIN   MORRIE BRISTOL   DAVID ALBERS

Three spaces above these names he had printed DUNSTON RIVIERA. Dotted lines connected Dunston Riviera to Cronin and Bristol.

"These are the three people who got screenplay credits for *In Contemplation of Death*," he said, tapping the lower names with his pen point.

"I know. Who's Dunston Riviera?"

"Not who, what. Dunston Riviera is an agency that has both Cronin and Bristol as clients."

"Who's Albers' agent?"

"We're not sure yet. Now, it's obviously going to take time to analyze these new data from Deltrediche and Mixler in detail, but let's do a quick once-over and see if by some wild chance we've accomplished something tonight."

Rep shuffled the pages that Deltrediche and Mixler had covered with scribbling. For three minutes he referred to them while making notes on his own legal page. When he was through, the big page looked like this:

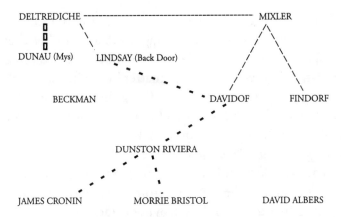

"The dashed lines mean we know your story was passed from one person to the next," he explained. "The dotted lines mean it could have been because there's a natural relationship, but we don't know yet."

"And you're saying Davidof is both the Hollywood contact of a senior editor at Back Door Press and one of the guys that Bernie Mixler showed the story to on his own."

"Deltrediche and Mixler said that, independently, and without any chance to collaborate. That may mean absolutely nothing. But it is very interesting that Davidof is also a client of Dunston Riviera. Having three writers on one screenplay is a bad sign. It often means that the first script ran into trouble."

"So maybe Dunston Riviera called in Bristol to rescue Cronin or vice-versa, and he needed some help in a hurry, and Davidof gave it to him in the form of my story."

"Maybe. Or maybe not. But that's what we accomplished tonight. We came up with some questions to ask that are a lot more focused than the ones we had before."

"Okay," Buchanan said with what Rep took to be a concessionary expulsion of breath. "You're not mailing it in. But how close are we to filing a complaint in court?"

"I have no idea. What we're a lot closer to is drafting a letter to the general counsel for Point West Productions."

"A letter saying what?"

"That information which has come to our attention and which we believe to be reliable suggests that his or her client is in serious trouble; that we would like some voluntary cooperation in investigating the matter in an effort to resolve these nagging questions without filing suit; and that in the meantime we demand that all relevant documents, floppies, e-mails, recordings, pixels and anything else pertinent to *In Contemplation of Death* be preserved."

"Won't that kind of letter have exactly the opposite effect? Won't they start deleting stuff from their hard drives and shredding first drafts and destroying evidence?"

Rep's eyes glowed at the prospect. For the first time that night he was truly happy.

"When you get back to your room tonight," he told his client fervently, "kneel down and pray that Point West Productions starts deleting hard-drive entries, shredding documents, and destroying evidence."

⊞ ⊞ ⊞

In his own room at the Hilton Midtown half an hour later, Rep kicked himself for overplaying his hand. The Davidof connection didn't have to mean a blessed thing, but he'd been so anxious to impress Buchanan that he'd let his exuberance run away with his judgment. He'd been so giddy that he'd almost walked out of the restaurant without his laptop, which Buchanan had had to retrieve for him. Now he had her up there with him and without a net.

He hooked his laptop up to the dataport on his phone and checked his e-mails. Then he disconnected the laptop and dialed his own office number to collect his voice-mail messages. They were routine, until the last one.

"Hey, Rep, Paul Mulcahy getting back to you," the recorded voice on the last message said. Mulcahy was a law school classmate, practicing entertainment law in Los Angeles. "I don't want to get into this in a recorded message, but call me right away, okay? Go ahead and use my home number if you have to."

Rep didn't have to, because Mulcahy was still at his desk in lotus land at seven-twenty, Pacific Daylight Time.

"That was a very provocative message," Rep said.

"I didn't mean it as a tease, because I don't really have any hard information for you," Mulcahy said. "But there's something you might want to know before you start messing around with Aaron Eastman and Point West. I don't think he's any boy scout. You're not the first guy to start asking questions about him recently. I have no idea what it is, but he's in something heavy with someone."

"What kind of questions are the other people asking?"

"Don't know, don't care. All kinds of off-the-wall stuff, from what little echoes came to me. All I'd bet on is that he's got something bigger than alimony and royalty disputes on his mind right now."

"Is Point West in financial trouble?"

"No idea. I have absolutely no clue what this is all about. I just don't know if I'd want to get mixed up with him right at this point in time."

"Thanks," Rep said. "Talk to you again soon."

He hung up. He wiped his forehead. He swiped moist palms on his pants. Then he turned his laptop back on and opened a new document. With the tentative, jab-style of typing he always used, he started drafting:

[NAME]
General Counsel
Point West Productions
[ADDRESS]
   Re: *In Contemplation of Death*
Dear _____:

 This firm represents Charlotte Buchanan, the author of *And Done to Others' Harm* (St. Philomena Press 1997). Information that has come to our attention and that we believe to be reliable leads us to believe that the recent Point West production

In Contemplation of Death borrowed significantly in theme, characterization, and plot line from Ms. Buchanan's novel.

He paused for a moment. He took a deep breath. Then he started typing much more quickly.

Chapter 6

By Wednesday, eight days after his initial conference with Charlotte Buchanan in Chip Arundel's office, Rep's mood had just about returned to its customary equilibrium and placid contentment. His nastygram to Point West had gone out Tuesday, putting the ball in the bad guys' court until at least sometime next week. He'd send a message to Mixler later in the day, reminding him that he still owed Rep a copy of the movie treatment for *And Done to Others' Harm*. And he'd told Buchanan to come up with a copy of the manuscript that Deltrediche had used for her multiple submissions. That figured to keep her busy for a few more days, anyway.

All in all, Rep didn't see any reason why he couldn't spend the rest of this week practicing real law instead of worrying about sullen heiresses and second-rate mysteries. His gait as he passed his secretary's desk at 8:40 a.m. was his customary purposeful stride rather than the uncertain shuffle he'd caught himself lapsing into recently.

"Debbie, if the trademark samples from Cremona Pizza don't come in with this morning's Federal Express delivery, please remind me to rattle their cage about it," he told the efficient young woman.

"I think the messengers brought it by on the early morning run," she called after him. "They put a package on your chair. It was damp, so I put some *ABA Journals* under it."

"Damp?" Rep muttered jauntily. "They didn't send whole pizzas instead of just the labels, did they? This may turn into a value-billing situation."

The brown carton on his chair was indeed wet at the edges and near sodden on the bottom. Not to mention more than a little ripe. As soon as he picked it up, Rep knew it hadn't come from Cremona Pizza. Whoever sent this had used ordinary mail, and hadn't included a return address.

The box was tough, with no perforations or other invitations to easy opening. When Rep finally got the end flap pulled off and began to work the contents out, his first thought was, *Why is some idiot sending me beef tenderloin?* Quickly, though, he realized that the thick, pinkish-gray, longish piece of meat with one end curled downward wasn't beef tenderloin. A dozen more grisly possibilities occurred to him in the few seconds before he identified it.

It was tongue. Calve's tongue, probably. Accompanying it, looped around each end and with a double handle connecting the loops, was a cat's cradle of twine. He had figured out the grotesque message even before he read the letters crudely cut and pasted on the scrap of paper that fell out of the box last: HOLD YOUR TONGUE.

My client isn't neurotic after all, Rep thought. *Neurotic isn't within a time-zone of what my client is. My client is nuts. Bananas. Crackers. My client is marsh-loon crazy.*

Rep had gotten a real death threat once in his career. It had come from an entrepreneur in Terre Haute who thought that he could use well known trademarks if he just put them on cigarette lighters and barbecue aprons instead of products like those the trademark owners actually sold. Rep had explained the unpleasant truth, with its implication that once Rep unleashed the pit bulls in the Litigation Department the man's company and most of his personal worth would become the property of Rep's clients.

"Your clients will never see a penny except from the fire insurance," the entrepreneur had assured Rep with a kind of fierce solemnity. "And you won't live to collect your fee, much less enjoy it."

Rep hadn't had the slightest doubt that that threat was real. Turning his ignition key that evening and for several evenings afterward, he'd wondered for a nanosecond whether his ideas would be separated from his habits before he got the car in reverse.

This hold-your-tongue stuff, on the other hand, screamed phony. A bad guy seriously interested in scaring Rep wouldn't have come up with something lame and literary. Like the Terre Haute entrepreneur, he'd take the direct and unambiguous approach. The garbage in the damp brown envelope was the kind of thing someone who'd seen too many movies and read too many hard-boiled private eye novels would dream up.

Charlotte Buchanan, in other words. He looked at the postmark on the envelope: New York, Tuesday morning. Charlotte Buchanan had concocted this inane prop and mailed it to Rep to reinforce his belief in her claim. Point West wouldn't try to warn him off unless it were guilty, so Buchanan had tried to make Point West look guilty by confecting a childish threat that she apparently thought Rep would be dumb enough to blame on Aaron Eastman's production company.

Even as he fetched an oversized envelope and sealed this mess inside of it, Rep knew the next four things he should do, and in what order. He ought to call Steve Finneman and tell him that he'd be getting a confidential memo later in the day about a potentially delicate situation. Then he ought to dictate the memo. Then he should call the postal inspector or the police, maybe both, and suggest that someone with a badge start dusting for fingerprints and interviewing Big Apple butchers.

After he'd done all of that, he ought to tell Miss Buchanan to find herself a new lawyer because she and Rep now had, to say it politely, a material conflict of interest.

He faced the implications of doing this for thirty-eight manly seconds before he flinched. He would be saying that the daughter of a major client's CEO was either a criminal or a head-case. And as sure as he was that Charlotte Buchanan had sent the package, his certainty owed more to intuition than evidence. This stunt was of a piece with the obsessive fervor that glowed in Buchanan's eyes and rasped in her voice and breathed through her prose—but hardheaded lawyers would dismiss that kind of stuff as two steps below astrology.

Maybe Buchanan had been idiotic enough to leave fingerprints on the envelope or the note, or maybe she'd crack under police interrogation. But would the police even check Buchanan's prints if Rep didn't tip them off about his own suspicions? Fingering Buchanan wouldn't exactly be a text-book example of savvy client relations. And even if the cops thought of Buchanan all by themselves, that would still open up the old Fortnum and Mason hairbrush can of worms, wouldn't it?

Because the closest thing Rep had to evidence, when you got right down to it, was Buchanan's effort to blackmail him. He couldn't disclose that coherently without revealing the basis for the blackmail, which meant he would have to risk not only disbelief but exposure and ridicule. He'd blown his chance when he failed to walk away at the initial hint of a threat. Now he couldn't tug at the first string on this explosive package without the whole thing blowing up in his face.

After thirty-eight seconds of uncomfortable reflection Rep went to the fourteenth floor lounge and buried the package in the back of the freezer. He salved his conscience slightly with the thought that he hadn't yet actually destroyed the package, but he knew he was just delaying that inevitable step. This situation wasn't going to get any clearer. If he didn't have the guts to come clean now, he wasn't going to find the necessary courage in three days or a week. He was suppressing evidence of a legal conflict of interest and, incidentally, a criminal act.

This was professionally unethical. It was legally wrong. And it was stupid, for the same reason that it was stupid for Cary Grant in *North by Northwest* to pull a knife out of a murdered diplomat's back, hold it up in plain sight, and then stand there looking at it like a moron for six seconds in front of a roomful of witnesses. Except that Cary Grant at least had the excuse of acting impulsively, whereas Rep was acting deliberately and intentionally.

Wow, he thought as shambled back into his office. *Unethical, illegal, and dumb. The hat trick.*

⌗ ⌗ ⌗

That noon he got a ham-and-cheese sandwich and a half-pint of skim milk from a deli on Market Square and consumed them while sitting on the generous edge of the massive Civil War monument dominating that locale. It was on the third bite that, just for an instant, he thought he saw his mother walking up Commerce Street.

It wasn't his mom, of course. His mother was—would have been?—fifty-two, and the data processor/keypuncher/file clerk striding back from lunch was in her early twenties. Rep's subconscious hadn't played this nasty little trick on his optic nerves for seven or eight years, and he couldn't be sure what visual cues had triggered it. That raw-boned, first-generation-off-the-farm hardness in her expression, maybe. Or the slightly old-fashioned hairdo, vaguely evocative of Mary Tyler Moore being perky for Lou Grant. Or the aggressive, shove-it-if-you-don't-like-it way she pulled on her cigarette and almost spat the smoke out, as if she couldn't wait for the next throat-searing nicotine rush.

Rep was five the first time this had happened. Walking down Washington Avenue in Evansville on a Saturday afternoon, his sweaty paw securely clasped by his Aunt Rita, strolling past all the small town mom-and-pop stores that still had a few years to live before the death sentences decreed by malls and superstores would be executed. He'd seen a woman from behind, about thirty feet in front of them. Dark brown hair in a shag cut that was probably unfashionable by then even in Evansville.

"There she is!" Rep had shouted in a paroxysm of excited joy as he broke his aunt's normally Houdini-proof grip. "There's mommy!"

And he'd pelted down the sidewalk, yelling "Mommy!" at the top of his lungs, drawing stares from other pedestrians but, curiously, no reaction from the woman he was yelling at.

His aunt, even in high heels, had caught him just as he overtook the woman and rounded to look her in the face. He saw the woman's startled glare just as his aunt grabbed his bicep and swung him off the ground. Before his feet hit pavement again he was already blubbering, not in anticipation of the physical punishment that he assumed would promptly sanction his insubordination, but in despair; for the woman's face bore not the slightest resemblance to the features in the soft-focus, five-by-seven gold-framed print at the back of his father's top dresser drawer.

The brisk, blistering swats that he feared hadn't come. Breaking sharply with Hoosier conventions to which she ordinarily conformed, his aunt had instead gathered Rep's sobbing, shaking frame into her arms, patting his back, stroking the hot tears from his cheek with the backs of her fingers, kissing his hair, and murmuring words of comfort along with the now superfluous assurance that, "That lady isn't your mommy, dear."

It happened sporadically after that, sometimes twice in a month and until late in his teens never less than once a year. It would always be a woman he saw from a distance, from behind. Always a woman with some incidental feature that reminded him of the head and shoulders and face inside that small gold frame. Even at ten or twelve, though more discreetly by then, he would walk away from a taco or a slice of mall pizza or a discussion of Larry Bird's prowess and follow women, get fifteen feet or so ahead of them, turn to look at their faces— and then feel his guts shrivel.

He had realized by then that the photo would scarcely help him know what his mother looked like now. Still, he clung to the black-and-white image because that was all he had. Visual memory apparently didn't work very efficiently when you were fifteen months old. At least his hadn't. Fifteen months was Rep's age the last time he'd seen his mother, and his own memory didn't provide the first particle of recollection about her.

Or of much else. He didn't remember the men or the strange woman coming to their home in 1971. He remembered a vague, undefined sense of something missing, but he couldn't recall when he'd first begun to feel it. He remembered understanding, at three or so, that he was living with his aunt, and that this was different from the way his playmates lived. He remembered his father telling him, in between endless sales trips in the black Buick Electra station wagon with the faux wood trim, that his mother had had to go away and he wasn't sure when she'd be able to come back.

And he remembered not knowing. What had happened? Where had his mother gone? Why? No one would tell him. They finessed his questions, stonewalled him, played dumb, until he'd finally stopped asking. The only thing he'd known— and he'd known this only because of delicate calligraphy on the back of that picture—was that on at least one day in her life his mother had been in Enid, Oklahoma.

In his mid-teens he'd entertained the traumatizing hypothesis that his mother had left his father for someone else. This was logically plausible but psychologically unsatisfactory, and he'd not only rejected it but punched out a chess club teammate (one of the few smaller than Rep, fortunately) who had dared to suggest that the theory might be tenable. The best he could do by way of alternative was a fantasy involving a secret mission to South Vietnam, which he didn't really believe but had gotten him through some rough nights. He had taken this fantasy to the point of seriously considering—

at five-seven and one hundred forty-four pounds—enlisting in the Marine Corps.

He had enrolled at the University of Oklahoma instead, to the consternation of relatives (his father was dead by then) who insisted that he could certainly have won admission to Indiana or Purdue. He had gotten the only two C's he received in his entire academic career during his second semester at OU, because that was when he did the leg-work required to find out what had happened to his mother (most of it, luckily enough for his grade point average, having happened in Oklahoma).

Eight months before her marriage to his father, twelve months before Rep was born, and two-plus years before the men and the strange woman had come to the door, Jeannine Starkey had driven a sky blue, 1962 Ford Falcon onto the dusty, beaten earth parking lot of a dry goods store about forty-five miles from Stillwater. A man named Luck Daniels had gotten out of the car and walked over to a Chevy pickup truck to talk with two men about selling them military grade fulminate of mercury, which he understood they planned to use to stop the war in Vietnam and end capitalist exploitation of third-world countries by blowing up the ROTC building at the University of Arkansas in Fayetteville.

Negotiations had not gone smoothly, mainly because the ersatz radicals in the pickup truck were plainclothes members of the Oklahoma Highway Patrol. When the Falcon peeled off less than a minute later with Daniels barely back inside, one of the cops was dead and one was wounded. Three minutes after that every law enforcement officer in five states was on the lookout for a sky blue Ford Falcon.

When Texas Rangers spotted it the next day, Starkey was no longer inside. She had gotten as far as a stand of scrub pine near the Texas border where, after four uncomfortable hours in a rancid, improvised sleeping bag, she had awakened to find herself alone with the Falcon gone and a note next to her. The note said, "Tell im yure kidnap'd. Blame me. Sory. Luck."

There was an informal nationwide moratorium on death sentences in 1971 because the United States Supreme Court was getting ready to make the death penalty briefly unconstitutional. Luck Daniels was a cop-killer, though, so that was pretty much a technicality. The Rangers had fired sixteen shots at him and thirteen had hit him, partly because of superior marksmanship and partly because they'd pumped the last four into the dying man's belly from three feet away.

Daniels' bullet-riddled demise wasn't the end of it by a long chalk, though. Not with a dead trooper and Starkey's fingerprints all over the Falcon's steering wheel and dashboard. Not to mention the note, which the precious idiot had left intact in the scrub pine when she'd hiked off in search of a ride to hitch.

She'd gotten her ride from a thirty-two year old traveling cleanser salesman named Thomas Reppert Pennyworth, who was very happy because he'd just been promoted to a territory in northern Kentucky near Indiana, where he had family. Whatever worldliness he possessed after more than ten years on the road had proven unequal to Starkey's animal sexuality. It had taken Oklahoma two years and three months, but they'd tracked down Jeannine Pennyworth (as by then she was), convicted her of murder, and (Oklahoma being somewhat delicate about running twenty thousand volts through women even if the Supreme Court would have let it) sentenced her to life in prison.

And so Rep knew. Knowing, he understood the evasions and the stonewalling. He imputed to motives of noble self-sacrifice the passage of nearly two decades without so much as a pencil scratch from Jeannine to the boy she'd carried in her womb for nine months and then nursed for twelve and nurtured until the knock on her door.

Still, he'd had to find her. Had to see her real face, hear her actual voice. Had to bar forever those fraudulent teases from his pitiless subconscious. He had burrowed even deeper into the public records of the State of Oklahoma's Department of Corrections, tracing in laconic, bureaucratic entries the course his mother's life had followed from the moment she'd left an Oklahoma City courtroom in handcuffs and leg-irons.

She had gone to the Women's Penitentiary in Norman. She had, over nine years, apparently done her best to violate every prison regulation she could, earning administrative punishment for everything from smoking without permission to insubordination to brawling. When not in disciplinary detention she had worked as a field hand, a laundress, and a highway maintenance crewmember. She had, somehow, sat still for enough classes (or maybe just been inherently smart enough) to earn her GED. She had applied for parole after seven years, which was denied after a parole board deliberation that had lasted about twelve seconds.

Then, after nine years of hard time, she had escaped. Walked away from a work detail and never been seen again by any Oklahoma civil servant conscientious enough to write it down.

Escaped? Rep had almost bleated when he'd found the entry. *A cop killer (as far as the law was concerned)? A criminal not savvy enough to destroy the most incriminating piece of evidence against her walks off a work detail and disappears without a trace?*

It could happen, he supposed. One of the things criminals learn in prison is how to be better criminals. No *America's Most Wanted* in the first years of the eighties. Not many computers. In her early thirties, even after almost a decade in the slammer, maybe she'd still had enough sexual charisma to seduce a recent parolee or a guard or a dumb farm boy into risking his (or her) life for a thrill or two.

But Rep knew that there was another possibility. It happened, brother, oh you better believe it happened. Look up *Cummins Prison Farm* in the *Readers Guide to Periodic Literature* if you don't believe it. Not from the twenties or the thirties, either, but the early sixties. Lip off once too often to the wrong guard. Catch that lead-weighted baton a little too hard or a few times too many in the wrong place. Die from internal bleeding or from having your brain turned to jelly and go into a quickly dug grave in one of the fields those field hands hoed, with *Escaped* covering the whole thing in the official records.

And so he still didn't know. Not for sure. He understood, all right. Understood why he was the way he was, why he shunned drama and embraced dull, normal, regular, predictable, unthreatening routine. Understood why he'd spent most of his conscious life seeking the approval of aunts, teachers, den mothers, girl friends, Melissa, and most other females, especially if they were older than he was. He understood, but he didn't know, and understanding made not knowing worse.

By the time he heard Steve Finneman's voice, Rep had finished his sandwich but he hadn't tasted a bite of it.

"This is an unusual culinary choice for you, isn't it, Rep?" Finneman asked as he sat down next to him. "I thought you usually ate someplace where it's air conditioned and you can get four different kinds of cheese with a six-dollar hamburger while you read the *New York Review of Books*."

"Variety, I guess," Rep said. "Wanted some sunshine, I suppose."

Finneman was pushing seventy, and had bristly hairs in his ears and coke-bottle horn-rimmed glasses and veined hands and a mottled, well-seamed face to prove it. He was six-two and still carried enough bulk to remind Rep that he'd played tackle way back when for a school in one of those states where in fall you can see nothing but wheat from your tractor's hood ornament to the horizon. Like the Japanese emperor under the shoguns, Finneman's absolute authority over the firm depended on his never, or almost never, using it. The two main things Rep knew about him were that he'd won the only case the firm had ever gotten to the United States Supreme Court, and he regarded similes as the essential form of legal argument.

"How's the plagiarism claim for Taylor Buchanan's girl going?"

"Okay so far. Still pretty preliminary. Gathering facts."

"Every case is different, of course," Finneman mused, "but I generally like to have my facts pretty much gathered before I write a demand letter. Chip seems to think you've written one in this case."

"It's more a first-shot-across-the-bow letter," Rep said. "Trying to open a dialogue. I sent him a copy. You too."

"I can't wait to read it. Charlotte was in the office late this morning to see one of the tax guys, and she was high as a kite, talking about how great that letter was."

"I'm glad she's pleased, but there's a long way to go."

"I thought there might be. Getting a client high as a kite when there's still a long way to go can turn into a problem later on."

"I take your point," Rep said respectfully.

"Taylor said something about a trip you took with the girl to New York this week," Finneman said.

"We both went to New York on the same day and had a meeting there," Rep said, not sure why he should be defending himself after apparently satisfying the client. "We didn't go together."

"Well now, I'd call that a distinction worth noting. Here's the thing, though. Chip isn't the firm's most secure lawyer, if you know what I mean. These M and A guys are like that. If we litigators lose a case, that just means we make some more money appealing the judgment. But if those transactional boys have one or two deals they've been counting on crater, all of a sudden they've lost a client and eight hundred billable hours overnight."

"Ah," Rep said with vast relief as the light dawned. "I should've told Chip about the trip to New York before I took it. I'll fill him in up front from now on."

"I'm glad you thought of that, Rep," Finneman said.

"There are some aspects of this case that might get a little delicate, depending on how things develop," Rep said.

"Another good reason to have Chip in the loop."

"There may be some things Chip won't be able to help me with, and would rather not know."

"I can see that," Finneman said in a familiar, almost sleepy voice that told Rep he'd grasped the essential subtext of Rep's comment. "In some cases you have issues come up that are kind of like this Civil War monument we're sitting on. The reason some of those gents are carved in stone behind us is that they locked up the pro-slavery members of the Indiana Legislature before they could vote the wrong way. If the Union had lost, they'd have been carved in the flesh."

"Words to live by," Rep said.

⸙ ⸙ ⸙

Rep got back to his office a bit late, so he was surprised when the cheerful, recorded voice told him that there was only one message waiting on his voice-mail. He played it, hoping he'd hear from the inside counsel at Cremona Pizza.

"This is Aaron Eastman," the message said instead. "I got your letter. First of all, thanks for not leaving a horse's head in my bed. Second, I'm in the Midwest tomorrow scouting locations and props for my next movie. If you're serious enough about this claim to blow off the whole day on practically no notice, meet me at the Air National Guard sector of the Indianapolis Airport at six-thirty in the morning."

That tore it. This was definitely not your typical, sturdy, four-square Midwestern copyright case. Things were moving very fast. Rep wasn't ready to spill the whole story to Arundel yet, but Finneman needed to see the hold-your-tongue package. Rep hurried down to the lounge to retrieve it from the freezer.

It was gone.

Chapter 7

"Admit it, this isn't what you expected," Aaron Eastman said.

"This isn't what I expected," Rep yelled.

He yelled because he was overcompensating for the roar of four throbbing engines that spun propellers outside windows to his left and right. He agreed because Eastman was right.

To start with, Eastman himself wasn't what Rep had expected. Thoughtlessly swallowing sitcom stereotypes, Rep had pictured the producer as short, bald, equipped with a cigar, and sporting a Rodeo Drive silk shirt open to the navel to show a gold medallion against graying chest hair. Instead, the man he'd met at the airport nudged six feet, wore his ample, light brown hair in an unpretentious but (Rep suspected) very expensive brush cut, and was dressed like a young CEO on casual day.

More to Eastman's point, Rep had expected to find Eastman waiting beside a Lear Jet or some equivalent aeronautic symbol of coastal opulence. The craft that Eastman had actually invited Rep to board was much older and much slower: a fully functional, World War II-era B-24 four-engine bomber, straight out of *Twelve O'Clock High*. The plane took off, to Rep's unconcealed consternation, with Eastman himself at the controls.

The vintage warbird showed every sign of loving restoration, but no concessions to spoiled modernity compromised its authenticity. Though Rep and Eastman were seated less than six feet from each other, for example, they were talking over throat mikes, because the cabin wasn't pressurized and they'd donned oxygen masks around two miles up. Even the pilot—the real one, who'd taken over at ten thousand feet—looked as if he'd just stepped out of a ready room. Rep felt that he ought to be seeing the man in black-and-white, the way he remembered World War II pilots before Ted Turner colorized their exploits.

The doughy-faced twenty-something sitting in the navigator's seat, on the other hand, struck Rep as stereotypically left coast and post-war. Eastman had introduced him as "Jerry Selding, production assistant and entourage *du jour.*"

"That takeoff was impressive," Rep said.

"Just showing off," Eastman said. "Bad habit. I had thirty hours logged on this boat before I even started thinking about *Every Sixteen Minutes.* And remember, these babies were designed to be flown through flak by ninety-day wonders, so it's not that big a trick."

"That's reassuring," Rep said. "But about six hundred feet down the runway I thought we might test Hemingway's theory about courage being grace under pressure."

"I'll tell you something no one ever mentions when they quote that line," Eastman said. "Our boy Ernie had a major thing about his mother—and guess what mom's name was? Grace. How's that for a creepy mental image?"

"Interesting," Rep said—albeit, not quite as interesting as being thirty thousand feet over Lake Michigan in a plane pushing sixty years old.

"I brought something for you," Eastman said, reaching awkwardly behind his back to tender a clutch of photocopied pages. "That's the product placement deal with Philip Morris for *In Contemplation of Death.* Signed it three months before principal photography started. Fifty thousand dollars, on the condition that the female lead spend at least twenty-four on-screen seconds smoking Marlboro Lights, with the pack 'conspicuously displayed.'"

"Good advertising for them and easy money for you," Rep commented.

"Not so easy as all that. You should've seen the attitude Shevaun Waltrip copped about it. Brat had her own condo at the Betty Ford Clinic before she was eighteen, but from the way she whined you would've thought puffing a cigarette was the next thing to mainlining horse. Anyway, that's why the lead character in that movie smokes. It was the fifty thousand bucks, not because we stole the idea of having a heroine with bad habits from your client."

"That doesn't come as a complete surprise," Rep said.

He knew this comment was tactically obtuse, but he couldn't stop himself from saying it. He suddenly wanted to seem worldly and with it. He was trying hard not to be blown away by Eastman and the B-24 and the Hollywood-confidential stuff. He suspected that bowling him over with this kind of just-between-us-insiders routine was exactly what Eastman was up to, and knew he had to resist it. The thing was, he couldn't help liking Eastman, who came across as less phony and more down-to-earth than half the partners at Rep's firm, and who could talk knowledgeably about flying four-propeller bombers in one breath and offer articulate literary banter in the next. And dammit, the B-24 was impressive.

"I'm not going to tell you your claim is a crock," Eastman said. "I gave you that product placement agreement to show you I'm on the level. I know Point West could be liable for what a lot of other people did, but I want you to start with at least the possibility that I personally am playing straight with you. Because we have some things to talk about."

"What do we have to talk about?" Rep asked.

"First thing you have to understand is, and I think you probably know this, I can't just throw a hundred thousand at your client to make this thing go away. Even if it would cost me six times that to defend it. One nuisance-value settlement and I'll have frustrated writers coming out of the woodwork, accusing me of ripping off every unsuccessful novel, short story, poem, and grocery list written in the last twenty years."

"Well," Rep said judiciously, "I don't think nuisance value is what Charlotte Buchanan has in mind."

"I believe you," Eastman said. "But suppose you weren't a solid, steady IP lawyer with a good firm—which I dug up from Martindale-Hubbel myself instead of paying a lawyer four hundred bucks an hour to dig it up for me. Suppose instead you were a typical plaintiff's lawyer, a bottom-feeding legal gunslinger taking your client for a ride on the cheap and planning down the road to sell her a settlement based on something out of Point West's petty cash box. Wouldn't you have said exactly the same thing?"

"I suppose so," Rep admitted. "But I probably would have said it with biting indignation and in a highly mortified tone, instead of dryly and concisely."

"Which brings me to the second reason we're having this meeting. Namely, to see if we can find a way to stop this trainwreck before it happens."

"I'm game," Rep said.

Swiveling in his co-pilot's seat, Eastman looked steadily at Rep. For two or three seconds, Rep felt the cool, gray eyes visible over Eastman's oxygen mask appraising him. Then, Eastman snapped his head toward the starboard window. Rep's eyes followed the gesture. Through thick glass designed to stop chunks of metal flying at lethal speeds, he saw a section of olive drab wing bouncing gingerly as if an unseen high diver were poised on its far end; saw the humps of the starboard engines; saw the wing and engines gilded by brilliant sunshine above, set off against blindingly white clouds below them; and sensed, rather than saw, the whir of two propellers whose mind-numbing lacerations of air almost six miles from earth was the only thing keeping them alive.

"Look at the *visual* there," Eastman instructed him.

"I see the power," Rep said in a good-student-trying-to-be-helpful voice.

"That's exactly right, you *see* the power," Eastman said. "People think movies are stories on film. Baloney. Mediocre Trollope is a better *story* than any movie ever made, including *Citizen Kane*. Stories in Hollywood are like cameras. You have to have them to make a movie, but they're not the point. Do you know what movies are?"

Rep figured by now that he didn't have the first idea, and if he had he wouldn't have dared express it until they were safely on the ground. He responded with a dignified negative.

"Movies are what paintings were before jet lag. Representational painting turned to dreck in nineteen-oh-three, at Kitty Hawk, North Carolina. Painting is about passion, passion is about people, and something standing still can't capture the *passion* of people who experience life at hundreds of miles an hour. Movies are passion dynamically captured. Movies aren't about telling, they're about feeling."

"Okay," Rep said. It occurred to him that this response lacked a little something, so he took refuge in what he hoped was an intelligent question. "What's the passion you're going to capture with those propellers?"

"The territorial imperative," Eastman answered. "Berlin airlift. Real beginning of the Cold War. Nineteen forty-seven. Russians blockade the city. Truman says, one, we stay in Berlin. Two, we will supply Berlin by air, like a besieged garrison."

"I saw a movie about that on television once," Rep offered brightly. "*The Big Lift*."

"You know what was wrong with that movie?"

"No," Rep said—superfluously, because Eastman was already answering his own question.

"They made the story the point. American airman in love with a fraulein but bitter because the Nazis were mean to him while he was a POW. Please."

"I see your point," said Rep, who didn't.

"The Berlin airlift was B-24s landing at Templehof Airport every sixteen minutes around the clock for months," Eastman said. "That had nothing to do with loving your enemies. That was about an ape four hundred thousand years ago pissing on sixty trees so all the other apes would know where not to come if they didn't want to fight. It wasn't some chick-flick muck about two women crying in a dark room. It was about defining territory, which is real important, because only the apes that defined their territory and made it stick lived long enough to have little apes—namely, us."

"Uh huh," Rep said.

"So I don't steal stories," Eastman said. "I don't care enough about stories to steal them. I probably paid the guy who did the first script for *In Contemplation of Death* twenty thousand more than I had to just because I couldn't be bothered to call his agent and string the negotiations out for two more days. Stories are just a detail to me, some guy punching keys."

Rep's response to this would have fallen short even of "uh huh" on the banality scale, but he didn't have to give one. The plane had started its descent somewhere around "we stay in Berlin," and a city had appeared on the lakeshore below them.

"Milwaukee," Eastman said, pointing at the modest industrial city. "Flying into General Billy Mitchell Field. Has to be the only airport in the country named after a military pilot who was court-martialed."

"Is Milwaukee the home front setting for *Every Sixteen Minutes?*" Rep asked.

"No. We're not scouting Milwaukee today, we're scouting Berlin. I'll explain while we're driving around. You have to see it while we talk or it won't make any sense. Meanwhile, tell me what your client needs. Not what your client wants. What your client needs. Then we'll see what we can do."

Rep had to think about the question for a few seconds. Without phrasing it quite the way Eastman had, Rep himself had been struggling with that issue ever since he'd gotten Charlotte Buchanan's case.

"What my client really needs is respect," Rep said finally. "She wrote a novel all by herself. She got it published. She woke up every morning wondering if she was famous yet. She wasn't. Her book sold fewer copies than *The Economic Report of the President*—even though it was slightly better written."

"I know it had to be a decent book," Eastman said. "More than decent, pretty darn good. Because otherwise she wouldn't have gotten an agent like Julia Deltrediche to rep it. But what you're really saying is that life ripped her off, and she can't sue life so she's using me instead."

"We're talking about what she needs," Rep said. "What she needs is to know that she isn't the only one in the world who thinks that what she did is worthwhile."

"You're not going to believe this," Eastman said thoughtfully as the B-24 jolted onto a runway in a remote corner of General Mitchell Field, "but I know exactly how she feels."

"I do believe it," Rep said. "Last night I rented *Red Guard!* on video and watched it with my wife. That was your *Titanic*, and people today should be talking about it in the same breath as *Spartacus* and *Ben Hur*. But when it came out it just seemed to slip under the radar somehow. It didn't make anything like the splash it should have."

"They should have called the video version *Aaron Gets the Shaft*," Eastman said. "Not that I'm bitter. Not much. First, Galaxy Entertainment Group spread rumors that I'd lost control of expenses and this was going to make people forget *Heaven's Gate* and *Waterworld*, even though *Red Guard!* was the first film that studio had released in ten years that was on time and on budget. Then they bumped the release from Thanksgiving weekend in ninety-five to Valentine's weekend in ninety-six, so that it not only came out with no holiday-weekend bounce, but it hit screens in a year with the strongest Oscar competition anyone can remember instead of the mediocrities that were up the year before. And on top of that the release date change meant *Red Guard!* was already old news by the time the ninety-six nomination ballots went out. There's more, but we'll have to let it go at that, which believe me is good news for you. It looks like the mayor's office has some fancy wheels waiting for us."

Before Rep had his oxygen mask off, Selding was out of his seat, helping Rep with his briefcase and laptop. A scant quarter-hour later Eastman was driving Rep in a jade green Dodge Viper west on Wisconsin Avenue in downtown Milwaukee. After schlepping Rep's bags and making sure that the Viper had come equipped with the sackful of Sausage McMuffins he'd ordered for Eastman, Selding had driven off in a Taurus with an aide to the mayor of Milwaukee to chat about the details of major film shoots in a city where that isn't an everyday occurrence. The jump from General Mitchell Field to Milwaukee's central business district isn't long, but Rep figured it probably took most people more than the eight minutes Eastman and the Viper required for the task.

"Don't let me hog the McCalories," Eastman said as he disposed of his third Sausage McMuffin. "It's been breakfast time on my biological clock for half an hour, but some of those are for you."

"No thanks," Rep said. The greasy thumbprint that Eastman had left on the rear-view mirror when he adjusted it looked like a week's supply of cholesterol all by itself.

"Look at that!" Eastman shouted suddenly. He wrenched the car into an improvised parking space on a side street and jumped out with a digital camera.

Rep looked. He'd been on a case in Milwaukee his first year with the firm, so he knew he was seeing the federal courthouse. Gray stone, elegant arches sheltering the porch, round towers framing the front, gothic spires along the sides. It struck Rep as lightyears better than the steel-and-glass box approach to federal courthouses that prevailed these days. It also looked pretty German. But it didn't exactly set Rep's pulse racing.

Eastman had shots of the building from four different angles before Rep managed to climb out of the car and catch up to him.

"Now I know how Emma Thompson felt the first time she saw Chatsworth while she was planning *Pride and Prejudice*," Eastman said when Rep panted into his general vicinity. "And look at *that!*"

He wheeled and pointed to a red brick building on the north side of Wisconsin Avenue. Rep would learn later that it housed the Milwaukee Club. Like the courthouse, it was noticeably Teutonic, though in a less monumental sort of way. The realization of what Eastman was up to crept slowly into Rep's brain, which was hard-wired to interpret undertakings that weren't quite so insane as Eastman's apparently was.

"Were you being literal up there on the plane? Are you seriously planning on having Milwaukee, Wisconsin stand in for late forties Berlin?" Rep asked this on the run, scurrying to keep up with Eastman, who was off to photograph the Milwaukee Club.

"Milwaukee, plus two days of second-unit shooting in Berlin itself, plus Industrial Light and Magic," Eastman said. "I can have six guys in Ike jackets and campaign hats walk down the steps of that courthouse, zoom in for a close-up that'll make you think you could reach out and touch the stone, and then when the camera pulls back for a long shot you'll see the building surrounded by bombed out rubble. I'm going to make an epic with a bankable cast, and I'm going to do it for under fifty million dollars. Because if Hollywood has a future, that's it. We can't go on making movies with nothing but bright orange fireballs and flying cows and famous buildings blowing up so that people who don't speak English will pay to see them. Guys in India and Italy and Canada can do that as well as we can, and for a lot less money. And we can't spend a hundred fifty million dollars making classic Hollywood productions when four out of five of them flop. We have to make fifty-million-dollar movies that look like they cost three times as much, and I'm going to show them how it's done."

Eastman led Rep back to the Viper only long enough to stow it in the parking ramp of the Pfister Hotel, down a block and across the street from the federal courthouse. Then they started walking.

Rep would estimate later that they walked six miles in the next three hours. When they finally got back to the Pfister, Eastman had snapshots of the Northwestern Mutual Life Insurance Company's headquarters, with its row of Ionic columns that would have dwarfed the Parthenon; the east façade of the Milwaukee County Courthouse, which could have stood in for some of the sets in *Triumph of the Will*; the Bockl Building; the Germania Building; Turner Hall; the Mackie Building, all white stone and improbable cupolas; the Mitchell Building, which wouldn't have looked out of place a hundred yards from the Brandenburg Gate; Mader's Restaurant, with acres of beer-hall gingerbread; and Milwaukee City Hall, which looked as if it had been transplanted brick by brick from Munich.

Along the way they talked about how to settle Charlotte Buchanan's case. An eavesdropping outsider, Rep thought, would probably have found their meandering discussion desultory and inconclusive. Rep, though, had an odd sense that they were making a kind of oblique and indefinable progress.

"I don't know," Eastman mused toward the end of their ramble, "you think she'd go for Guild arbitration? Bullet-proof confidentiality agreement, no transcript and no appeal? Even if she lost it'd be a kind of respect."

"I don't like our chances if the arbitrators are members of the Screenwriters Guild, since they couldn't help thinking about the next time they might have a shot at working for you. Maybe we could look at using Guild rules and standards with a neutral panel. But we'd still have to have some discovery."

"Boxcar discovery would be a problem. Might be able to work something out, though. Tell you what. Do you think she'd be willing to just talk to me? See if we can get on the same wave-length?"

"I'll ask her," Rep said.

They were tramping by now through the dark recesses of level 5 of the hotel's parking ramp, approaching the Viper. Eastman clicked the locks up from ten feet away, and Rep quickened his steps until he gratefully sank aching legs and weary muscles into the front passenger seat.

He was comfortable for just about one full second. Then he saw something that had him sitting up tensely. Eastman must have seen the same thing because he reacted at the same moment.

"Get out!" he barked.

Rep got out. In a hurry. So did Eastman.

Rep's neural reflexes had gotten well ahead of his logical processes, so it took him a couple of seconds to understand what he'd noticed and why it had spooked him. The trigger was a spotless rear-view mirror, without the greasy thumb-smudge Eastman had left on the way downtown. No smudge meant someone had wiped it clean after Rep and Eastman had left the car. Someone wiping the mirror clean probably meant someone worried about fingerprints—*ergo*, someone who'd been doing something inside the car that he (or she) didn't want anyone else to find out about later on.

"Bomb, you think?" Rep asked as Eastman joined him about eight feet behind the car. He was astonished at the casual way he asked this chillingly plausible question. He shouldn't have been feeling calm. He should have been struggling to control his bladder.

"Doubt it," Eastman muttered. "Too public a place, and they wouldn't have known how much time they'd have."

"What, then?"

"I have a pretty good idea. Let's see if I'm right."

Striding decisively forward, Eastman swung the trunk lid up. He searched the inside of the trunk methodically, then lifted the pad on the bottom and probed at length through the spare tire well and the tire itself. After a good ten minutes, he came out empty-handed, and slammed the trunk lid disgustedly.

He stepped around to the passenger door that Rep had left open. Frowning with concentration, he thrust his fingers deeply between the back and seat cushions, then under the seat. He shook his head.

Now he opened the glove compartment. He fingered the maps and the owner's manual and the registration. Then, triumphantly, he beamed and pulled himself from the car's interior. He was holding a small, brown envelope, perhaps one and a half inches by four.

"What's that?" Rep asked.

"About enough happy dust for two good lines, unless I miss my guess," Eastman said. "Under the circumstances, though, I don't think we'll bother with a chemical analysis." He sprinkled white powder on the pavement in a space three cars away. He tore the envelope into tiny fragments and flung them toward the wall.

"I think we can go now," he told Rep.

Rep acquiesced, even though he found scant comfort in Eastman's joining him in the Reasonably Respectable People Who've Recently Destroyed Criminal Evidence Club. He didn't have any better ideas, and even if he had he was too busy trying to sort things out to argue. *Was Charlotte Buchanan that nuts? Was this part of the same amateur campaign as the hold-your-tongue nonsense? If not, how had a couple of thousand dollars' worth of cocaine found its way in the last three hours into a car provided by the Milwaukee mayor's office? If so, how had she managed all this cloak and dagger stuff, breaking into a locked car and cleaning up fingerprints when she was through? Did Eastman suspect Buchanan? Did he have any idea that Rep suspected her?*

Rep was still thinking when they pulled out of the ramp onto Mason Street, turned right onto Jefferson, and headed back toward Wisconsin Avenue.

"I think if we take a left on Michigan we can pick up a freeway along the lakefront that'll basically take us right to the airport's back door," Eastman said. Rep nodded.

They had just crossed Wisconsin and, even with Eastman at the wheel, hadn't yet hit thirty miles an hour when Rep noticed the flashing red and blue lights. A motorcycle cop was pulling them over. Conscious though he was of perfect innocence, Rep felt an icy tremor in his gut. Looking through the windshield, he noticed another motorcycle cop waiting at the Jefferson/Michigan intersection, and saw what he would have bet was an unmarked car pulled up on the opposite side of the street.

"Duh, what a bore," Eastman said to himself, popping the leather-wrapped steering wheel impatiently with the heel of his right hand. "On the other hand, this may have a perverse entertainment value."

He had his driver's license and the Temporary Car Loan form supplied by the mayor's office ready by the time the cop reached the driver-side window. The policeman examined them gravely for a very long thirty seconds.

"May I see the registration, also, sir?" the officer asked then.

"I'm not sure we have one. The car's a loaner, just for the day."

"Yes, sir," the cop said. "Would you mind just opening the glove compartment and seeing if there's a vehicle registration in there?"

"Of course, officer."

Eastman opened the glove compartment. He had barely begun to finger the documents inside when the cop brusquely intervened.

"Excuse me, sir, would you mind if I looked through the glove compartment myself?"

Only in the most technical sense was this a question. Everything in the cop's tone, clipped delivery, and body language made it an order.

"Why no, officer, I have no objection whatever to your looking through the glove compartment yourself. You have my knowing, intelligent, complete, and unqualified consent to do so."

The cop frowned at this, his expression suggesting for the first time that he wasn't sure he was still in control of the encounter. He recovered quickly.

"Would you gentlemen please step out of the car?"

Rep and Eastman obeyed. Rep noticed that they were picking up unabashed stares from most of the pedestrians in the vicinity. Rousts apparently weren't all that common in this part of downtown Milwaukee.

The cop slipped into the driver's seat, leaned across to rest his right elbow on the passenger seat, and spent what seemed like five solid minutes searching every atom of space in the glove compartment. His expression when he pulled himself back out of the car suggested a constipated elephant just after *coitus interruptus*.

"Thank you, sir," he said to Eastman. "The, uh, reason you were stopped was an illegal lane change back there the other side of Wisconsin Avenue. Since you're a visitor to our city, we'll just let it go with a warning. Enjoy the rest of your stay in Milwaukee, and please drive carefully."

The motorcycle seemed to belch angrily as the officer made a u-turn and sped away. Rep and Eastman slipped back into the car.

"We were set up," Rep said.

"I was set up," Eastman corrected him as he made a thoroughly signaled swerve into the driving lane. "Someone planted sky-powder in the car and then dropped a dime on me."

"Well Hemingway would've been proud of you. Your performance epitomized grace under pressure. Without your consent, by the way, that was a completely illegal search."

"In the legal textbooks, maybe," Eastman said. "Not in court. After the first three times they have a film held up because a star gets busted for possession, producers become experts on criminal procedure. If I hadn't consented, he would've held us up 'til one of his buddies had a chance to fetch a warrant, or maybe he would've found some excuse to make a custodial arrest so he could search the car without a warrant."

"His buddy couldn't have gotten a warrant."

"Sure he could. The cop busting our chops would have made a prearranged signal that supposedly meant he'd seen traces of something suspicious when I opened the glove compartment, and one of his pals would've run to a tame judge."

"But there wasn't anything suspicious for him to see," Rep protested.

"Right. But none of this folderol would matter unless there had been. I don't care what you learned your first year in law school. On the streets, the real rule about search and seizure is, if you find something, the search was legal—at least 'til you get to the court of appeals; and if you don't find anything, who cares?"

They had by now made their way to an almost empty freeway. Eastman was cruising along at precisely the posted speed limit.

"I'm thinking this isn't the first time this kind of thing has happened to you," Rep said.

"You can't make movies without making enemies."

"Did you make any enemies with *Red Guard!*?"

"Must have." Eastman shot Rep a quick, sly look. "After all, I made at least one with *In Contemplation of Death*, didn't I?"

"If you did, I apparently made the same one."

"Whatever," Eastman said jovially as he pulled a computer disk from his shirt pocket and handed it to Rep. "Tell you what, I'll make you her hero by the time you see home again. Here's something to keep you company on the plane ride back to Indianapolis. That has the twelve official drafts of the script for ICOD, as we called *In Contemplation of Death*. In chronological order, with completion dates."

"Message: You have nothing to hide and you want to do the right thing."

"Right," Eastman said. "Look. You and I know I could've bought your client's story for twenty-five thousand bucks plus two percent of the net, and since there was never going to be any net that means I would've had it for less than one-tenth of one percent of my budget. You've got my ideas about an exit strategy for this mess. Make my pitch to your girl, and let's see if we can make the clients happy for once, instead of making the lawyers rich."

"What can I tell you?" Rep said. "I'll call her."

❁ ❁ ❁

And he did. The moment he could reach a pay-phone in Indianapolis, he dialed Charlotte Buchanan's home number. He got her answering machine and left a message. Then, impulsively, anxious for her approval, he dialed her office number at Tavistock.

"Ms. Buchanan isn't in," an efficient voice told him. "May I take a message?"

"I've already left a message for her at another number," Rep said. "Do you expect her in later today?"

"No," the secretary said. "Actually, she's visiting our facility in Kohler today and isn't expected back here until tomorrow afternoon."

"Kohler," Rep said lamely after an uncomfortable pause. "As in, Kohler, Wisconsin."

"That's right."

"Which is within driving distance of Milwaukee, isn't it?"

"About an hour away," the secretary confirmed.

"Right," Rep said, more to himself than to her. "No message."

He limply hung up the phone. His shoulders drooped as he walked to his car.

Chapter 8

"Hey," Melissa said delightedly at 4:25, "you're home early."

"I didn't even stop by the office to check messages," Rep said. "I had nine-point-four billable hours in by three-forty-five this afternoon. I was afraid if I worked any more today my pension might suddenly kick in and mess up all our tax planning."

"Somehow you don't seem as, I don't know, *buoyant* as I'd expect from a guy who had nine-point-four billable hours booked and was still home in time to spend an extra one-point-five non-billable hours with me."

"I'm a little preoccupied. There were some developments today."

"Spill," Melissa said, making sure that he caught the glint in her eyes.

"I'm really not supposed to."

"Pretty please?" She added her impish smile to the mischievous glint.

He spilled.

"So," he concluded, "now the fat's in the fire for sure. I have to write a memo explaining this whole thing without making myself look like too much of an idiot."

"Why?"

"So the firm can disengage itself from this case."

"Again, why? Because the nice man gave you a plane ride and therefore no one who works for him could be a plagiarist?"

"No," Rep said. "Because we can't press a claim for Charlotte Buchanan while at the same time suggesting to her father that she needs professional help before she literally takes a shot at Aaron Eastman."

"I don't know," Melissa said. "I think you might be jumping to conclusions."

"Nothing would make me happier than to have you talk me into believing that," Rep said. "But I don't see it. There's too much coincidence. I put the hold-your-tongue package in the freezer early yesterday morning, she's in the office late that morning, and it's gone with no explanation by mid-afternoon. Then Eastman gets set up in Milwaukee when she just happens to be within convenient driving distance. The hold-your-tongue thing maybe you could pass off as a bad joke. This stunt today, though, makes me think Charlotte is spiraling out of control."

"It's what happened today that I'm having trouble with," Melissa said. "Charlotte could've done the childish threat with the string and the meat. But today someone tried to frame a guy for possession of cocaine."

"Right. I've seen the look in Charlotte Buchanan's eyes when she gets worked up about this and, believe me, she's more than capable of it."

"Psychologically capable, maybe, but how about nuts and bolts?" Melissa asked. "I suppose it's not that much of a trick to buy cocaine, even in Indianapolis, and anyone would know about wiping fingerprints off. But how did she follow you without being noticed? If she didn't do that, how did she know where the car would be? How did she know you and Eastman were going to be in Milwaukee, for that matter? And how did she finesse her way into a locked car without leaving any sign that she'd forced her entry? When I was a kid you could open a car lock from the outside by fishing through the door seal with a bent coat hanger, but I don't think that trick works with any car built in the last ten years."

"I don't know how she managed it," Rep conceded. "But someone did it, and who else is there?"

"Well, let's think about that. Based on your description of today's episode, I'd say Aaron Eastman did a fairly remarkable job of keeping his cool."

"Grace under pressure personified," Rep agreed. "When I commented on it he told me stuff like this had happened to him before."

"Well, there you are. Unless Charlotte's grudge goes back longer than we think there's apparently someone else in the picture. After all, didn't that one guy who called you back say that Eastman was involved in some kind of shadowy stuff a lot more sinister than a plagiarism claim?"

"Yeah," Rep said, shrugging without enthusiasm.

"I mean, think about it," Melissa continued. "The most remarkable thing about your meeting with Eastman today was that it happened at all. Aaron Eastman must get plagiarism claims all the time. There can't be many of them that he deals with by inviting the claimant's lawyer onto a bomber for a face-to-face chat. So why did he put this elaborate move on you?"

"Maybe because he suspects there really is something to Charlotte's claim and he has to take it seriously."

"But he denied that and you thought he was being honest with you, right?"

"True," Rep admitted.

"If you're right, there has to be another reason. Maybe Eastman just wanted to size you up. Maybe there is a harassment campaign against him, and what he suspected was that Charlotte's claim itself was part of it. Maybe he wanted to brace you to get a gut feeling about whether you were in this for Charlotte or were part of a bigger machination."

Rep had the unpleasant but not unfamiliar sensation of certainty diminishing.

"If he did think that," Rep said, tracking Melissa's reasoning, "then this hypothetical other player in the background becomes more plausible."

"A lot more plausible candidate than Charlotte Buchanan for copping white powder and burglarizing late-model sports cars."

"But now we're taking coincidence to the quantum level," Rep said. "Charlotte Buchanan happens to get me involved with a guy who happens to have another enemy whose attack happens to dovetail with her attitude. What would one of your students get for a plot like that?"

"C or C-plus, depending on grammar and diction," Melissa said. "I'm an easy grader. Which is about what I would've given *And Done to Others' Harm*. The kindest thing I can say about it is that it's nothing special."

"I didn't think much of it either," Rep said.

"And that gives me even more trouble than coincidence. How did Charlotte get an agent like Julia Deltrediche to represent her?"

"Eastman said the same kind of thing," Rep admitted. "He said he knew the story was good because otherwise Deltrediche wouldn't have been handling it."

"So we have anomalies even if we make Charlotte the villain," Melissa said. "Look, I have an idea. Why don't you give me the disk that Eastman let you have and pop out for some Chinese? I'll run through the script versions and see if any brilliant insights work their way into my brain. After dinner you can join me. Put off your memo until we've done that and you've had a chance to sleep on it and maybe talk to Charlotte Buchanan about today."

Rep's nod was wearily minimal. But he handed her the disk.

⚙ ⚙ ⚙

It wasn't long after that—5:15 or so—that Chip Arundel walked into Rep's office. Rep had dutifully sent him a memo about the Eastman meeting. Such obsessive i-dotting and t-crossing might suggest simple conscientiousness to the credulous, but not to Arundel. The way he figured it, this sniveling little IP wimp was actually trying to turn a throwaway claim into a major splash. And the only possible reason for doing that would be to replace Arundel as the billing partner for Tavistock, Ltd.

Arundel poked around Rep's desk and thumbed through stacks of papers on the credenza. If there were a note, a phone message, a calendar entry, or a scrap of paper so much as hinting that more was going on between Rep and Charlotte Buchanan than Rep's desiccated little memos suggested, he intended to find it.

He came up with nothing. A bit nervous now, he checked the doorway to be sure the secretaries were gone. Then he opened Rep's desk drawers and pawed through them. Nothing but paperclips and ballpoints rewarded his efforts. He turned his attention to the cabinets underneath the credenza. He was in the midst of a fruitless quest amidst legal pads and packages of Post-Its when a noise at the door startled him. Jumping, he slammed the cabinet door. Slammed it forcefully enough to make a thick tome titled *Corbin on Contracts* tip over on the bookshelf above the credenza. He wheeled around to find himself facing the cleaning lady.

"Oh," he said. "Hi."

Nodding, the gray-haired woman emptied Rep's wastebasket and favored his desk and chair with three or four desultory whisks of a feather duster. Then she left, making exactly the same noise going out as she had coming in.

Arundel took a second to get his breathing under control. Marathon nine-figure merger negotiations were one thing, but petty burglary was more nerve-wracking than he'd bargained for. Deciding that there was no point in searching further, he lifted the fallen volume to put it back in place against the other texts on Rep's bookshelf.

As he replaced it, he noticed something stashed behind the books. Curious, he pulled it out. It was a videotape in a cardboard sleeve. The title on the label read *The Discipline Effectiveness Program.*

Arundel shrugged and put the tape back in place. He hadn't even known Rep had kids.

❀ ❀ ❀

It was after 11 p.m. when Melissa, still bent over the glowing screen of her computer, heard Rep come into the living room. She'd been going through the scripts alone, on her antique laptop. After they'd shared shrimp chow mein, Rep had explained that he had to get to something on their Dell, and that was the last she'd seen of him until now.

"I'm going to have to crash," he said apologetically. "I've been up since five, and I have to be up by six tomorrow to catch a puddle-jumper for Traverse City."

"What's in Traverse City?"

"A trademark claim for a client that has to see me between trips to Germany."

"Day trip?"

"It better be," Rep said. "If I bill time on two Saturdays in a row I'm going to get a reputation for diligence."

Melissa glanced at her watch.

"I had no idea it was so late," she said. "You go ahead. I'll be in soon."

"Did you find anything?" Rep asked.

"Pretty much variations on what we've already seen," she said. "But I noticed something funny about half an hour ago and I've been playing with it ever since. The disk says it's almost full, but the bytes for the script versions I've found on here don't add up to that much space."

"Which means there's something else on the disk that isn't listed in the directory," Rep said.

"Right. And just out of perverse curiosity I've been trying to find it. I think I'll give it another twenty minutes."

"Okay. I'll try to stay awake."

Less than ten minutes later she turned up the unlabeled file. Adrenaline racing, wondering if this could be the smoking gun that showed plain theft by Point West Productions from Charlotte Buchanan, she brought it up on the screen. She found herself reading a treatment for a movie that apparently had nothing to do with *And Done to Others' Harm* or *In Contemplation of Death*. At least she thought it was a treatment. It was clearly a pitch for a movie, intended to excite interest from studios and agents and people with money. It had the same basic elements and the same breathless style as the handful of treatments she'd read while researching popular culture.

On the other hand, she'd never seen a treatment with footnotes before. And this one had quite a bit more detail than the customary "*Basic Instinct* meets *Dumb and Dumber*" approach. Names and dates and numbingly thorough descriptions studded the text. It read like a treatment written by someone incredibly anal who was really into the story.

The story itself was a political thriller. Its working title was *Screenscam*. It involved a president of the United States who had gotten several million dollars in campaign contributions from the Red Chinese Army through an intermediary, only to find himself under investigation by a Congressional committee that seemed to be getting inside information from sources in the Chinese government. In between trysts with a zaftig intern, this president had gotten the troublesome Chinese source terminated—literally—by agreeing with Chinese communist officials to pressure a corporate entertainment conglomerate into burying a promising movie due for distribution by a studio the conglomerate owned.

The movie that got buried sounded a lot like *Red Guard!* And when all else failed, the conglomerate had completed the interment by sabotaging the Oscar prospects for its own movie. *Red Guard!* again, based on the Rep-spill she had extracted a few hours ago. Except that this went way beyond anything Eastman had told Rep, featuring sinister computer hackers, bribed mailroom workers, and black-mailed vote-counters.

No one as thoroughly steeped in deconstructionist theory as Melissa was could be easily impressed by any form of narrative fiction, but Melissa nevetheless sat back, stunned at the audacity of the plot. Reality had long since overtaken fiction on the scandal escalation front. Stealing nuclear secrets was old hat. Trading high-level security classifications for money from foreign governments wouldn't seem like a new idea to anyone who'd read the *New York Times* in the last decade or so. And chubby interns with a penchant for sucking cigars and other things now pretty much defined *cliché*.

Rigging the Oscars, though, was something else altogether. Even in scandal-fatigued *fin-de-siècle* America, no one could be blasé enough to shrug that off. Letting a foreign power dictate trade policy or human rights policy was one thing. Giving another government veto power over America's preeminent cultural icon would be like fixing the World Series. Which, come to think of it, had happened once.

At least.

And they'd made a movie about it, hadn't they?

Suppose *Screenscam* was being planned as a cinematic *roman à clef* supposedly depicting what had actually happened to *Red Guard!* ? That could maybe get happy dust planted in your glove compartment all right, at least if the wrong people thought it might actually happen.

Rep was snoring deeply when Melissa slipped into the bedroom to tell him. She decided it could wait until morning.

Then she thought again. In the morning Rep would be up super early, and Melissa might still be fast asleep. And he'd kiss her lightly on the eyelid and slip out without waking her. She wasn't going to let him spend a Friday in Traverse City, Michigan, possibly write precipitate memos or e-mails, even conceivably talk to Charlotte or Eastman, without the benefit of this juicy little tidbit she'd picked up. She went into the study to write a quick note she could Scotch tape to his laptop case, where he couldn't possibly miss it.

His legal pad was still out, lying next to the computer. In small letters in the upper right-hand corner he'd printed, "Jennifer Payne, C/land ScenePlay, Fri-Sat, Doubletree Suites on Wabash." After a few seconds of denial, she quickly grasped the possible implications. An empty spot in her diaphragm quickly gave way to blank anxiety and building anger as Melissa sank into the chair in front of the computer.

Murmuring, "No, no, no," she snapped the machine back on. Figuring out Rep's password was just a matter of time. She knew that he changed it monthly, rotating through the first names of nineteenth-century vice-presidents. DeWitt, Hannibal, and Chester drew blanks, but Adlai (for Adlai Stevenson, vice-president to Grover Cleveland) did the trick.

Rep had gotten sixteen e-mails in the less than one hour since he'd announced he was going to bed. And she couldn't help noticing (well, *she* could have helped noticing, but she didn't) that the first one was from a correspondent calling herself (or, ungrammatically, himself) Bienfessee.

Melissa wasn't going to read Rep's e-mail—the kind of e-mail that, she now began to suspect, he generally used his firm's laptop to retrieve, precisely so she wouldn't be privy to it. But if he'd spent several hours indulging himself in a childish fetish while she was wading through dreary redrafts of badly written working scripts for a second-rate movie for his benefit, she was going to be big-time honked off. And hurt. With a few mouse-clicks she called up the last five sites visited from the computer.

The list did absolutely nothing for her disposition. The Disciplinary Wives' Club. Shadow Lane. WHAP! (Women Who Administer Punishment). Sex.sociality.spanking. Christian BDSM. In many other contexts it might almost have been funny, but she wasn't laughing.

She was, instead, standing up and sweeping Rep's attaché case and legal pad furiously to the floor as she choked back angry tears. *How could he? How the blankety-blankety-blank COULD he?* In a scarlet-tinted instant fantasy she rousted him from bed, pulling the sheet out from under him to dump him on the floor like the husband in some screwball comedy from the forties, venting her rage and hurt at him, and then just as implausibly beating him up. Just slapping him silly. *No,* she thought bitterly, *he'd probably LIKE that.*

This brought a mordant laugh, and the laugh rang down the curtain on her cathartic fantasy. She let out a long, cleansing breath and felt her temperature drop. She picked up his attaché case and legal pad and replaced them beside the computer. She went mechanically through the process of shutting down the computer as she allowed herself a few wholehearted sobs. By the time the screen went blank, depression had replaced rage. When she climbed into bed a few minutes later, she left the maximum possible amount of sheet space between herself and her childish, timid, self-absorbed husband.

Chapter 9

Friday was when it all finally hit the fan.

Rep reached Charlotte Buchanan on his digital phone around 8:00 Friday morning, roughly halfway through a ride in what was apparently the only cab serving Traverse City International Airport.

"So how was Kohler?" he asked as casually as he could manage.

"The part I saw was heavy on toilets," she said.

"Something to be said for convenience, I suppose."

"The sales meeting was at The American Club, which is a five-star resort with a world-class golf course. Or so they tell me. Personally, I've never been able to see the point of golf, especially on a cloudy day. So after the crack-of-dawn plant tour I begged off my morning foursome, which basically left me free until two o'clock. Unfortunately, the only other thing to see in Kohler, Wisconsin—and I mean the *only* other thing—is the Kohler Company's museum of bathroom fixtures. So I'm now a mini-expert on the history of toilets."

"Yesterday was a bit more productive for me," Rep said. "I spent most of it with Aaron Eastman. We should talk."

"Great, let's talk. Shoot."

"Not over a digital phone," Rep said. "We could end up sharing our thoughts with anyone in two states who has a police scanner or a short-wave radio. How about Monday at the office?"

"No good. I transitioned from road warrior to program marketing support about three months ago, and Monday the first program I've really contributed to is being presented. That shoots the whole day. Plus I have to put some major face time in at THQ on Saturday and Sunday helping the presenters put the finishing touches on it, so I can't even come by your office over the weekend."

Rep was dismayed to realize that he'd understood every syllable of Buchanan's suit-speak, and wondered if he were turning into Arundel-Lite. "THQ" was Tavistock Headquarters, and the stuff about transition from road warrior meant that she was now working on putting promotions together for salespeople to use instead of traveling on sales calls herself. Rotating Buchanan through key departments would be a standard way of grooming her for a senior executive position in a few years.

"What it comes down to," Buchanan continued, "is I'm pinned to Tavistock and the house until Tuesday."

"Tuesday it is," Rep said. "Nine-thirty?"

"Fine."

Rep tapped his phone antenna pensively against his cheekbone for a few seconds after ending the call. Yesterday afternoon he'd learned that Buchanan had spent the day within easy driving distance of Milwaukee. Now it transpired that none of her Tavistock colleagues could verify that she'd actually been in Kohler for much of the morning and the early afternoon. For a delicious moment he imagined trying to break her story by cross-examining her about the history of toilets.

⌗ ⌗ ⌗

"I'm *not* upset," Melissa said as she strode at forced-march pace through the thicket of bookshelves that separated Reed University Library's tech support office from its tech support supply room.

"Don't tell me you're not upset," Krieg panted in her wake. "In the last ten minutes I've heard you utter two profanities, one blasphemy and a barnyard obscenity. That wouldn't get me through the first page of the average junior term paper, but it's about a year's quota of foul language for you. Reppert's acting like a jerk, isn't he?"

"No," Melissa said. She bent over an open file drawer and began to look for boxes of number 14 printable acetate, but she found it hard to maintain the modest concentration that this straightforward chore demanded.

I understand his little hobby, she kept thinking. *His own small vice. I'm not going to begrudge it to him, and I'm not going to get all pissy about how he shouldn't need anything but me. Everyone uses fantasies during sex. Heaven knows I do, and some of them are a lot wilder than anything WHAP! ever dreamed up, I'll bet. But if he were going to kiss off Charlotte's case for the night, why didn't he just invite me to bed instead of having me do busywork while he enjoyed himself solo? And even if he had to surf through cybersmut, how could he make an appointment with someone while he was at it—especially without telling me? And is it really just an appointment or is it a date? Maybe I'm seven pounds overweight— okay, twelve pounds—and maybe I'm marking time as a techie and teaching a just-for-fun course once in awhile when I should be getting super serious about finishing up my Ph.D., dissertation, but still—*

She stopped, because her fingers had, without conscious help from her brain, stumbled over a thin box of number 14 printable acetate. And because the inside corners of her eyes were starting to smart. Self-pity was far more addictive for her than marijuana. She could wallow in it deliciously for hours if she let herself. Also, Krieg was saying something else, and Melissa supposed she should at least pretend to be listening.

"I don't know if this helps, Melissa, but sometimes I think men just have no conception that certain feelings women prize even exist. It's not *insensitivity,* it's *nonsensitivity.*"

That's very helpful, Melissa thought, while turning what she hoped was an interested expression toward Krieg. *Why don't you write it up for the Publication of the Modern Language Association?*

"On my last go-around with Tavistock, for example—out-sourcing AV, remember?"

"Yes," Melissa said. "Make change your friend."

"Right. Well, one of the younger guys who was going to lose his job kept coming on to me. I interpreted it as anxiety-displacement, about his career, you know, and tried to be sympathetic without letting things get to the point where I'd have to check Indiana's age-of-consent statute."

"Uh-huh," Melissa said. *Punchline?* Melissa thought.

"It turned out," Krieg said with a fatuous chuckle, "that all he wanted was my grass connection in California. His video editing skills had already gotten him a grunt job with a production company in L.A. He wasn't interested in my body at all."

"Imagine that," Melissa said.

"I'm not suggesting that he should have been," Krieg assured Melissa. "It's just that any woman would see instantly that it was a very rotten kind of thing for him to do, and I don't think he even spotted the issue."

"Louise," Melissa said patiently and with the complete sincerity of a naif lying in a good cause, "even though Rep is a man, he hasn't done anything rotten."

"That's the kind of thing you'd say even if Reppert had committed full throttle coitus with a cheerleader swinging from a trapeze in your living room while you fixed dinner in the kitchen," Krieg said, leaning forward and lowering her voice almost to a whisper. "But I for one will not gainsay your construct."

"Thank you," Melissa said. "That's very non-objectivist and counter-patriarchal of you."

While Krieg was smiling demurely in gracious acceptance of this compliment, another female voice intervened from twelve or fifteen feet away.

"Ms. Pennyworth, there you are," the voice half shouted. "We need your help."

"Not now, dear," Krieg interjected protectively. "Whatever it is, it can wait. Is this help with a paper or something for one of my classes? You have a one-week extension, effective immediately. Don't bother Ms. Pennyworth. Go have a smoke or whatever it is people your age do to relax these days."

"I don't smoke," the newcomer said apologetically, shaking girlish bangs. "I'm not in any of your classes, and this isn't about a paper. We have an emergency request from a major donor for a movie from the videotape collection, and none of us can find it."

"What's the title?" Melissa asked.

"We're not sure. They thought it was *Death Came in Green*, but nothing like that is listed anywhere. It's an English mystery from the 1940's, set partly in a hospital."

"That sounds like *Green for Danger*," Melissa said instantly. "Some people would find it a little dated, but I think it's lots of fun. The library does have a copy, and it may be indexed under suspense or even comedies instead of mysteries."

"*Is* it a comedy?"

"With the British sometimes it's hard to tell."

The searcher thanked Melissa profusely and hurried off. The expression on her face suggested that she'd thought seriously of genuflecting first.

⌗ ⌗ ⌗

"That pizza isn't to eat, Ms. Masterson. It's evidence in a trademark case."

"I know that," Masterson told the receptionist who was finishing an early lunch of nuked lasagna at 11:58 in the fourteenth floor lounge. "I was checking to see if anyone had stolen the frozen yogurt I brought for my own lunch and hid behind the pizzas in the hope that it would still be here when I finally get a chance to eat it."

"You mean we have to add petty theft to our list of associate grievances?" asked Arundel, who had entered the lounge in time to get the gist of Masterson's answer. "You folks have an impressive array of morale problems for people making six figures a year eighteen months out of law school."

Savvy beyond her years, Masterson understood that Arundel meant this as a friendly comment.

"I've had my lunch pilfered three times in the last month," she said. "It's incredible. You think you know the people you work with, but obviously we don't."

"You're onto something there," Arundel said. He was securing his fifth cup of coffee for the day, intended to wash down a catch-as-catch-can lunch that he, like Masterson, would be eating at his desk. "Take Pennyworth, for example. He came here straight out of law school, been here ever since, made partner a little over a year ago. Admittedly we either had to make him a partner or fire him, and if we'd fired him we would've had to find somebody else to do trademark and copyright work, so it wasn't like we plumbed to the bottom of his soul or anything. Even so, you'd think after that length of time you'd know someone as well as you know Rule ten-b-five."

"And?" Masterson prodded, baffled by the subtlety of the oblique signal she assumed she was receiving.

"I'm almost embarrassed to admit it," Arundel said. "I had no idea that there were any little Repperts running around. But apparently there are."

"Well, no, actually, there aren't," a now thoroughly baffled Masterson said. "He and his wife don't have any kids. I had to do without a secretary for half a day last week because mine was making a list of all the children of lawyers in the firm for a museum outing this summer. He didn't have any on it."

"You don't say," Arundel said in his most professional brush-off tone. "My mistake, then. Well, enjoy your yogurt."

Half an hour later, as he sat at his desk wading through the dense prose of a client's annual 10-K report to the Securities and Exchange Commission and through an equally dry turkey on whole wheat, Arundel thought two things.

The first was, *There are people making thirty thousand bucks a year who eat a better lunch than I do almost every day.*

The second was, *What in the world was Pennyworth doing with that tape hidden in his office if he and his wife don't have children?*

At twelve-forty-three, he brushed crumbs from his charcoal gray vest, adjusted the white French cuffs that matched the collar on his otherwise royal blue shirt, and strolled with studied nonchalance to Rep's office. He felt he could be reasonably sure of privacy until the end of the lunch hour. He secured the *Discipline Effectiveness Training* tape and returned to his office with only a faint sheen of sweat along his upper lip to betray his nervousness.

He called the firm's AV department and said that he'd need a television and VCR as soon as possible. A drone whose voice he didn't recognize and whose name he didn't register promised to have it to him by two o'clock.

✤ ✤ ✤

The great thing about small town airports, Rep thought when the cab dropped him off at Traverse City International just before two p.m., is that there's hardly ever anyone in them. A lonely attendant staffed the pristine ticket counter for Quad State Airlines, unencumbered by any snaking line of passengers anxious to check in for the 2:50 flight back to Indianapolis. Rep approached in solitary splendor, rashly entertaining hopes of eating something more nutritious than a candy bar between getting his seat assignment and boarding the plane.

Then he checked the monitor on the wall behind the slight, ear-studded gent at the counter and realized why he had the place to himself. DELAYED flashed opposite his flight number, right were 2:50 should have been.

"Why is it—"

"Weather," the attendant said in bored haste, as if he'd had this conversation two or three dozen times already today.

Rep glanced at the abundant sunshine streaming through the windows and the blue sky visible outside them.

"Thunderstorms in Toledo," the attendant said wearily. "Our plane there can't take off to come here, and that's the plane that's supposed to take you to Indianapolis."

"When—"

"Update at three," the attendant sighed. "No promises."

"Are there any airlines connecting to Indianapolis whose planes can fly in the rain?" Rep asked.

There were, but the options they defined didn't strike Rep as happy ones. He could wait here for several hours and connect through O'Hare, wait there for over an hour, and (if he were very lucky) get into Indianapolis around nine tonight. Or he could wait here for several hours and connect through Pittsburgh, sitting there for over an hour before getting into Indianapolis, if he were very lucky, around ten. Or he could rent a car, drive five hours plus, and get home maybe by eight.

He decided to wait for the Quad States update at three.

Which was why, after checking his messages at the office and leaving word for Melissa on the answering machine at home, he had a chance to call Paul Mulcahy in L.A. When Mulcahy's voice-mail recording had finished, Rep left a message asking for information about Mixler and about Selding, the young guy who'd been with Eastman yesterday.

❀ ❀ ❀

"Bye, Ms. Pennyworth," a voice behind the counter said as Melissa strolled past on her way home, around 2:15. "Thanks for your help with the video."

"Sure," Melissa said. "Did you find it all right?"

"In suspense, just like you said. We had it messengered over to the patron by ten."

"You had a messenger run it out to someone?" Melissa asked, astonished. Even in the labor-intensive world of academics, this was extraordinary. "That must have been a very major donor."

"Well, a very major donor's daughter. Charlotte Buchanan."

Melissa stopped. With no greater stimulus than this off-hand datum, the fundamental fact about her husband suddenly burst through the resentment and irritation she'd been accumulating since late last night: Rep was a *mensch*. He wasn't a jock or a stud or a world-beater, but he was someone you could count on. He got up in the morning and he did his job. He did what he was supposed to do and tried not to hurt people along the way. She wondered if maybe, somehow, some way, she had jumped to conclusions last night.

And with that thought, the last stray flotsam clogging her formidable intellect disappeared. Everything she'd heard from Rep in the past twenty-four hours marched through her mind with the unerring precision of a drill-team, except much faster, and dovetailed with what she remembered of *Green for Danger's* plot.

"Excuse me," she said, reversing her course. "I want to check a couple of things."

⌗ ⌗ ⌗

Arundel's jaw hadn't actually dropped, but he was doing a bit of heavy breathing as he got into the tenth minute of *Discipline Effectiveness Training*. He knew stuff like this *existed*, of course. But actually seeing it, there on the screen in his darkened office, knowing its provenance, challenged his *seen-it-all-nothing-surprises-me* self-image. He dug a phone list out of his desk to find the number for the firm's head computer guru.

His own phone rang just as he found the number. He grabbed the receiver and snapped his name. His caller didn't identify himself and didn't have to, for it was Finneman.

"Tempus-Caveator, Inc. just filed a thirteen-d on Tavistock," he said. "Conference room one."

Those who spend their time doing useful things instead of merely moving around money that other people have earned would find it hard to imagine the galvanic effect that this laconic message had on Arundel. Finneman was saying that a very large corporation had just officially notified the Securities and Exchange Commission that it had acquired more than 5% of the stock in Tavistock, Ltd., with the intention of influencing management and control; in plain English, that it was undertaking a hostile takeover of the company. Chip Arundel was going to war.

Before he went to war, though, Arundel clicked off the video and called the head computer guru.

⌗ ⌗ ⌗

At exactly three o'clock, Quad State Airlines informed Rep that it was still raining in Toledo, and that the next update would come in about an hour. While Rep was getting ready to seethe about that, his phone beeped insistently. He answered to hear Mulcahy's voice.

"So you're going on with the Eastman thing anyway," Mulcahy said.

"True," Rep sighed. "Do you have anything on either of those guys I asked about?"

"I never heard of Selding, but it's funny you asked about Mixler. The word is that he's been greenlighted for about a year on a made-for-TV movie about Margaret Thatcher. They're talking about Cameron Diaz for the lead."

"What, they couldn't get Jennifer Aniston?"

"Word is Jennifer's English accent has gone south since she married Brad Pitt. They didn't think she'd be credible in the scene where Thatcher faces down a troop of IRA gunmen and rescues Prince Andrew."

"I thought Mixler was an agent or a sub-agent or something," Rep said.

"Well sure, but in his heart everyone in Hollywood is a producer. Every Key Grip and Best Boy on every film being shot spends his spare time fantasizing about how he'll rig the points when he's finally executive producer on a major project."

"How did Mixler manage to make his fantasy come true?"

"No idea," Mulcahy said, "but he must've impressed someone fairly far up the food chain at Galaxy Entertainment Group."

"Wasn't Galaxy the studio that Eastman was working with on *Red Guard!*?"

"Yeah. He made the deal before Tempus-Caveator bought Galaxy. And it's a good thing he did, because apparently no one at T-C thought *Red Guard!* was worth much of an investment."

"Okay," Rep said. "Thanks."

He was about to turn the phone off because his battery was running low, but he noticed an envelope icon on the screen, indicating that a voice-mail message was waiting for him. He retrieved it.

"Mr. Pennyworth?" said a whispered voice that Rep recognized as belonging to Paul Calvin, a clever-with-machines type in the firm's AV department. "There's something I think you should know. Mr. Arundel asked for a TV and VCR earlier this afternoon. Then a little later, he called the Systems Administrator here and said he wants a record of all the internet connections you've made with your firm computer over the past year."

❀ ❀ ❀

It took Melissa until 3:45 p.m. to find the *Life* magazine article from August 10, 1962. It was the last item on the list she'd made of books, articles, videotapes, and vertical file materials extracted by the Reed University Library for Charlotte Buchanan.

"Tragedy at NASA," the headline read. In appropriately somber tones, the article described how four space program workers had died of anoxia because without realizing it they had gone to work in a chamber filled with pure nitrogen. Breathing it felt the same as breathing air, but it didn't bring any oxygen to their lungs. They had gradually grown drowsy, fallen unconscious, and died.

Melissa didn't get a speeding ticket on the way home, but only because the Indianapolis cops were sleepy that day.

⁂ ⁂ ⁂

Dispatched in haste from Conference Room I, Mary Jane Masterson scurried into Chip Arundel's office a little after 5:00. Arundel had sent her to retrieve a printout of pending regulatory proceedings involving Tempus-Caveator, Inc. that he remembered getting a week or so before.

The cardboard sleeve for the *Discipline Effectiveness Training* videotape inevitably drew her eyes. Intrigued, she flipped on the VCR and in fifteen seconds had seen enough to leave her astounded at her good fortune.

"Talk about fireproof," she whispered in awe. "If I play my cards right, I have just officially acquired an asbestos-covered butt."

⁂ ⁂ ⁂

Rep was about to call home again at 5:20, in the hope of actually talking to Melissa instead of just leaving a message for her, when the triumphant announcement from Quad States Airlines echoed through Traverse City International Airport. The flight from Toledo had called within range! It should be here in twenty minutes! They'd do a quick turn-around and try to have their Indianapolis-bound passengers in the air by six o'clock! A mere three hours and ten minutes late! They were very sorry for the inconvenience! Would passengers please proceed immediately to the gate!

Rep proceeded. He put the leather carrying case holding his laptop on the x-ray machine's conveyor belt at the security checkpoint. He dumped car keys, loose change, digital phone, and watch into a plastic basket and handed it to an attendant. He stepped without incident through the metal detector. He retrieved his belongings from the basket. He stepped over to the x-ray machine to pick up his laptop. He noticed an attendant hovering over it.

"Is this your computer, sir?" the blazered gentleman asked.
"Yes."

"Would you mind if we checked it a little further?"

"No, of course not."

The attendant lifted the case to a table, stood it on its base, and ran a small, white, rectangular cloth over the zipper and the handles. Rep waited patiently. This happened about once every four or five times that he traveled by plane— generally at smaller airports, where people didn't have enough to do and felt they had to justify some Airport Authority's heavy investment in high-tech toys.

The attendant put the cloth into a scanner. About five seconds usually passed between this step in the ritual and the part where the attendant said thank you and nodded Rep on his way. This time, though, the interval was more like fifteen seconds, and when the attendant looked up from the scanner he didn't say thank you.

"Would you turn the computer on, please, sir?"

"Certainly."

Rep pulled the laptop out of its case and started to open it up.

"Uh, not here, sir," the attendant said hastily. "Would you mind taking it into that small room over there to turn it on? This gentleman will show you the way."

The gentleman in question had appeared silently behind Rep's left elbow. He was about six-three, even without the Smokey-the-Bear hat he was wearing. He thoroughly filled a double-breasted gun-metal blue uniform coat featuring many brass buttons and a Sam Browne belt. And a badge. Rep noticed a holstered pistol, a can of Mace, and a pair of handcuffs on the belt.

"This way," the guy said. He didn't say "sir," and if he had he wouldn't have meant it.

Rep followed the state trooper out of the security area, down a short hallway, and into a windowless room. Another man was waiting for them in the room. He was in mufti, but he had one of those haircuts that says football coach, marine, or cop. The uniformed trooper repeated the request that Rep turn on his computer.

He did so, noticing both men reflexively flinch as he pushed the gray button that would coax the machine to life. Green lights came on. The black screen dissolved into rapidly blinking numbers and letters. A little electronic fanfare played, as if the computer were quite pleased with itself at managing to make its circuits hum.

The two men looked at each other.

"Okay?" Rep asked hopefully, taking care to keep any smart-alec tone out of his voice.

The state trooper responded by undertaking a methodical examination of the laptop's carrying case. The guy in civvies gazed with studied neutrality at Rep. After a good five minutes of turning the laptop case inside out, the uniformed trooper spoke.

"Sir, the reason you were asked to come in here is that the security scanner picked up traces of an explosive called PETN on your computer case."

"People sometimes use PETN to blow up airplanes," the plainclothesman said.

"The people who blew up the airplane over Lockerbie a few years ago used PETN packed inside a laptop computer," the uniformed trooper said.

"I see," Rep said.

"So the question, then, would be," the cop in mufti said, "why your laptop case has these traces."

"I have no idea," Rep said.

"Well," uniform said, "has anyone besides you had access to your computer case in, say, the last two weeks?"

"Um, sure, I guess," Rep said. Melissa, for example. Eastman, Selding. Buchanan. Other clients, including the one he had just seen. His secretary. Most of the lawyers in the office, if you got right down to it. Most of the non-lawyers, for that matter. Not to mention the odd cabbie and bellhop.

"We'll be wanting a list," mufti said.

Rep felt blood draining from his face. With a mental shudder he imagined people like the folks in front of him going to his clients and his colleagues and saying *Just a few routine questions. Nothing serious. We found something funny on your lawyer's bag and we were wondering if you might be a terrorist.*

"Gosh," Rep said, "I can't do that. I mean, just start naming people on speculation because a machine beeped."

"We're going to have to insist," mufti said.

"Excuse me," Rep said, blustering a bit in indignation at this gross deviation from everything he'd taken the trouble to learn in Criminal Procedure I at a top-rated American law school, "but you're not in any position to insist. You can't just hold me here for questioning without arresting me."

"Okay," uniform shrugged. "You're under arrest."

"On what charge?"

"Failure to provide proper cooperation and assistance to law enforcement authorities in the course of a legitimate criminal investigation," mufti said.

"Is that a crime in Michigan?" Rep asked in genuinely interested astonishment.

"It's a crime in this room until a judge says it isn't," uniform said.

"Look," Rep said, "this is ridiculous. I have a plane to catch in less than half an hour."

"I wouldn't be counting on that," uniform said. "You have the right to remain silent, *et cetera*. You know, like from *NYPD Blue*."

"I know the rest," Rep sighed. "I'm a fan."

Chapter 10

Melissa had sworn that she'd never do what she was about to do. She sat at Rep's computer in their den at six o'clock Friday night and got ready to read his e-mails.

She just didn't see that she had any choice. She had gotten home to find a message from Rep on the answering machine saying that his flight was delayed and he'd update her when he knew more. But no update had come, and when she dialed his digital phone number all she got was an invitation to leave messages that a satellite would pass on when and if it felt like it. She normally took this kind of thing in stride, but Charlotte Buchanan's case wasn't a normal situation. Especially after what she'd learned in the library this afternoon, the tension pooling in her gut had gradually congealed into worry, and the worry was starting to feel a lot like fear.

But she couldn't exactly call the police, could she? *Yes, officer, well you see there's this English movie, and then I found an article in a 1962 issue of* Life *magazine....* So, conscience-stricken but resolute, she pulled up the last e-mail Rep had gotten, which had come in after they'd both gone to bed.

Rearward,

I read your post. That's terrible. I don't have anything for you now, but I'll keep my ears open. Hang in there.

Rosie Cul

Melissa blinked. Post? Then she remembered the web sites he'd visited while she was reading bleary-eyed through lame working scripts—the sites that had sent her to bed in tight-lipped indignation. It took nearly twenty minutes for her to navigate through the unfamiliar waters, but she found the sex.soc.spanking bulletin board and scrolled quickly to a posting by Rearward at 7:45 yesterday evening:

> Big problem. Someone has learned my name and is spreading information about my interests to people who don't share them. It's gotten to the point where others may be hurt. I need to know if anyone has been making inquiries about me in the past year or so. Please do *not* post responses but e-mail at the following address: repcent@husker.com.
>
> Rearward

It took a few seconds for the implications to penetrate. When they did, though, Melissa sat back open-mouthed for a moment, awestruck. Rep wanted the information he sought so badly that he had told what could not be told; spoken what must forever remain unsaid. He had revealed himself, offered his most vulnerable flank. He had given his actual, real-world e-mail address to who knows how many casual net-surfers, one or more of whom might be able almost instantly to put his actual name and face with it.

Despite Rep's injunction not to respond with an answering post, Melissa checked two screensful of bulletin board entries following Rep's. Many of them shrieked with outrage at the wanton invasion of privacy Rearward had indicted. Most expressed unqualified sympathy and support for him. But none of them actually offered any information, and she realized that this kind of stuff wasn't going to get her anywhere.

She went back to the e-mails sent to Rep and reviewed them in reverse chronological order. The fifth one she came to set the bells off in her head.

Rearward:

> I wouldn't ordinarily respond to this type of thing, but the situation you describe is very bad. The entire system and all the good it does depends on respecting each other's privacy and space. (Or to put it another way, from certain points of view it's bad for business.) I do have some information that may be helpful to you, but I'm afraid I can't e-mail it—after all, we aren't completely sure who's reading your e-mails, are we? I'm leaving tomorrow for the Chicagoland Scene Party this weekend, but I'll be back in L.A. on Monday. Call one of the numbers on my web site and we'll set up a secure way to communicate.
>
> Jennifer Payne

Melissa was still far from mastering the lingo, so she didn't know that people who shared Rep's, er, interest and actively tried to meet others with the same inclination described themselves as being "in the scene." Even so, she had no trouble connecting this reply with Rep's note about "Jennifer Payne" and the "C/land Scene Play." The only problem this left was that she didn't know what to do now.

Well, yes, she did, actually, but she was having trouble making herself do it. It wasn't being afraid, so much. It was more that she just couldn't imagine herself doing it. She remembered almost weeping with rage and frustration in the none too ample trouble-lane of I-80 when she was 19, staring fecklessly at the jack and the tire iron while her father, who could have changed the flat in ten minutes, told her that by-God *she* was going to do it, not him, because someday she was going to have to change a tire when there wasn't any man around to help her and she'd better know how. It was the same kind of thing. She hadn't been afraid of getting her hands dirty. It was just—what, me? change a *tire?*

Then the computer pinged and an envelope icon appeared in the lower right-hand corner. She had mail. Or, rather, Rep did.

Trembling a bit, she brought the new message up. It had hit the machine at 4:37 p.m.

> Mr. Pennyworth:
>
> Big time change of plans. Big news. You need to get face-to-face with Aaron Eastman pronto. As in yesterday. He'll be in northern California, at the St. Anthony Hotel in Pomona Sunday night, supposedly trying to line up some Silicon Valley financing Monday for his next flick. (This is from a *very* reliable source, and it's on the money.) He's just gotten some very critical information, and you need to strike while the iron's hot. (Sorry for the cliché, but I'm writing this in a hurry.) I won't be reachable, but I'll try to get word for you at the St. Anthony. I've already had someone make a reservation for you for Sunday night.
>
> Charlotte Buchanan

Back to the web sites. Sex.soc.spanking didn't have the information Melissa was looking for, but Disciplinary Wives Club did. The Chicagoland Scene Party would run from four o'clock this afternoon through noon on Sunday. DWC helpfully provided a hot-link for anyone who wanted to go directly to the Scene Party site and sign up. Melissa clicked.

Three minutes later she had filled in all the blanks on the screen. She had identified herself as Aunt Stern, which she thought was kind of clever for spur of the moment and everything. She had given Rep's e-mail address, because that cat was pretty much out of the bag. She had blanched when she'd filled in her credit card data, despite the banner saying that if she really turned out to be a woman, 70% of the $300 fee would be rebated to her. The screen arrow rested on "SEND," and her index finger hovered over the mouse. But she hesitated. It wasn't the money that was holding her up. It was the thought that that credit card had her name on it—not Rep's or a crafty *nom de guerre.*

Irritated at her own continuing timidity, she impulsively dialed Louise Krieg's number, as a recollection of their chat this morning vectored into the pattern her mind had already formed from the data she'd been gathering.

"Happy Friday night," Krieg said delightedly after Melissa identified herself. "I'm just about to get blitzed. Care to join me?"

"Can't," Melissa said. "I have a quick question. You said there was someone in Tavistock's AV department who ended up getting a job with a production company in L.A. What was his name?"

"All I can say is it's a bloody good thing you asked that before I fired up my little white friend here. Let me think. Tall, neatly bearded, mellow schtick, longish hair—Selding. That's it. His name was Selding. Jerry or Harry or something."

"Thanks," Melissa said. She clicked SEND at the same moment.

Chapter 11

The first thing Rep saw after the cell door slammed was a guy coming toward him out of gauzy shadows made of gray light filtered through dank air. A big guy and bald, with a scarred, misshapen pate. Applied to him, "knuckle-dragger" would have been barely metaphorical, and "mouth-breather" relentlessly literal. A loose leather vest worn over a sleeveless top exposed arms where tattoos featuring snakes and skulls rippled. His expression suggested indignation at someone else being chosen to play Uncle Fester in the last *Addams Family* remake, and it seemed to Rep that he had a point.

"Welcome to jail," the guy grunted through a yellow, picket-fence smile. "Let's play house."

That's when Rep woke up. He was still in the airport's windowless interview room. The uniformed state trooper and the bullet-head in civvies were conferring in a corner with their backs turned toward Rep, as they had been when he'd dozed off.

They had done this periodically during Rep's sojourn in the room. At other times, one of them would step outside with a portable phone that they apparently shared. Most often, though, they would confront him together, either to ask him questions or to speculate, ostensibly between themselves but patently for his benefit, on the impossibility of an intake judge being found anytime before nine o'clock

Monday morning—sixty hours from now, as Rep verified with a glance at his watch.

He hadn't made any phone calls, although they'd told him he could make one. He hadn't called Melissa because he didn't want her name to figure any more prominently than it had to in the report these guys were going to write. And he hadn't called a lawyer because if he'd known one who lived in Traverse City, and had had his home phone number, and had been lucky enough to reach him, and if that lawyer had possessed the legal acumen and street-smart craftiness of Clarence Darrow, Louis Nizer, and the O.J. Dream Team combined, the very best advice he could possibly have given Rep at the moment would have been, "Keep your mouth shut."

Rep was accomplishing that without any help. Not so much because he had any police court savvy to spare as because this evening's trauma seemed to have shut down several of his mental circuits. He could no longer generate the cerebral energy to take a writeup on a client's bill, much less answer challenging questions.

The door opened and another man came into the room. He was wearing a navy blue sport coat over an open-necked white dress shirt and khaki slacks. Rep sighed inwardly with relief at this indication that the man had about as much imagination as the average can of tuna fish. *God preserve me from imaginative lawyers*, he managed to think.

The man introduced himself. Rep didn't bother to note his name but he picked up the title: Assistant United States Attorney. A couple of the sputtering synapses in Rep's brain coughed back to life. Not assistant district attorney for whatever county Traverse City was in. Not corporation counsel. Not deputy Michigan attorney general. Not anyone paid by the State of Michigan or any of its appendages, as Trooper Smokey and Coach Bullet-head were. Rep's custodians had passed the buck to the federal government.

Gee, Rep thought, *now I'll have an FBI file. Just like mom.*

The guy held out his hand as he pulled up a chair across the table from Rep—friendly, first-time-in-this-bar kind of way. Rep found himself shaking the hand, not by conscious choice but by almost involuntary reflex. The guy smiled—friendly, new-face-at-the-Kiwanis-Club kind of smile.

"So. What's the problem?" he said.

Rep didn't say anything.

"Look, this is just routine. We're not talking SWAT teams at four a.m. PETN, if that's what it really is and that machine didn't blip when it should've blinked—well, PETN is serious stuff. We just need to follow up in a discreet and professional way. You can understand that. You're a professional. You'd do the same thing. So what's the problem?"

Rep didn't say anything.

It went on like that for quite awhile. Solicitude. *Can we get this man some coffee, maybe?* Low-key carrots. *Just give me something to chew on. Coupla names and we'll call it a night.* Low-key sticks. *I don't wanna go the grand jury route. Which do you think would bother your clients more—five-minute chat in the office or a piece of paper with Latin on it?* Humor. *You don't need immunity, do you? 'Cause I'm definitely not gonna make it back for last call if that's what's holding us up.* A break now and then—the guy had a taste for Diet Dr. Pepper without ice—followed by little snatches of OK-fun's-fun-but-dammit-this-is-serious. *You know what you're acting like, don't you, partner? You're acting like someone who's been through the mill and has something to hide. You want me to walk out of this room thinking that's what you are?*

Rep kept on not saying anything and eventually it was ten-fifteen. Coach Bullet-head, who had been outside with the door closed, came back in and tapped the Rotarian Assistant United States Attorney on the shoulder. They walked outside and when they came back in thirty seconds later the Rotarian didn't bother to sit back down.

"Okey-dokey, pal, don't say I didn't try to do it the easy way. We're not holding you. You're free to go. But I'd get myself a frequent-flyer card with Quad States if I was you. I have a feeling we're going to be seeing each other again soon. And when that U.S. marshal comes by with that great big lucite-covered shield on his coat pocket and that bulge under his left armpit and that grand jury subpoena in his right hand, don't be surprised if he strolls right into the middle of a conference with your senior partner and your biggest client."

Rep stood up and retrieved his laptop. They insisted on keeping the case, so he gathered the bulky accessories stored there into an awkward bundle that he pinned under his arm: power cord and modem connection, plus the recharging unit for his digital phone—umbilical baggage that his ancestors had conquered a continent without but that he desperately needed for a low-key, Midwestern trademark and copyright practice. The laptop case had been his only luggage, so he had to pull out a legal pad and a thin correspondence file as well.

He was astonished at his good luck when he found someone still tending the Quad States counter. By 10:26 he had secured a ticket on the flight back to Indianapolis at 9:10 Saturday morning. Now all he had to do was find an airport hotel with a vacant room, wait twenty minutes or so for its shuttle, jolt through a half-mile ride that for some reason would take ten more minutes, check in, call Melissa, take a shower—with any luck at all he could be asleep before midnight.

He turned away from the desk to find Trooper Smokey waiting for him.

"I can give you a ride to the Day's Inn," he said. "I mean, missing your flight and all. I don't have any chits, but if you send the receipt in the airport authority can reimburse you."

What, the whole sixty-nine-ninety-five? Rep thought. He came very close to telling Trooper Smokey contemptuously to skip it.

But he didn't. He took a deep breath and after the exhalation the guy he saw wasn't Trooper Smokey. He was someone who got up every day to do his job just as Rep did, except that his job meant facing physical danger and nasty people so that guys like Rep could make five or six times his salary by pushing papers across a desk in air-conditioned offices.

"Thanks," Rep said. "That'd be great."

Six minutes later the trooper dropped him off outside the Day's Inn lobby, exactly half a mile from the terminal and a snappy one hundred fume-choked yards from a noisy, arc-lighted Budget Rent-a-Car facility. Rep was in his room by 10:40.

He found that he couldn't plug in both his laptop and his digital phone without moving the bed. Not feeling up to anything quite so ambitious, he connected the laptop and put the phone on his pillow so that he'd remember to recharge its battery before retiring for the night. He was surprised to get the answering machine when he called home, but he left a message updating Melissa (who he supposed was taking a shower) and figured he'd try again after checking his office messages and e-mails.

While his computer was booting up he flipped on the room TV and began banzai channel-surfing in search of white noise. He clicked past CNN and MSNBC without a flicker of attention. He wasn't physically tired but he didn't have an ounce of mental energy to his name. The ordeal of arrest and interrogation and the exhilaration of surviving them left him pumped and drained at the same time. He was looking for pure eye candy, mental junk-food.

He found it. *Entertainment Tonight!* Coming up not at the top of the hour but in three minutes, after two last beer commercials and a final wrap-up of the Tigers' game against the Indians. Perfect.

Rep propped himself up in bed, dialed his computer into his office, and started reviewing e-mails. The one from Charlotte Buchanan was four down the list. He reached it at the exact moment *Entertainment Tonight!* introduced its first story.

"A lot of people wouldn't call what we bring you on *ET!* hard news," a male anchor who seemed to be smiling in spite of himself was saying. "Well, tonight is an exception. We lead off with a copyrighted story featuring Lisa Goldman that we ran on today's first *ET!* edition at six o'clock Pacific Time tonight."

A perky reporter appeared on the screen in front of what looked like a very large but strangely rural airfield.

"We're here in Oshkosh, Wisconsin, home of the Experimental Aircraft Association Airfield and Museum, which every August becomes the busiest airport in the world during the annual EAA Fly-In," she was chirping. "So why are we here in June? Because the EAA is home to many vintage aircraft including, over there on the flight line about a hundred yards behind me, a very early Sikorsky Whirly-Bird, one of the first choppers to be used by the U.S. military. Don't worry, we're about to get a closer look. Word is that producer Aaron Eastman has more than a cameo role for this baby in mind in his current incubating pet project about the Berlin airlift, *Every Sixteen Minutes.* Aaron is joining us—"

Aaron had in fact moved into the frame, but Rep scarcely noticed. Distracting him was a bright orange and black fireball that suddenly engulfed the Sikorsky chopper. The accompanying explosion drowned out several of Ms. Goldman's next words, and *ET!*'s censor had by now taken care of several more.

"Holy BLEEP what the BLEEP is this BLEEP?" she was shrieking—not at all perkily—by the time she was audible again. She was still shrieking, from pretty much a prone position, when *ET!* cut the tape and went back to the anchor.

In the last half-second before he started moving very fast, Rep simultaneously heard something about PETN and finished reading Buchanan's e-mail.

He clicked off the television. *Charlotte Buchanan is supposed to be trapped in Indianapolis 'til Tuesday! What's with the weekend jetset number?* Clumsy with haste, he fumbled once before clicking FILE and pointing his mouse at EXIT AND LOG OFF. *NO! I have to disconnect the phone line first!*

He brought up the icon of two computers talking to each other and clicked DISCONNECT. *PETN in Oshkosh! How far is Oshkosh from Kohler?* Back to FILE, back to EXIT AND LOG OFF. *Where's Melissa? Why does LOG OFF take so bloody long? Where did 'where's Melissa?' come from, Melissa's in the shower.* Click on SHUT DOWN THE COMPUTER. Sit and wait fretfully while his laptop took its time obeying the command, like a truculent toddler reluctant to go to bed. PLEASE WAIT WHILE THE COMPUTER SHUTS DOWN. *Like I have a choice.*

Finally a blessedly blank screen. Shut the computer. Unplug the computer. Detach the modem cord. Roll them up any which way. *Do I have the room key? Who cares?* Scoot toward the door cradling legal papers and miscellaneous electronics, like a high-tech vagabond. *Am I forgetting anything? No.* YES! *My phone!* Retrace his steps. Stuff the phone and charging cord into the ungainly bundle under his arm.

Out of the room at last. *Wait, should I go back and try Melissa one more time? No, I'll call her from the road, if I still have enough juice on this thing.* Elevator might take forever, hoofing it down the stairs instead. Front desk, lobby empty except for a couple of weary stewardesses and one other guy, presumably a passenger on whatever flight they'd serviced.

"Change of plans," Rep stammered to a desk clerk who couldn't have cared less. "Checking out of two-oh-nine."

He scribbled his name across the bill and, when the clerk fumbled while separating copies, impatiently took the thing from the man's hands and ripped the leaves apart himself. Then he hurried out of the Day's Inn and started stumbling toward Budget Rent-a-Car. Across dark pavement, gravel, verge, mud, and all but invisible car bumps, it seemed a lot longer than a hundred yards. While the clerk waited for an antique printer to spew out his rental contract, Rep turned his phone on to try Melissa again.

He saw in the tiny screen's green glow that he had a voice-mail message. He decided to check that first. BLIP-TALK. The message was from hours ago.

"Rep, this is Melissa. I think you were right about Charlotte and I was wrong. We need to talk right away. Call me as soon—"

The voice stopped. The screen went blank. His battery was dead.

"All right," the clerk said. "Initial here, here, here, here, and here, and sign here and here. That's one mid-size sedan, slot B-four. Will you be needing anything else?"

"Yes," Rep said. "A pay phone. And directions—" He stopped himself before he could say "directions to Oshkosh, Wisconsin," amending this to "and Michigan, Indiana, and Illinois highway maps."

Clutching maps, now, along with everything else, he waddled toward the pay phone that the clerk pointed out in the corner. He called home and got the answering machine again. His wife liked long showers, but not this long. Hammering in his head as he made his way toward slot B-4 was *Where's Melissa?*

Chapter 12

Melissa figured she might as well have a neon sign on her back flashing FAKE when she checked into the Doubletree Suites on Wabash Street in Chicago around eleven Friday night. Her wardrobe didn't include the kind of exotica that she assumed would be *de rigeur* in the arcane *demimonde* she was about to enter. Not a single leather teddy, latex camisole, or black rubber hood to her name. Her most promising improvisational effort involved a suede vest with cross-bodice laces over a dark green satin blouse, but she concluded sadly that looking like a game show host in drag wouldn't fool anyone at the Chicagoland Scene Party. She ended up in an eggshell blouse and basic black skirt. It struck her as something you'd wear to teach phonics to the Brady Bunch, but it was the best she could do.

The Doubletree's lobby directory was discreetly silent about the Chicagoland Scene Party. This nonplussed Melissa, who wasn't sure she could get up the nerve to ask the desk clerk where in the Pentagon-sized hotel she should go to find the event. As it turned out she didn't have to.

"There is a special, limited-interest, invitation-only event being held in the southeast corner of the second floor," he said with studied neutrality after handing her a cardboard folder with a plastic key-card inside. "If you aren't pre-registered for it, you may find it more convenient to avoid that area."

"Um, whereabouts in the southeast corner?" Melissa asked.

"The Wilmot Proviso Salon and the Ostend Manifesto Ballroom," he answered, explaining further that naming function rooms after nineteenth-century documents generated during the debate over slavery reflected the Doubletree's commitment to promoting education in American history.

After stashing her modest luggage in her room and trying (again) without success (again) to reach Rep on his digital phone, Melissa went down to the second floor for what she expected to be a low-key, risk-free reconnaissance. Whatever the Scene Party had on its schedule for tonight must surely be over by now, she reasoned. She could get the lay of the land, find her bearings, and then count on a good night's sleep to give her the courage for a full-scale assault Saturday morning.

This Doubletree didn't have corners, strictly speaking, and Melissa didn't have a compass, so it took a long and circuitous walk to bring her to the vicinity of the Wilmot Proviso Salon. She realized she was finally there when she spotted a long, skirted table with a banner that read "STOP Here for CSP Registration" hanging from the curtain behind it. An oversized rendering of an open hand with black fingers and a bright-red palm surrounded by throb marks emphasized the verb.

Melissa hesitated. It didn't look—or sound—as if the night's events were over after all.

Three people waited behind the table. The nearest was a woman who leaned over it while she talked with her two seated colleagues. She looked eight to ten years older than Melissa. Her full-skirted, navy blue dress seemed at least as matronly and plain vanilla as Melissa's outfit. What Melissa could see of the clothes worn by the other two attendants seemed equally unremarkable. So far this was about as exotic as an assistant librarians' convention—and Melissa was still scared out of her wits. The leaning woman turned toward Melissa with a warily curious smile.

"Can I help you?" she asked.

"Er, yeah, I guess," Melissa said. Freezing for an awful moment, she took a breath and decided to plunge ahead. "I guess I need to register, don't I?"

"Name?" the woman asked politely, moving to seat herself behind two low-cut cardboard boxes marked A-L and M-Z respectively.

"Pennywor—" Melissa began before she remembered her assumed identity and caught herself. "Er, that is, Aunt Stern."

"Oh, I *like* that," the woman said. "Yes, here you are. You're a top, I'm guessing."

Melissa guessed the same thing. The woman pulled out a completed form and a plastic-encased, pin-on name tag. Next to AUNT STERN on the name tag she put a sticker that matched the throbbing hand from the registration banner. As soon as Melissa had affixed the name tag, the woman held out her hand.

"I'm Margaret Keane," she said, pronouncing the name "cane." "Welcome to the Chicagoland Scene Party."

"Thank you," Melissa said, shyly shaking the proffered hand.

"And since you clearly are a woman and have now registered, you're entitled to a seventy percent rebate on your fee. May I just have your Mastercard for a moment so I can do an imprint on the credit voucher?"

Only for a second or so did Melissa consider the possibility of shrugging off $210 so that she wouldn't have to produce a credit card with MELISSA PENNYWORTH stamped on it. Whatever credibility she had—and she didn't think she had much—would evaporate instantly if she pulled a stunt like that. Besides, she'd already given them her credit card number and the name that went with it over the computer. She produced the requested piece of plastic, followed by a driver's license with her photograph. A minute later she got them back with a customer copy of a credit slip, as if she'd just returned a Coach handbag to Marshall Field's.

"Now," Keane said. "You seem a bit new to our little group. Would you like me to show you around a bit while you get your feet wet?"

"That would be wonderful," Melissa said, heartily meaning every syllable.

"Excellent," Keane said. "Why don't we start in the dealer room?"

Melissa followed her new-found guide through the Freeport Doctrine Foyer into the Wilmot Proviso Salon. Still half expecting something out of Fellini, Melissa was again surprised to find ordinary looking people milling about in dress no more unconventional in general than that sported at the typical Reed University Faculty Tea—rather less so, if anything. There were, to be sure, a few nurses in starched, white uniforms, a pre-Vatican nun or two, and one tall, severe lady who looked like Mary Poppins in need of Preparation H. On the whole, though, the women strolling along the aisles between the dealers' booths looked pretty much like Melissa; and the men looked like—well, like Rep would probably have looked if he'd been here.

For a gut-chilling moment, in fact, Melissa wondered if Rep actually were here. A glimpse of something out of the corner of her eye made her think of him, and she asked herself if he'd come here after all; if that explained the "flight delay" he'd reported this afternoon, and her inability to reach him since; if he'd been lying to her so that he could sneak off to this thing. A closer look erased this suspicion, for the face she'd spotted belonged to a woman of stately *gravitas*, near or past fifty, in a goldenrod blouse and midnight blue skirt that might have dressed a British prison matron or an American cub scout den mother.

The wares offered by the dealers, on the other hand, did markedly distinguish the Chicagoland Scene Party from your run-of-the-mill convention of hardware distributors or systems management executives. They offered videos—*Training Mark and Lisa* and *The Best of British Spanking, Vols. I to VI* were some of the titles that Melissa noticed; books like *The Compleat Spanker* and *Disciplined Husbands, Satisfied Wives*; and pamphlets addressing such catchy topics as *The Spencer Spanking Plan, How to Keep a Permanent Record, The Definitive List of Spanking Scenes in Movies and Television,* and *Friday Night Conduct and Deportment Review.* Audiotapes that Melissa saw in passing promised *Interview with Pam, a Disciplinarian* and *Jennifer's First Session (Live Recording).* You could drop anywhere from six to eighty dollars on these items.

Then came the implements. Fortnum and Mason hairbrushes from London—"Genuine $55.00" according to the sign next to them. Long, rectangular, wooden paddles with tapered handles like those that Melissa's mother assured her had been used in grade schools and high schools in the sixties. Larger versions of these with holes drilled in them, identified as "Spencer Paddles." Unusual scourges consisting of round wooden handles with six thin, flat, wooden strips attached to them, certified by accompanying placards as "Canadian Birch GUARANTEED." Razor strops, riding crops and quirts. Forked strips of leather twenty-six inches long and identified as "Actual Scottish School Tawses." These ran $60 each. Oval paddles in black and red leather that looked like vaguely sinister, oversized Ping-Pong bats—bargains, these, at $39.95. More rectangular paddles, except that these were leather instead of wood. Most of them were $65, but some had fur-like padding over the leather on one side, which jacked their price up to $75. One dealer seemed the envy of his neighbors because he offered a limited selection of oval paddles made of wedding gown white kangaroo leather. While Melissa was watching he sold one of them to a middle-aged man for $225.

By the time Keane had led Melissa down two full rows, the displays' shock value had declined dramatically for her. She began to wonder, in fact, if perhaps she had gotten a bit too used to the surroundings. Snatches of chat between dealers and buyers that would have floored her twenty-four hours ago—"a nice, crisp pain," "very even distribution over the entire lower half of the buttocks with each stroke"— didn't have much more effect on her now than would sales patter for a filing system.

"That red leather hand paddle is one I've had particularly good luck with," Keane commented as they finished up the last aisle and headed for the Ostend Manifesto Ballroom. "You simply can't wear it out, and it produces dramatic coloration without ever breaking the skin."

"Maybe I should try one," Melissa said.

"Let me know if you decide to. I can get you a discount."

"You're being awfully nice to me," Melissa said. "I mean, it looks like you have nearly two hundred people here, and I'm just someone who signed up at the last minute. I really appreciate it."

"When you inflict pain for a living I think it's a good idea to be nice whenever you have the chance," Keane said. "But that's not my only motive. Do you mind if we step over here out of the traffic? I'm dying for a cigarette."

"No, please, go ahead."

The Ostend Manifesto Ballroom was far less crowded than the dealer room. On a platform at the far end, a tall, amply bosomed woman was demonstrating, as a poster on a nearby easel promised, "How to Administer a Proper Caning." Her measured rattan strokes were at the moment falling on a sofa cushion but were nevertheless evoking considerable interest. A number of presumed tyros lined up at the platform stairs, waiting to try their own technique under the woman's tutelage—one more manifestation, Melissa thought, of Americans' fascination with self-improvement. In the far corner, a tripod-mounted video camera pointed at a red velvet backdrop also attracted a modest crowd, presumably interested in watching or making what the sign over the backdrop called "Video Personals." Dotted around the rest of the ample floor were knots of people sharing drinks and conversation, and showing off new wares they had bought in the dealer room next door.

"What's your other motive for being nice to me, if you don't mind my asking?" Melissa asked after Keane had ingested two restorative lungfuls of Virginia Slim Menthol smoke.

"Don't you see it?" Keane demanded, sweeping the room with her left hand. "Look around. At least four men for every woman. Maybe five. A woman who's genuinely into the scene is a pearl of great price. Your value is greater than rubies—and Ruby don't come cheap, *badda-bing*. Seriously, you're worth your weight in gold."

"I see," Melissa said. "Well, if I'm all that valuable, there's something really big you might be able to help me with. One of the main reasons I came here was to meet Jennifer Payne. Do you know her?"

"You really are new, aren't you?" Keane asked.

"What do you mean?"

"Jennifer Payne is a legend in the scene. She was there before Shadow Lane, before Blue Moon, before we had any respect at all."

Melissa wondered if this was a very long time ago. She had had time to give only cursory thought to this question when the prison matron/den mother in the goldenrod blouse and blue skirt approached.

"Hi, Maggie," the newcomer said, wiggling her index and second fingers at Keane. "Share. Please. I'm about to go into severe withdrawal."

Keane shook a cigarette loose. The den mother gratefully took it and accepted a light. She was wearing what Melissa could tell up close was a very expensive blond wig, pulled back into a petite French roll off the back of her neck. Melissa's upclose view confirmed that the woman had to be over fifty but nothing sagged much, even though the corners of her eyes and the top of her forehead said she had no face-lifts in her past.

"Who's your new friend?" she asked as blue-gray smoke dribbled out of her mouth.

"This is Melissa Pennyworth," Keane said as Melissa's jaw bounced off the 100% Herculon deep-pile carpet covering the floor of the Ostend Manifesto Ballroom. "Her *nom de jeu* is Aunt Stern, which I think is just as clever as it can be."

"You sound like you've checked her out pretty thoroughly."

"Credit card, driver's license and a half-hour of casual talk," Keane shrugged.

Shifting her cigarette to her left hand, the newcomer turned to Melissa.

"You'd be Rep Pennyworth's wife, then," she said. "I'm Jennifer Payne."

"I don't know what to say," Melissa managed as she shook Payne's hand.

"Well, it's pretty much up to you," Payne said. "But what it comes down to is that you're buying and I'm selling. So if I were you what I'd say is why your husband needs the information he went public on the net in order to get. I'd tell the truth and I'd make it as complete as possible."

The silence that followed lasted less than five seconds. To Melissa, however, the interval seemed not vastly longer, exactly, but outside of time altogether, as if it existed in some kind of zone from theoretical physics where time didn't pass at all and there was nothing except space and consciousness. She remembered one other moment like this, from a soccer game when she was eleven: her only breakaway, defenders and teammates alike somehow flatfooted on the field behind her, nothing in front of her but the net and the goalie and eighty feet of grass; not thinking, not calculating, just doing; her Nikes *thokking* against the ball, her feet automatically crossing to follow the sphere's bouncing roll, her eyes telling the goalie she was going to shoot left, the goalie's eyes wide and mouth O'ing as her arms and legs spread, *thok* again to the left, the goalie darting in that direction, then Melissa planting on her *right foot*, pivoting her body, in perfect, instinctive synch with the ball, and *THOK!* with her *left foot*, shooting to her own *right*, against the direction of the goalie's desperate lunge, and the ball bounding into the net.

This was exactly like that. A zone where perceptions and nerves and instincts and mind and body all merged into one autonomous being. Keane must have known Melissa was coming from shortly after she signed up. She must have told Payne. Why? Payne must have asked her to. Why? Because Payne thought Rep might be coming to this event in response to Payne's message. Keane had gone to the trouble to be sure Melissa was who she said she was. Why? Because Payne didn't want to reveal herself to someone else. So. The best answer—not the only one, no certainty, but the *best* answer—was that Payne really was on Rep's side and Melissa could trust her.

Melissa told Payne everything she knew. Payne nodded, smoked hungrily at first and then more languidly, and toward the end gave Melissa little feminine touches of acceptance and encouragement, fingertips on elbow, upper body inclining a bit toward her. When Melissa had finished, Payne didn't spend any time thinking things over. She just started talking.

"This is worse than I was afraid it was," she said. "I wish I could help you more, but here's the little I know. Your husband was right. Starting several months ago, I picked up a lot of queries on the net and some on my own e-mail trying to find out particulars about a spanking enthusiast who used the play name Rearward. Obviously, I wasn't the only one getting them. I assumed it was either blackmail or lonely hearts stuff, and either way it had to be squelched, but the net is so huge and unregulated that there's no way you can squelch anything for sure. All you can do is ream the inquiring party out and tell everyone you know not to respond."

"Right," Melissa said.

"Here's the small amount of help I can give you. One of the people asking this was using the play name Fessephile. That happened to be a name used by an ex-client of mine. That's the information that I was promising to pass on to your husband."

"I don't know if I dare ask this," Melissa whispered, "but can you tell me the ex-client's real name?"

"I'd love to but I can't. We don't do photo i.d.'s in my business. He always contacted me and came to me under his play name. He paid in cash. He contacted me either by phone from a number that's not in any cross-directory I could find, or from an e-mail address assigned to John Smith. I'm not kidding."

"How about a physical description?" Melissa pressed.

"Male. Not young. That's about it. I'm really sorry, but that's just the way it is. I've dealt with thousands of guys, and my last contact with this one was a few years ago. I couldn't picture his face to save my life."

"Well, you really have helped," Melissa said. "If you think of anything else, can you get in touch with me?"

"Count on it," Payne said. "Will you be staying at this through the weekend?"

"No, I'm going to leave as soon as I get a night's sleep," Melissa said. "I have what I came for, and there are a lot of other things to do now. But you know Rep's e-mail address."

"Right," Payne said. "Good luck. Maggie, I must owe you at least a pack by now. Don't let me forget."

The other two women moved off, and Melissa began to make her way toward the far side of the room, where she could exit without going back through the Wilmot Proviso Salon. Sketchy as it was, Payne's information was filling in some blanks. Or at least raising some possibilities. Why had whoever did this gone after Rep? Maybe they hadn't been going after Rep *per se*. Maybe they'd been going after a category that Rep happened to be in—copyright lawyer in Indianapolis, for example. Which is what you might do if you were, say, Charlotte Buchanan and wanted a lawyer you could hold a club over. Except that the one thing Payne was absolutely sure of about Fessephile was that he was male. But maybe—

"Excuse me," a male voice said, interrupting her thoughts and her determined stroll. "You look like you're lost in concentration."

"I'm terribly sorry, I didn't mean to run into you," Melissa said, although in fact they hadn't made contact.

"Don't think a thing about it. Are you enjoying the party?"

"Uh, sure."

"Great event, isn't it?"

"Absolutely," Melissa said. She wanted to skirt away, but the man wasn't moving out of her path, and the line for Video Personals blocked her retreat. The man was a little taller than she, balding, dressed in the Rodeo-Drive-casual-shirt-and-slacks-that-cost-more-than-two-Brooks-Brothers-suits look that she associated with the West Coast. His name tag featured a glowing buttocks icon and identified him as Packbrat. He was holding one of the wedding gown white paddles, and making sure she could see it.

"Did you make it to the scene party in Palm Springs last October?" he asked.

"Er, no, actually, not," Melissa said. She tried without success to sidle around him. "Listen, I was heading off to meet someone, so if you don't mind I'd—"

"I see that top symbol on your tag," he said, ignoring her feckless brushoff. "Goes with your name."

"Uh, golly, thanks. Look, I really—"

"In my admittedly limited experience a lot of women who say they're tops are actually switches. Would that include you, by any chance?"

"No."

"You do know what a switch is, don't you?" the man asked then. His tone was still friendly, still signaling pick-up banter, but the question seemed to have a bit of an edge.

"Yes," Melissa said, getting ready to guess if she had to. She had felt awkward and then irritated. Now she felt threatened. She'd been faking it all along, and Keane had seen through her effortlessly. But Keane had turned out, miraculously, to be on Melissa's side. This guy now seemed determined to call her bluff as well, and he gave no hint of being on her side "I'd love to discuss this with you further, but—"

A sharp, no-nonsense, feminine voice interrupted her.

"You are being remarkably rude to this lady, young man," the voice said. Melissa glanced over her shoulder to see Payne striding up to them with Keane in her wake.

Packbrat, though he was certainly no longer young, clearly understood that he was the one being addressed. Blush red ran up his neck and cheeks and over his bald spot. In less than two seconds his eyes looked in four directions, the last one down. He backed up a step and reflexively raised both hands in a gesture that was simultaneously placatory and defensive.

"I, I'm, that is, I'm sorry," he stammered. "I didn't mean to."

"You're not nearly as sorry as you're going to be," Payne said. "We're going to get to the bottom of this right here and now—and I mean that quite literally."

Melissa opened her mouth to demur, but a sharp squeeze above her elbow from Keane preempted any comment.

In three quick paces Payne reached a banquet table strewn with empty plastic glasses and nosh remains. She pulled a straight-back chair away from the table, flipped it around with one hand, and braced its back against the table edge.

"All right," she said, glaring at the man. "Come on over here and get what's coming to you."

A tense, exciting stillness started in the center of the little group and began radiating outward through the Ostend Manifesto Ballroom. The buzz of conversation diminished and gradually died away. The tinkle of ice against plastic faded.

Packbrat stood for five or six seconds in wavering hesitation. No one made a move toward him. If anything, in fact, people backed away. He had an unimpeded path to the exit. All he had to do was turn ninety degrees or so, and then five or six normal steps would have taken him through a door into the corridor.

But he didn't turn. He didn't protest. He closed his eyes, gulped air into his lungs, then took a step toward Payne. Then, eyes open now, another step, and another, and he was standing two feet away from her, in front of the chair.

"Give me that paddle you've been flouting in everybody's face," Payne said, holding out her right hand.

Flaunting, not flouting, Melissa thought automatically, but she immediately reproached herself. As long as Payne was saving Melissa, she could use any diction she wanted to.

Jerkily, Packbrat lifted the white leather paddle and held it out, handle first, to Payne. She took it from him, then unbuttoned the right cuff of her blouse and began deliberately rolling the sleeve up toward her elbow.

"Do you understand why you're going to be disciplined?" she asked.

"Yes." This came out as a strangled murmur, barely audible to Melissa.

"Why? Tell me."

A long mumble from Packbrat followed.

"Say it clearly, so that we can all hear you," Payne snapped as soon as the mumble stopped. "'Because I was rude to a lady who is a guest at this event.' Say it. Now."

"Because I was rude to a lady at this event," Packbrat managed in a spiritless voice.

"And why am I going to take the time and trouble to discipline you for that offense?"

"For my own good and benefit," Packbrat said mechanically.

"That's right. For *your* own good and benefit. You're going to get the paddle, you're going to get it in front of all these people, and you're going to get it good and plenty. We are *not* going into one of the private rooms. You were rude in public, so you can take your medicine in public. I'm going to take this paddle, and I'm going to spank you until you can't sit down. I'm going to turn you over my knee like a naughty schoolboy, and I'm going to give you a sound spanking on your bare bottom."

She paused. As her words sank in, Melissa heard gasps and excited whispers from around the room. She felt tension increasing around her, the way you feel a thunderstorm coming in about seven minutes before it hits.

Packbrat said nothing. The next words Melissa could make out were again Payne's.

"Pull down your pants," Payne said. Packbrat's hesitation lasted perhaps half a second, but that was enough for Payne to shout, "Now!"

Packbrat was fumbling with his belt and trouser snaps before the echoes of that syllable had died away. He lowered his trousers and his underpants at the same time. His shirt-tail hid most of his bottom, but what Melissa could see of his posterior was as unerotic as she could imagine anything being.

Regally, Payne sat down on the chair. She raised her right arm almost full length above her shoulder.

"Please assume the traditional position," she ordered.

As Packbrat obeyed, Melissa saw why Payne had braced the chairback against the table-edge. He was no schoolboy but a full grown man, and his awkward descent across Payne's lap forced her hard against the back of the chair. The table actually moved a couple of inches under the strain. Melissa had a vision of the table not being there, and of all the awful solemnity Payne had managed to generate dissolving into slapstick as the chair tipped over backwards.

"Is she really going to beat him because of me?" Melissa whispered to Keane.

"You bet. This is the real thing."

"I can't let this go on. That paddle looks like it could really hurt."

"It *will* really hurt," Keane said. "Spankings are supposed to hurt. But this wouldn't be happening if he didn't want it to happen. Men pay Jennifer Payne hundreds of dollars to do this to them, and this one is getting it for free."

Payne had pulled Packbrat's shirttail up to expose his bottom fully, which added nothing to its aesthetic appeal. *No man who remembers disco should ever wear bikini briefs,* Melissa thought. Payne now had her left arm secured around Packbrat's waist.

"There's no sense feeling sorry for yourself," she said. "You've got this coming and you know it. Are you ready?"

Melissa didn't hear Packbrat's response, but Payne apparently did. She swung the paddle down and smacked his bottom sharply. It didn't seem to Melissa that Payne had hit him as hard as she could, but it wasn't any stage-swat either. Melissa heard an emphatic *WHAP!* and saw a coppery mark on the lower half of Packbrat's bottom, across both of his cheeks. He gasped.

Payne immediately raised the paddle and smacked Packbrat again, and again, and then again. By the fourth *WHAP!* the beginnings of a grunt tinctured by a high-pitched squeal had supplemented Packbrat's gasps. Payne paused.

"What happens to naughty boys who don't mind their manners?" she asked briskly.

Packbrat managed a panting response, and by the time it was out his bottom had flattened under the paddle again at the start of a second flurry of smacks, which looked and sounded harder than the first four.

"That's right, they get spanked," Payne said, punctuating her commentary with repeated stimulus of Packbrat's abused rear end. "They get *WHAP!* spanked *WHAP* on their bare bottoms *WHAP! WHAP!* in front of *WHAP!* all *WHAP!* the *WHAP!* people they've *WHAP!* offended by their *WHAP!*

WHAP! WHAP! childish *WHAP!* juvenile *WHAP!* boorish *WHAP!* misbehavior *WHAP!*"

Increasingly urgent "AAAGH!s," "WHOA!s," "YIIIPE!s" and "OH BOY!s" now mingled freely with loud, fervent, and urgent promises of behavioral reform from Packbrat. His toes repeatedly tattooed the carpet in spastic, three- or four-beat rhythms.

None of this seemed to move Payne. The paddle continued to descend relentlessly. At one point, in fact, Payne brought the paddle down across the backs of Packbrat's thighs, saying crossly, "No squirming! Take your punishment like a man!" The occasional comments Melissa heard from the spectators—running the gamut of originality from "YES!" to "You go, girl!"—offered apparently unanimous approval for the vigor and enthusiasm Payne brought to her task.

"He can stop it anytime he wants to," Keane whispered to Melissa, grasping her firmly on the bicep. "All he has to do is say, 'Mercy.' She'll stop instantly, and he knows it."

Melissa realized that Keane had grabbed her again because Melissa had unconsciously stepped toward the chair where Payne was spanking Packbrat. Melissa, however, had no further thought of intervening. The sheer, nervous energy of the moment had pushed her, and she was a bit alarmed by her reaction. She was watching a grown man being beaten in a grotesque parody of what she would consider child abuse if this were a genuine parental spanking. She figured it ought to be repulsive and nauseating, and at one level it was. But she also found it exciting. And not only exciting, she realized with a guilty start, but something else: funny.

I can't help it, she thought defensively, *it IS funny!* Such high seriousness brought deadpan to such ridiculous conduct. It was like watching the chorus from *Oedipus Rex* break off in mid-verse and go into a Three Stooges routine.

Finally, Payne paused again. Packbrat panted in labored UNNHH!'s for a few seconds before Payne spoke.

"All right," she said in an almost tender voice. "Have you learned your lesson?"

"YES!" Packbrat assured her. "I have! I promise I have!"

"I hope so. Is there anything you'd like to say before we finish your spanking and you start your corner time?"

"Yes," he sighed. "Yes. I—I deserved that spanking. Thank you for disciplining me."

"You're welcome," Payne said, as several spectators applauded. "Now, here's one for good luck—*WHAP!*—and one on general principles—*WHAP!*—and one to make sure you don't forget—*WHAP!*"

"Thank you!" Packbrat said, very quickly. He actually said this in response to each of the climactic swats, but only the ultimate expression of gratitude was audible over the paddle's reports.

"You're welcome. Now, before you pull your pants back up, go over there and kneel on the floor with your nose against the wall, and just think things over while you reflect on your punishment."

Packbrat slipped from Payne's lap to his knees. Grabbing the tops of his pants, but careful not to pull them up, he labored to his feet, shuffled awkwardly to the nearest wall, and knelt there in the penitent attitude prescribed.

After Packbrat was in position, Payne stood up and walked over to Keane and Melissa, pulling a black, felt tip pen from the pocket of her skirt as she did so. She rested the paddle on the table nearest them and on its surface wrote in an elegant, cursive hand:

Date—June 27
# of Strokes—4 dozen+
Reason—rudeness
Administered by—Jennifer Payne

She handed the paddle to Keane.

"Give him about ten minutes against the wall," she muttered. "Then tell him his punishment is over and he can pull his pants back up—and give him back his paddle."

"He'll treasure this," Keane said to Melissa, gesturing with the autographed paddle. "He'll put it in his trophy case."

"If I were you," Payne continued to her soul sister, "I'd make sure he doesn't get alone with any inexperienced girls. He's liable to be dangerous for the rest of the weekend."

"Right," Keane said.

"As for you," Payne said to Melissa, "I think you'd better make tracks in a hurry." Taking Melissa's arm herself, she began to walk her toward the dealers' room.

"I intend to. I'm going straight back to my room."

"No. At least not any longer than it takes you to get your suitcase. Check out. Right now. Find another hotel, then go back home tomorrow after you've gotten a good night's sleep."

"Why?" Melissa asked.

Payne sighed as she continued to urge Melissa ungently along.

"This will take some explaining if you're really going to buy it," she said, "so I guess I'll have to give you the long version."

"Okay."

"What you just saw isn't my standard routine. My specialty is more the strict but loving older sister, more in sorrow than in anger, 'I'm terribly sorry, honey, but rules are rules and I'm afraid you're just going to have to have a spanking,' hugs before and after, that kind of thing."

"I see. I guess."

"A lot of clients, though, don't necessarily want your specialty. They have particular scenes they like to act out, almost scripted routines that they want to follow. It's my job to draw that out of them and accommodate them."

"Well, sure," Melissa said. "I mean, being a professional and everything."

"Exactly. Now, it so happens that none of the lines you heard just now were terribly original. Including Packbrat's lines. In fact, I've been through that whole routine before—with Fessephile."

"You're saying Packbrat is Fessephile?" Melissa demanded.

"Yes. There were minor variations, of course, but parts of the scenario were word for word. It refreshed my recollection. The memories came flooding back. I'll have Maggie check the registration data, and by the time you're home tomorrow I will have e-mailed you Packbrat/Fessephile's real name."

"So that, by some incredible coincidence the guy who tracked Rep down was the same guy who started hitting on me tonight after you and I talked about him?" Melissa commented, raising her voice to make it a question.

"Nothing coincidental about it. Your husband went public with his query, and someone who wanted to badly enough could have found out that you had signed up for this event at the last minute. Fessephile was here to find out if someone was on his trail, and it was natural for him to suspect you—especially after he saw you talking to me. He accosted you so that he could check out his suspicions."

Melissa nodded while she took a deep breath. Payne's theory made sense—and it made Melissa's skin crawl. What if Payne hadn't happened to be watching over Melissa like a discreet bodyguard when Packbrat had checked out his suspicions?

"You've been enormously helpful and very kind," Melissa said, "and I don't want to seem skeptical. But can you really be sure about his identity? You said yourself you've done this for thousands of men and couldn't remember a particular face."

"I can't remember clients' faces," Payne conceded. "But I never forget a bright red, well spanked bottom."

Chapter 13

As soon as he made it onto I-635 South out of Traverse City, Rep verified that the last milliwatt of juice in his digital phone battery was gone. He glared in dismay at the useless hunk of plastic and silicon in his hand. He was desperately anxious to reach Melissa, not only to update her but even more just to hear her voice. Now he couldn't, unless he pulled off the highway and used a payphone. Which he wouldn't let himself do, because if he did—if he stopped relying on sheer momentum, gave himself a few minutes to reflect on how insane his enterprise was—there was no way he'd talk himself into continuing this mad, Quixotic trek through four states to thwart the nefarious plans of professionals coldly proficient enough to blow up helicopters and plant cocaine in locked cars.

He was wondering if things could possibly get worse when he saw the cop car in his rear-view mirror. It was about two hundred yards behind him. No red and blue lights flashing, just a looming, distinctive profile in Rep's wake. His eyes flicked automatically to the speedometer, where he was relieved to see the needle hovering closer to sixty than sixty-five. He cut it to fifty-eight anyway, just for luck. Half a minute later the cop apparently lost interest. The squad car pulled into the left lane and blew past Rep, presumably in search of less vigilant prey.

Air exploded from Rep's lungs as he realized that he'd been holding his breath. White-knuckled fingers on each hand had been gripping the steering wheel to a point just short of molecular fusion. *I'm not cut out for this*, Rep thought in near despair. He hadn't done anything wrong (lately), but a nothing—a squad car randomly patrolling the interstate—had had him shaking like a novice crack mule approaching Customs.

This won't cut it, he thought then. *I've got to do something constructive.*

He decided to stop thinking.

It worked. Like a machine—well, like an unshaven, cranky machine that had been up since five o'clock Friday morning and tended to jump whenever a car with lights on its roof happened into view—he cruised without incident through northwest Indiana, threaded his way through Chicago on the Skyway, paid the sniveling little penny-ante tolls on I-94 north of the city, managed the transition in Wisconsin from I-94 to I-43 and then to State Highway 41. He pulled into Red and Flora's Lake Winnebago Motor Court in Oshkosh, Wisconsin a little after seven a.m. Saturday. (Though lacking some of the ambience of, say, a Holiday Inn, Red and Flora's had the inestimable commercial advantage of promising a vacancy on a sign big enough for Rep to see from the highway as he approached the first Oshkosh exit.)

While Rep was busy not thinking during the odyssey, his mind had worked steadily, just below the conscious level. Fatigue, fear, and aggravation had stripped away the preconceptions, suppositions, and conventional wisdom that typically impair logical processes. Rep would reflect later that it was like working on a crossword puzzle with wrong answers for two or three critical clues across. You flounder until you finally realize the answers are wrong and erase them. Then, with a string of blank squares unbroken by vagrant mistaken letters, clues down that had been baffling you for half an hour suddenly become limpid and five minutes later the puzzle is done. By the time he got to his room, Rep had figured two things out:

(1) He'd been played for a chump from pretty much the beginning of this case, and he thought he knew how it had been done and who had done it; and

(2) Something very bad was going to happen unless he did something about it in the next twenty-four hours.

This meant that he couldn't afford more than six hours of sleep, even though he felt like twelve would've been more like it. And those six hours were going to have to start pretty fast.

He plugged his digital phone in to recharge. He called Melissa on the room phone and told the answering machine that he was in Oshkosh and would have to explain more later because he was just about to crash. Then he called what looked from the Yellow Pages like the three most luxurious hotels in the Oshkosh area and asked for Aaron Eastman. After going 0 for 3 he gave up and called the number he had for Eastman's production company. He reached a security guard who politely explained that it wasn't yet 5:30 a.m. on the West Coast. Expressing unqualified agreement with this temporal observation, Rep talked the guard into connecting him with Eastman's voice-mail.

"This is Rep Pennyworth," he said after the beep. "We have to talk in a big hurry. Call my digital phone number and leave a message about where and when."

Then he recited his digital phone number. And climbed into bed. And fell instantly and gratefully into an untroubled sleep.

⊞ ⊞ ⊞

By nine o'clock that Saturday morning, the meeting in Conference Room I at Rep's firm was ninety minutes old and Tyler Buchanan still wasn't there. Steve Finneman and Chip Arundel led a generous sampling of the firm's senior litigators and transactional lawyers. Mary Jane Masterson joined an even more generous selection of the firm's grunts.

The chief financial officer and sundry top executives from Tavistock, Ltd. took up most of the rest of the space around the massive walnut table filling the cavernous room. But Buchanan himself, Tavistock's board chairman, chief executive officer and largest single shareholder, The Man, whose immediate and undivided attention to Tempus-Caveator's hostile takeover bid was indispensable, remained unaccounted for.

This absence was by far the morning's most portentous event, and it had Arundel's belly tied in knots. There was nothing he could do about it at the moment, though, so with superficially unruffled calm he had spent over an hour dealing with other things.

"All right, we're working on poison pill and we have white knight on hold for the moment," he said. "There will be an emergency meeting of the board at five o'clock this afternoon to consider issuing up to one hundred million additional shares of stock, with priority buy options for shareholders of record as of December 31st of last year. That takes care of the corporate side. Now we need something for the litigators to get their teeth into. Something really juicy on Tempus-Caveator. Something a court will enjoin a tender offer for if they don't put it in the proxy statement. What have we got?"

For several seconds only foot shuffling answered this comment, and Allen Edmonds wingtips rubbing against deep pile Herculon don't make much noise. Then, after the polite interval her seniors were entitled to had run, Masterson spoke up.

"Tempus-Caveator was on the witness list for the Thompson Committee hearings in the United States Senate a few years ago."

"You mean the campaign finance scandal thing that didn't go anywhere?" Arundel asked. "Hype-city for months, then it closed on Saturday night?"

"That one," Masterson confirmed. "Foreigner out of nowhere with a sudden security clearance at the Commerce Department; mysterious calls made from a payphone across the street from his office; dirty money back-tracked from a bagman at a presidential reception through shady characters in Indonesia all the way to some woman colonel in the Red Chinese Army."

Behind the fleshy lids that hooded them, Finneman's eyes flicked with interest at the pertinence of Masterson's comment and the self-confidence in her tone. Not cringing in the background, waiting to see what more senior people would say so that she could agree with them, but actually speaking up on her own. He began to wonder if she might not have the raw material to be molded into a partner in a few years after all.

"I thought the whole point of that thing was that the dirty money was foreign," Arundel said. "Tempus-Caveator is a vicious, bottom-feeding, low-life corporate predator, but it's a vicious, bottom-feeding, low-life *American* corporate predator. Where did it fit in?"

"Not clear. They resisted the subpoena, the committee didn't insist and they ended up not being called."

"So what, then?" Arundel snapped.

"So not long before the scandal broke," Masterson said calmly, "Tempus-Caveator wasn't Tempus-Caveator yet. It was Tempus, Inc. and Caveator Corporation, two separately owned companies. A lot of people expected the Justice Department to jump on their merger with both feet, but they got a pass. If you start putting two and two together—"

"I love it!" Arundel said triumphantly, his lips parting half an inch in a rare show of human emotion. He turned to the litigator sitting to Finneman's right. "Hit it. Pedal to the metal. Get on that baby and drive it right into the ground."

"What proof do we have at this point?" the litigator asked.

"Proof is your department," Arundel said. "I'm in charge of allegations. Come back here at one p.m. and *you* tell me what proof we have. Don't disappoint me."

"Restroom break," Finneman said then, displaying yet once more his genius for sensing latent consensus. He unobtrusively accosted Tavistock's CFO during the general shuffle out of the conference room.

"Where's Tyler?" he asked.

"Can't raise him," the CFO said uncomfortably. "He's gotten the messages and he knows where to come."

"Let me ask the question more clearly," Finneman said with a jovial Midwestern twang right out of summer stock. "Where the *hell* is Tyler? This is the most important issue Tavistock has faced in twenty years. If we don't play this right, you and he and everyone he's worked with at that company could be out on your collective rears in three months. Now where is he?"

The CFO stopped and pulled Finneman ungently into a recess off the corridor, between two secretaries' desks.

"Charlotte has disappeared," he whispered. "Before this takeover attempt came up she was scheduled to be in the office all weekend working on a huge presentation. She played hooky at home yesterday morning, and no one has been able to find her since mid-afternoon on Friday."

"Charlotte Buchanan, Tyler's daughter who has a copyright infringement claim being investigated by this firm?" Finneman asked with a thoughtful gaze.

"Charlotte Buchanan, the one thing in the world that is more important to Tyler than Tavistock, Limited," the CFO said.

❀ ❀ ❀

"So that's the basic story from Chicago," Melissa said around eleven-fifteen Saturday morning, as she concluded the twelfth minute of her series of voice-mail messages for Rep. She had already covered everything from the plot of *Green for Danger* to the scene party run-up. "Except, oh, God, how could I do this, I forgot one of the most important things. By the time I was ready to leave Chicago this morning, Margaret Keane had called and told me that the real name of the guy who came on to me was Bernie Mixler. Okay, *that's* the basic story. And there are a couple of things that really don't add up for me. I mean, more than a couple, but a couple *really* baffle me. Like, why was Jennifer Payne so nice to me? Why did she take such an active interest in this problem in the first place, for that matter? I mean, she said it was because interfering with internet privacy was bad for her business, and I guess it is, but that doesn't seem good enough to explain her becoming my guardian angel while I was at this, this, uh, scene event, I guess you'd call it."

A beep told her that she was nearing the end of recording time on this call, so she said that she'd hang up and call back with some more.

Which she did, but only after several minutes of reflection. There was one more facet of the problem that was gnawing at her, but she didn't trust herself right away to put it into words. Finally she felt she had enough of a handle on it to dial Rep's number again.

"My last comment is a little hard to articulate," she said when she knew she was recording again. "It's kind of oblique, because what made me think about it is all the literary theory I've been wading through for my entire adult life. I know this isn't news to you, but the all-time insight of the last fifty years is supposedly that nothing has any intrinsic meaning. We read *Moby Dick* and anything we think it means is a construct that we impose on it, based on our sex and class and race and background and so forth. And supposedly that's the way it is with everything, not just novels. So we're not even supposed to say 'reality,' we have to say "'reality,'" with quotes around it, because there is no independent reality, everything we think of as 'reality' is our own construct and so forth."

She paused and exhaled a long breath, as if she were getting rid of exhausted smoke from a joint. This was actually coming out very well, but she wondered if it would make the slightest sense to Rep—or anyone else who hadn't been buried for term after term in the rarefied arcana of literary deconstructionism. There was nothing to do but go on, though, so that's what she did.

"Anyway, what struck me as I was coming back from Chicago this morning was that this is basically a crock. What I mean is, it may be that everything I know about what's going on, and everything you know, and everything any other particular person knows is a construct that we each put together, influenced by all these factors I mentioned. But somewhere in this mess there's a reality that none of us has constructed out of our own prejudices and perceptions and that's completely independent of what we choose to understand about it. There's a reality that actually exists and that doesn't really care very much what any of us happens to think it might be. And that reality is that someone is trying to kill someone else. And they're going to bring it off unless someone else does something about it." She started to choke and willed herself back under control. "Well, Rep, you're trying to. I don't know if you can do it, but it's about the bravest thing I can imagine, the way you're doing it, and I don't care what happens or what anyone else thinks, I am so proud to be married to you."

❀ ❀ ❀

Why would anyone deed a collar? Rep thought as he fought his way up through cottony layers of sleep at (as he later learned) one in the afternoon. *And what college is Doan U?*

The big, hostile guy merely repeated the question, more threateningly and with hunks of Rep's bedclothes in his fists.

"Doan U know 'bout collar I deed?"

Oh I get it, Rep thought, *another jail dream. I've been to this movie before. Time to wake up.*

He woke up. Someone very angry was in his face.

"Don't you know about caller i.d.?" the very angry someone reiterated.

Uh-oh, Rep thought, *it isn't a dream. This is very bad.*

"Here," a voice behind the angry guy said. The next thing Rep knew a glassful of cold water had splashed in his face. He sat up quickly in bed, sputtering and suddenly awake enough to recognize Aaron Eastman.

"You're way out of your league, junior," Eastman said. "My company switchboard has state-of-the-art caller identification—not that we needed anything more than star-sixty-nine. The security guard who answered your call got the number for this place, so I was able to track you down instead of giving you a roadmap so you could find me. The maid is very trusting with her pass-key, so we didn't even have to 'loid your lock."

"If I hadn't been too tired to see straight when I called I would have left the motel number myself," Rep said. "We have to talk."

"You bet we have to talk, you bush-league shyster," Eastman hissed, his nose about an inch from Rep's. "We have to talk about helicopters blowing up less than three hundred feet away from me, and exactly what else your loony-tunes client has in mind."

"That's exactly it!" Rep said excitedly. "It's not Charlotte! I have that much figured out, but there are some blanks that you have to fill in."

"The only thing I plan on filling in at the moment is the space between your rectal cheeks, and I'll be using a size ten Ferragamo loafer with tooled leather welts to do it. The one doing the talking here is going to be you, and the first thing I want to hear is the name of whoever is running you and that broad who thinks she's Martha Grimes."

"That's just the point," Rep insisted, a hint of impatience coloring his voice. "No one is 'running' us. Someone is trying to make you believe that."

"Well they're doing a real good job. Since early yesterday evening I've had a singed scalp and a lot of nervous backers who are wondering if it's going to be bad luck to put money into one of my pictures. You know a lot more than you've told me so far, and when I walk out of here we're both going to know it. So start spilling your guts."

Rep's reaction to this, while understandable, was perhaps not as constructive as it might have been. He could discern a tincture of panic along with the clearly unfeigned anger in Eastman's voice, and he supposed he would have felt the same way. Rep found it exasperating, though, when people refused to heed perfectly reasonable analyses, i.e., Rep's; and while he had to swallow his irritation when the recalcitrants were paying clients or senior partners or Melissa, Eastman wasn't in any of those categories.

"This is ridiculous and it isn't getting us anywhere," Rep said with more than a touch of petulance. "Now here's the protocol. We're going to quit blustering and shouting and grabbing each other's clothes. We're going to sit down like two reasonably intelligent adults and have a calm, rational dialogue about this thing. I'm not saying another word until we're agreed on that, so you might as well just back off and start impersonating a grown-up."

The shape of Eastman's lips suggested that something including "sniveling little weenie" was about to come out. Before he could speak any actual words, however, the guy who'd handed him the water glass intervened.

"Hey, chief," he said, holding up Rep's digital phone, still plugged into the outlet. "Think this might be worth a try? Just as a start?"

Eastman blinked once in astonishment, then a second time in understanding as he saw panic wash across Rep's features. At that point the rictus into which his own face had frozen relaxed into something nearly serene.

"That idea is colossal," Eastman said with relish. "The guy who hired you must be a genius—if I do say so myself."

Rep hadn't had a particularly good look at the other guy yet. What glimpses he had managed around Eastman's shoulders had vaguely suggested one of those fourth-cowboy-through-the-saloon-door types from fifties and sixties westerns. The guy now unplugged the phone, turned it on, and gazed lovingly at the screen.

"Guess what, chief," he said. "This guy has mail."

"Gimme," Eastman said eagerly, leaping at the phone.

"Hey!" Rep protested, "you can't do that!"

He scrambled out of bed, grabbing for the phone. He found himself immediately back in bed, his chest smarting from the guy's casual right jab and blood seeping from throbbing nostrils as a by-product of the gentleman's efficient left elbow. When Rep opened his eyes five or six seconds later, he saw Eastman holding the digital phone up to his ear. The other guy, now seeming a bit more like the second-cowboy-through-the-saloon-door, looked like he really wanted Rep to hop out of bed again. After deliberate and mature consideration, Rep decided not to.

Minutes dragged by without this static tableau changing much—rather like a high concept European art film, Rep would think later. Rep himself didn't dare move. The cowboy watching him seemed tensed in coiled, ready stillness. And Eastman just stood there with the phone to his ear, listening. He didn't pace or scratch himself or adjust his posture, except to shift hands and ears on the phone now and then. The only thing that changed much was his expression, which changed a lot. It began with impatient interest, then progressed gradually through surprise, astonishment, incredulity, and gape-mouthed dumbfoundedness. The climax came when Eastman's lips snapped primly closed under a pinch-faced look like Rep's aunt used to get when she saw a girl in a mini-skirt, and a deep blush crept from the Hollywood hotshot's jawbone to his scalp.

Cripes, Rep thought as the clock ticked on, *I hope we're not in analog roam.*

Finally Eastman pushed what Rep fervently hoped was the END button and brought the phone down.

"I swear," he said in a fervent voice, "the next time some screenwriter brings me a script full of Midwesterners who don't do anything but smoke pipes, hunt ducks, and eat apple cobbler, I'm going to drown him in the ranch dressing tureen at Spago's. Joey, go get us three big cups of black coffee, and maybe some high-sugar pastry for the counselor here."

"Yeah, sure thing," Joey said, looking and sounding far more dubious than his words. He hesitated more than once on his way out, but he finally made it through the door, leaving Rep and Eastman alone.

"Who's Steve?" Eastman asked.

"Probably Steve Finneman, the senior partner at my firm," Rep said as Eastman nodded.

"He left a message for you. He said that Tempus-Caveator Corp. has launched a takeover bid for one of your firm's big clients. He also said that Charlotte Buchanan has suddenly gone missing and has to be found quick."

"Blitz my writs," Rep said to an Eastman momentarily baffled by this lawyerly ejaculation. "Give me that thing. I have to talk to Steve right now."

"You may want to hear some more before you call him," Eastman said. "Most of what I listened to was from your wife. She's had herself quite a little twelve hours or so."

"What do you mean?" Rep asked urgently.

"This is going to take a while," Eastman said. "I'll give it to you while you're dressing and freshening up."

Not quite half an hour later, Eastman and Rep had not only exchanged every scrap of relevant information they each possessed but had consumed between them thirty-two ounces of coffee and two cinnamon rolls larger than some eastern states. Rep had found time between mouthfuls to call Finneman and share what clues he had to Charlotte Buchanan's whereabouts. He had also explained to Eastman the theory that had formed itself spontaneously in his mind while he was driving to Oshkosh—a theory that, as he pointed out with some satisfaction to Eastman, the information from Melissa and Finneman backed up.

"Melissa I can see," Eastman conceded. "But why Finneman? What do Tavistock's corporate problems have to do with this?"

"The source of all the problems—namely, Tempus-Caveator. What I think has people doing nasty things to you right now is that you're shopping a project about Tempus-Caveator tanking *Red Guard!* You're accusing T-C of sinking an epic film it suddenly found itself owning so that a grateful Chinese government would shut off information damaging to the incumbent administration, with the pay-off for Tempus-Caveator being a critical antitrust pass from that same administration. Charlotte Buchanan moves into your orbit, and suddenly her dad's company has trouble with Tempus-Caveator too. Do you think it's just coincidence?"

"An elephant stomping through the savanna crushes a lot of earthworms in five years," Eastman said, shrugging. "That doesn't mean one earthworm has anything to do with another one. Charlotte Buchanan is making problems for me, so if you're right Tempus-Caveator should be helping her, not hurting her. Give me a logical reason why T-C's attack on me should make it want to take over Tavistock."

"It doesn't come to me right away," Rep admitted. "How did Tempus-Caveator kill *Red Guard!?* Is all that stuff in your treatment about hacking into computers to fiddle the Price-Waterhouse certified count really true?"

"That's speculation," Eastman said. "The truth is I don't know how, I just know what. They did everything they could to kill the movie, including making sure it came up empty on Oscar night. But how they brought it off, aside from the scheduling games I already told you about, I don't know."

"Okay, so we have to work on that one," Rep said. "Still, by my count there are now something like seven reasons why Charlotte Buchanan isn't the one who blew up your helicopter. With number seven being, whatever else you might think about her, it's hard to see her carrying water for Tempus-Caveator."

He smiled with the quiet, practiced confidence that his impeccable reasoning justified. The smile that Eastman offered Rep was just as quiet and just as confident, but not quite as friendly, somehow.

"That's very interesting," he said. "But I can think of one reason why you're totally full of it."

"Huh? What are you talking about?"

"Her e-mail to you. She knew I'm due in northern California Sunday night to prospect for cash. How did she know that? She wanted to get you out of Indianapolis over the weekend when the takeover battle started. Why? Just an interesting coincidence?"

"I think I can get you answers to those questions, actually, but it might take a little time," Rep said, hoping he could improvise as furiously as he was bluffing.

"Well I want to hear this, it ought to be good," Eastman said, glancing at his watch. "But I'll tell you what, you're going to have to get it done by five o'clock this afternoon, because that's when I have to drive to the airport to pick up Selding, who's flying in from L.A. with his laptop full of key information about these Silicon Valley money guys."

With Eastman's words, a tidy little Gestalt whole popped fully formed into Rep's consciousness. It was a model of craftsmanlike perfection, every mortise dovetailing perfectly into the corresponding tenon, every dowel countersunk into its apertures in a model of flawless joining, every metaphor unmixed and apropos. Rep didn't have time to analyze it; all he could do was go with it.

"I'll tell *you* what," Rep said, pointing his finger at Eastman and feeling a rush like he hadn't had since he'd thrown two blue chips at three aces showing with red cards up and black ones down in his own hand. "I'll tell you what. Give me one more piece of information, and before you leave for Pomona I won't just explain it to you, I'll prove it to you."

"I've been bluffed by experts, son," Eastman said, grinning wickedly. "You're on."

Chapter 14

The majestically arcing faceted glass ceiling and the clean architectural lines defined in light blue and industrial gray were busily trying to make Jerry Selding think he was someplace halfway civilized. He wasn't fooled, though. No matter how much United Airlines had tarted the place up, it was still Terminal 1 at O'Hare International Airport, and Selding still hated it.

As he tramped out of that terminal and began in earnest his epic, marathon, Trail of Tears trek to Terminal 4, Selding tried to avoid thinking about how many times he'd been through O'Hare in the past two years and how many times he'd be here in the next two. You can fly *over* the country from L.A. without hitting Chicago, but it seemed to Selding that whenever you flew around *inside* the country you had to touch down at O'Hare at some point along the way.

The burden that had already started a nagging little ache in the back of his right shoulder did nothing to improve his mood. Selding had checked his Travelpro bag all the way through to Oshkosh, but ever since leaving the storage lockers he'd been lugging his laptop—a Dell Latitude Pentium II in a massive black leather case bristling with zippers and flaps. It was big and dorky by Beverly Hills' elegant standards, but the price was right: he'd neglected to return it to Human Resources when Tavistock Ltd. pink-slipped him, and he'd just kept on using it since. Not that that made him any happier about toting the thing. In his view, laptops (along with portable phones and pagers) were *fin de siècle* gray flannel suits, badges of conformity—and Selding was as tied to his as any of the sales reps or middle managers or CPAs sharing the endless corridor with him were to theirs.

Finally he found himself approaching the Terminal 4 security area. He always thought of the same, limp joke as he neared the end of mind-numbing hikes like this: *If I just kept walking a little longer, I could skip the plane and reach Oshkosh on foot.* A woman hustled past him, in such a hurry that he checked his watch to be sure he wasn't running late himself. He wasn't, of course. People just seemed naturally to pick up their pace when they got this close, as if it were terribly important to spend an extra two minutes in the departure lounge instead of idling them away in the line to the x-ray machine.

Above such mindless herd instincts himself, Selding sauntered wearily into line. He put his laptop on the conveyer belt, stepped to the metal detector, and emptied keys and change from his pockets into a Tupperware bowl. He prepared to step between the magnetic sensors that would verify he was unarmed.

"Excuse me, sir," the guard at the table said, stopping him in mid-pace. "Is this pipe-cleaning tool yours?"

Selding glanced up. *Did anyone under sixty actually smoke pipes anymore?* The woman was holding a roach clip, and she was doing it with a knowing glint in her eye. Pipe-cleaning tool, right. She knew what it was as well as he did.

"No, of course not," Selding snapped. *Cripes, I couldn't possibly have done something that stupid, could I?* He took a deep breath, and spoke with a bit more control. "No, it isn't mine."

"One of the other passengers saw it on the floor and thought you might have dropped it," the woman said, shrugging and adopting a don't-blame-me expression. She set the implement down on the table. "Pass on through."

He walked without incident through the metal detector and retrieved the black leather laptop bag now at the secure end of the conveyor belt. His gate was one of eight grouped together on a concourse off of Terminal 4's main corridor— second-rate, low-service gates for affiliated, regional carriers. He'd be flying in a plane with propellers instead of jets, but at least Eastman wouldn't be at the controls.

He figured he had a good twenty minutes before they'd start boarding and he wanted to go over the opening scene storyboard for *Every Sixteen Minutes* one more time, so he found a chair and pulled the laptop out of its case. There wasn't an outlet in sight, of course, and even if he'd spotted one it probably wouldn't have been hot. Airports in the age of portable electronics had gotten cagey about making electricity too accessible in departure lounges, he'd noticed. He guessed that they didn't want passengers tripping over proliferating mares' nests of power cords. Selding figured it wouldn't be a problem, though. The battery still ought to have some muscle left.

He pushed the ON button. Nothing happened. So much for *that* theory. He tried again. Nothing. Not the slightest pulse of green light or the hint of a valiant beep.

Disgustedly, he snapped the lid shut. The battery probably wasn't charging back up all the way anymore, which meant this was the beginning of the end for it. A new one would cost $250 or more, and he bet he'd have to go to the computer equivalent of an antique store to find one.

He surveyed the departure lounge again, in a more determined search for a functional outlet. Five minutes and several irritated looks from fellow passengers were enough to convince him that the only possibility was set low in a wall around the far corner of the lounge. To get to it he'd have to shift a four-seat bench, and to do that he'd have to induce movement from a beefy Chicago Blackhawks fan who looked like he didn't care much for guys with earrings. And of course if he managed all that he still might find out that the thing wasn't supplying current anyway. He was on the verge of surrendering unconditionally to these formidable obstacles when he heard a woman's voice behind him, trying to get his attention.

"Uh, yo," he said, turning around. The lady was short and old—late twenties anyway, maybe early thirties—with dead ordinary brown hair. Her best feature was lively green eyes. Her shape was okay, he guessed, but it wouldn't have gotten a second glance on the coast. On the other hand, she had at least avoided that supermodel skinniness that was so common in California these days and that frankly tended to creep Selding out. (He wouldn't say it out loud to anyone, but he thought he was a fairly normal guy and his idea of a sexy woman didn't involve something that looked more like an anorexic adolescent male.)

"You looked like you might be looking for a place to fire up your computer," she said. She raised her own laptop case slightly in a vaguely empathetic gesture. "There's a Northwest Airlines Admirals Club room between gates eight and ten with work carrels, power strips and data ports. I've just come from there. If you're really desperate, you can come down with me and I can sign you in as my guest."

What a great pick-up line! Selding thought. *The third millennium way to hit on perfect strangers!* It was tempting, in a way, especially if she was also going to Oshkosh. But he figured he wasn't ready for that level of commitment with someone who could have babysat for him.

"That's really nice of you," he said with the mellow, coastal warmth his voice had acquired since his relocation. "But I don't think I'll have time to get there and back before they start boarding. Thanks anyway, though."

"Sure," the lady said.

O'Hare to Oshkosh was thirty cramped, unpleasant minutes of actual air time. Selding hated every second of it. It was with vast relief that he pulled his laptop out of the overhead compartment and ambled across the tarmac to

Oshkosh's tidy little terminal building. He never thought he'd be so glad to see Eastman in his life.

Eastman was all smiles, so friendly and palsy-walsy that Selding wondered for a moment if he were about to be fired. He decided instead that Eastman was just softening him up for some other really stinky job he had in mind.

"No more cattle car traveling for you for at least a little while, tiger," Eastman told him while they were waiting at the luggage carousel for his Travelpro. "You've earned a few perks. We've got a limo to the Paper Valley Hotel, which admittedly ain't the Century Plaza but it's the best place for a hundred miles in any direction. Plus, the hookers are a lot cheaper and instead of AIDS they'll give you stuff they treat with penicillin. There'll be room service waiting for you when we check you in. They don't do free range chicken out here, but that's okay because you've lived around here and you can probably still handle the local cuisine."

"You don't know how good that sounds," Selding said.

"Also, that chick from *Entertainment Tonight!* who thought she'd have a permanent bad hair day after our helicopter went blooey is still hanging around. She's looking for inside stuff, and if she thinks you'll give her some you might get lucky. If that's your speed."

"What can I tell her?"

"We'll talk about it in the limo. You might squeeze her a little bit, too. See if she's gotten cozy with the local law and found out anything about the explosion we don't know. That's on top of getting a line on another Sikorsky helicopter, which just became another entry on your to-do list."

"Right."

The limo ride was heaven. The martini was heaven. The prospect of trying his luck with the chick from *Entertainment Tonight!* was intriguing. The thought that, sometime around noon tomorrow, Aaron Eastman would be in that B-24 heading for Moneyland, leaving Selding for at least three unsupervised days with a luxury hotel room and a decent expense account—that thought was almost enough to compensate for the brutal hardships of a coach seat from the coast and a commuter flight connection. When Eastman showed him into Room 622 at the Paper Valley Hotel just before six o'clock, Selding decided that, on the whole, the world had once again become quite satisfactory.

As soon as Selding's door closed, Eastman quick-stepped to his own suite, 649. His laptop sat, open and glowing, on the work table in the suite's front room. The e-mail window open on the screen displayed a provocative message:

> Saturday, 4:12 p.m. CDT
> From: Jerry Selding[jselding@pointwest.com]
> To: Aaron Eastman
> Re: You've Got Mail
>
> Dear Mr. Eastman:
>
> Rep was right. If I could do this to Selding, Mixler could have done it to Charlotte. And did.
>
> Melissa Pennyworth

Rep and Melissa Pennyworth sat on a couch about eight feet from Eastman's computer, looking rather like teenagers babysitting for a child whose parents had returned a tad earlier than expected. He grinned at them in gracious concession.

"Where did you pull the switch?" he asked.

"At the security checkpoint," Melissa said. "I went through ahead of him, with a general issue Tavistock laptop and case that were identical to his. I left something I said he'd dropped with the attendant to divert him for a second, and that was enough for me to take his case and leave mine after they'd both been through the x-ray machine."

"So now he's sitting in his room with your laptop?"

"No, I switched back on the plane. As soon as he stowed the one he had in the overhead compartment, I opened the compartment right behind his, pulled the laptop he had stowed over to my area and put the one I had—which was his—in its place."

"Which gave you time before you boarded the plane," Eastman mused, "to find a data port and send me this e-mail."

"Right."

"But you were able to do that only because I gave your husband Selding's log-on password. How did Mixler know Charlotte Buchanan's password?"

"Selding told him," Melissa explained. "They both worked at Tavistock, they both had the Dell computers Tavistock gave to its employees, both computers used Tavistock-tailored software and operating systems that the company had licensed, and they both at least started out with company-issued passwords generated according to the same formula. Selding knew that if his password was 'jselding' then Charlotte's was 'cbuchanan.' She could have changed it, of course, but in most places only the techies bother with that. And even if she had, he probably still had friends back at Tavistock and could have found out the new one if he really wanted to."

"I see," Eastman said. "Of course if he'd turned the computer on he would have instantly spotted the switch. How did you know he wouldn't do that?"

"I deliberately ran the battery down on the one I switched with his."

"And you were lucky that he didn't find a working outlet."

"Well," Melissa conceded, "you need a little luck. But Mixler wouldn't necessarily have had to count on that. If our theory is right, he met Charlotte at O'Hare, and he could simply have kept her busy himself while an accomplice sent the e-mail."

"Not too bad," Eastman said. "It'd be kinda fun to figure out a way to show that on the screen."

"And one more thing," Melissa said. "You might want to have someone look into whether Morrie Bristol has anything going at the moment with Galaxy Entertainment."

"The Morrie Bristol who was the worst of the three screenwriters for *In Contemplation of Death*?" Eastman asked. "Why?"

"Because he's the only one of those three who's also a published novelist," Rep said. "I've left voice-mails with a couple of my buddies in the New York copyright bar to confirm it, but it won't shock me to the soles of my shoes to learn that Julia Deltrediche is his agent."

"That might be worth looking into at that," Eastman conceded.

"Which brings us to the most interesting question," Rep said. "What are we going to do now?"

"I don't know what you're going to do," Eastman said, "but I need sixty million dollars to make a movie with. I'm flying to northern California—except a little earlier than planned."

"Excellent," Rep said.

Chapter 15

"So how did it go?" Eastman asked Selding. "Did you make the earth move for her?"

Hemingway again, thought Selding, who wasn't entirely uneducated.

Eastman's question came at a bad time—specifically, at 11:20 Saturday night, as Selding was stumbling irritably out of a limousine that had delivered him to the EAA airfield. He nevertheless managed to answer it without overt insolence.

"Uh, no," he mumbled. Longing still for the air-conditioned atmosphere richly textured with tobacco smoke and redolent of alcohol that he had just left at the Paper Valley Hotel's bar, he pressed fingertips against temples in an effort to force the loathsome fresh air out of his head. "She said she doesn't sleep with sources."

"Hadn't she ever seen *All the President's Men?*" Eastman asked.

"Guess not. I was scoping out the local talent when I got your beep."

This anodyne comment was a triumph of discretion, for Selding had to concentrate fiercely to keep impolitic thoughts from tumbling out of his mouth. Eastman's message from forty minutes ago still echoed obscenely in his head: "Bad news, buckaroo. Attitude alert in Silicon Valley. Change in plans. Early command performance in Pomona.

Car on the way." *Just please don't call me 'buckaroo' again*, Selding thought now.

"Well, don't take it too hard, buckaroo," Eastman said. "After the opening weekend for *Every Sixteen Minutes* the local talent will be taking numbers outside your apartment— and I'm talking about the local talent in Beverly Hills. Let's climb on board so we can get our seat backs and tray tables in their original upright and locked positions."

That startled Selding, as it suddenly dawned on him that they weren't at the EAA Airfield to wait for a hastily arranged chopper to buzz them down to O'Hare where they could catch a real plane for the coast. Instead, they were going to make this improvised journey in Eastman's current toy, that bloody B-24. *Duh*, he thought disgustedly, just before he found himself being ungently hoisted into the thing.

When his eyes had adjusted enough to the dim red light inside to see Rep Pennyworth already ensconced snugly in the navigator's seat, he said something a lot stronger than duh. Thirty seconds later he noticed Eastman slipping into the cockpit and he realized that the certifiably wacko ego-maniac he worked for was actually planning to fly this crate himself all the way to northern California. The string of epithets he let loose with mentally at that point would have guaranteed an instant R rating for any film that dared to include them.

"Where's the real pilot?" Selding demanded, as rage and frustration finally overtaxed his normally inexhaustible capacity for toadyism.

"Probably bopping that *ET!* skirt you struck out with," Eastman said genially as he flipped switches and set propel-lers spinning. "I couldn't raise him on short notice."

"What's the big emergency, then? Why couldn't you just fly out tomorrow around noon, like you'd planned?" *And why do I suddenly have to be in on it?*

"Blame the shyster here," Eastman replied. "His client found out about the money meeting, and seems to have gotten her Ivy League-educated rear end out there with mischief in mind. So we have to improvise a quick and happy solution to her little controversy before she makes a nuisance of herself."

"Found out how?" Selding bleated.

"That's one thing you're going to help me get to the bottom of. I need some extra eyes and ears working on that full time, because I'm going to have my hands full getting the shyster and his client straightened out before the software princes start strolling into my hotel room Monday morning. Plus one more thing. There's buzz that our boy Morrie Bristol had one of his lame post-modern *angst* novels optioned at Galaxy and they're actually going ahead with it. I need you to check that out, too."

"I don't follow," Selding said, as a distant warning bell tinkled faintly in his head.

"Then just settle back and enjoy the ride while I run through this twenty-six point preflight checklist and then chat with the gents in the control tower."

Less than five minutes later they were in the air. Looking over at Rep as he thought Eastman's comments over, Selding bucked up a bit. It did make sense when you thought about it, he reflected. He wasn't a mere gofer, or even just a techie who could scan pretty pictures onto computer screens. When you got right down to it, he was actually a pretty impressive guy. He could really see Eastman thinking that the glittering little flicker of danger in the depths of Selding's dark brown eyes would help a *schlepper* like Buchanan's lawyer here see where the dictates of prudence might lie. Not to mention that other matter. Eastman wouldn't believe how clever Selding could sound about that one if he decided to. This had possibilities.

"Mask time, boys and girls," Eastman said. "Ten thousand feet in thirty seconds."

Selding had by now learned to handle the oxygen mask and throat mike adroitly, but he still hated the things.

Grudgingly he slipped his on and fingered the mike into position. He waited until he'd filled his lungs twice before he risked bellyaching.

"Couldn't you just cruise around eight thousand feet all the way to the coast?" he asked. "It's not like this is a seven-twenty-seven or anything."

"Maybe not, but we're way too big for that altitude. I'll be surprised if they let us stay below twenty thousand feet once we're cruising."

The plane throbbed through the night. Selding did *not* wonder what it would have been like to be riding in one of these things on a night bombing run over Germany, waiting for cannons to belch flak from below and Messerschmidts to come screaming out of the sky above. Nor did he think about the emotions that must have run through men preparing to rain anonymous death on unknown thousands beneath them. Selding's idea of history was the Reagan administration. What Selding thought about was being co-producer of a movie with world class distribution before he was twenty-nine.

He was pulled from his reveries, such as they were, by the lawyer (Pennyworth, he remembered). Quite suddenly, it seemed, Rep stretched his body, rubbed his eyes with the heels of his hands, and yawned so deeply that Selding could tell he was doing it even though the oxygen mask covered his nose and mouth.

"Sorry," Rep said after the performance. "I have no idea why I'm so tired all of a sudden. I got plenty of sleep, and I've only been out of bed since two this afternoon."

Selding shrugged more or less sympathetically as he stifled a yawn of his own. A hideous thought—not a thought, really, just the suggestion of the beginning of an idea—fluttered briefly across his consciousness. He repressed it.

"I'm feeling it a little bit myself," Eastman said. "Shouldn't be, though. We're getting pure oxygen. We ought to be feeling peppy and wide awake."

Selding tried and failed to suppress another yawn. He'd done two lines of pure Columbian nose candy less than ninety minutes ago. No way *he* should be sleepy.

"Maybe we should bag this flight," he suggested, a nervous edge coloring his voice despite himself. "Turn back and try it again after everyone has had a good night's sleep."

"No can do," Eastman said. "Don't worry. I'll get us there."

The lawyer yawned again, then lowered his head and shook it with impatience. Selding felt drowsiness begin to overtake him. The hideous thought—and by now it was a full-blown thought, all right—didn't flutter across his consciousness this time. It vibrated through his whole body with a terrible clarity.

"Maybe there's something wrong with the oxygen tanks," he said—a bit faster than he usually spoke. What colored his voice this time wasn't nervousness but panic. "Maybe that's why we're all nodding off."

"If there were something wrong with the tanks you'd have known about it long before now," Eastman scoffed reassuringly. "When you breathe you're getting something through your nose and into your lungs, right? Therefore, there's nothing wrong with the tanks."

"Maybe they made a mistake when they recharged them," Selding said, his voice rising. "Maybe they didn't put oxygen in them. Maybe they charged them with something else instead."

"Why would they charge them with anything but oxygen?" Eastman demanded.

"That's interesting," Rep volunteered. "My wife was just telling me yesterday about a movie called *Green for Danger* based on that. It takes place in a hospital, and the murderer kills someone by painting a tank of nitrogen green so that the anesthetist would think it was an oxygen tank. The patient gets nitrogen instead of oxygen, and dies of asphyxiation."

"I think we could tell if we were getting nitrogen instead of oxygen," Eastman said sarcastically.

"We couldn't, actually," Rep said. "There was an incident at NASA during the early days of the space program, back in the sixties. Some workers went into a sealed chamber filled with pure nitrogen. They couldn't tell the difference. To them, it was just like breathing air. But they weren't getting any oxygen so they passed out and died, just like the patient in the movie."

"I really think we should get down below ten thousand feet," Selding said, his urgent tones contrasting sharply with Rep's matter-of-fact commentary.

"Can't do it," Eastman said flatly.

"I understand your concern," Rep said soothingly to Selding. "Long before we lost consciousness we'd start having brain cells die from oxygen deprivation. We could be losing major IQ points somewhere over the Mississippi."

"WE'VE GOTTA GO BACK!" Selding suddenly yelled, displaying an energy level scarcely suggestive of oxygen deprivation. "SOMETHING'S WRONG!"

He settled back amid a pregnant silence. He looked at Rep, who returned the gaze with polite curiosity. He looked at Eastman, whose head swiveled to stare directly back.

"Buckaroo," Eastman said evenly, "is there something you'd like to tell me?"

Selding twitched. The spasm didn't limit itself to any particular part of his body, but shook him from great toe to forelock.

"Let's just go back and get down," he begged. "Then we can talk all you want to."

"We can talk all I want to up here," Eastman said. "And I'm going to Pomona, California unless you tell me why I shouldn't." He paused for four long beats. "Tell me now. Tell me why you think there's something wrong with the oxygen tanks."

"I WANT ON THE GROUND!" Selding yelled. "I WANT ON THE GROUND NOW! I SO WANT ON THE GROUND!" He gasped on the last syllable, short of breath. His face turned bridal veil white.

"Talk," Eastman said calmly. He waited again, through what were now shallow, ragged breaths magnified by Selding's throat-mike. Then he continued. "You know, it could be that there isn't something wrong with all three tanks. Did you think about that? It could be that what was supposed to be wrong was discovered, and fixed for two of the tanks. That would be a kind of poetic justice, wouldn't it? One of those noir things, kind of a *Double Indemnity*/*Postman Always Rings Twice* biter-bit kind of number, wouldn't it?"

"I DIDN'T DO IT!" Selding yelled.

"Who did do it?" Eastman asked.

"I don't know who did it," Selding wept desperately.

"Then we'll settle for what 'it' is," Eastman said. "Talk fast—while you can still talk at all."

"Okayokayokay," Selding said, very rapidly. "Understand, I had nothing to do with it. I only heard about it third-hand. The only guy I know was involved was Mixler."

"I'm waiting for 'it,'" Eastman said calmly.

"All right, you're right. The plan—what I heard was the plan, but I couldn't believe it, I thought it was just a sick joke—was that they'd substitute nitrogen for oxygen on the tanks in this plane. It was supposed to happen at the last minute, just before you took off tomorrow. So that on the way to the coast, you'd, uh, you'd all, um—"

"On the way to the coast," Eastman interjected helpfully, "everyone on board the plane would pass out. The plane would lose radio contact and then eventually crash, like that professional golfer's plane a few years ago. Pilot, crew, and all passengers dead. Aaron Eastman and his mischievous ideas about a movie-à-clef implicating politicians and Tempus-Caveator Corporation in a plot to rig the Oscar awards and incidentally cover up treason are all conveniently gone. Evidence of the crime destroyed by the crash. Chalked up to oxygen system malfunction. Perfect crime."

"Right, you can see why I didn't believe it," Selding said, as Rep and Eastman took off their oxygen masks. Selding did the same. "Are we below ten thousand feet yet?"

"We've never been above seven thousand feet since we left the ground," Eastman said. "You've been conned, my friend. Some day I'm going to do a movie about the power of suggestion."

"You don't really believe any of that stuff I said, do you?" Selding said, flashing a nimble smile. "That was just a gag to get you to go down."

"All right, counselor," Eastman said, "it's showtime."

"Uh, right," Rep said, acknowledging that he was now officially on. "You see, er, Mr. Selding, while that's an understandable position for you to take under the circumstances, it really isn't in your best interests."

Selding responded with what the *New York Times* customarily refers to as a barnyard obscenity signifying disbelief. Then, as exasperation distorted what had up to then been Rep's rather bland expression, he expanded on this commentary.

"Look, you've got nothing. Absolutely nothing. Everything I said just now is hearsay."

"It's not, actually," Rep said in a mildly puzzled tone. "In a criminal prosecution against you it would be an admission by a party—namely you—which is specifically defined as *not* hearsay by Rule 801(d)(2) of the Federal Rules of Evidence. And even if it were hearsay, it would be a declaration against penal interest, which is admissible as an exception to the hearsay restriction under Rule 804(b)(3)."

"Oh," Selding said.

"So maybe this will go faster if I handle the legal stuff and you handle keeping your mouth shut. I'll mostly skip over some of the obvious things, like your breaking down just now, and hit the subtler stuff. Like traces of PETN on my computer bag, which you handled only a few days before a helicopter that you'd had contact with blew up—helped along by PETN. And the fact that you had to help Mixler switch laptops with Charlotte at O'Hare, because you had the standard-issue Tavistock model just like she did, and you knew the basic approach to passwords."

"You're skipping that?" Selding asked.

"Right. See, the main thing is, only in Hollywood would this B-24 crash that someone had in mind be a perfect crime. In the real world, you couldn't count on all the tanks being completely destroyed by the crash, so you couldn't count on the FBI not figuring out that they were filled with nitrogen instead of oxygen. Especially when a helicopter blew up a hundred yards from the victim less than forty-eight hours before the crash. So you'd have to assume a murder investigation, and you'd have to have a scapegoat."

"And you're saying the scapegoat they have in mind is me?" Selding demanded.

"Of course not." Rep shook his head. He hated it when he got schoolmarmish with people, but sometimes he just couldn't help it. "The scapegoat is Charlotte Buchanan. Mixler lured her to Pomona."

"I thought your theory was that he did that so he could pull the laptop switch at O'Hare and send an e-mail message that was supposed to be from her," Selding objected.

"The question is, why did he want to send that e-mail? And the answer is that he wanted to implicate her—and me, but that's incidental—in Aaron Eastman's planned murder. That's why Mixler had her run down a video of *Green for Danger* and check out an article about the NASA tragedy. When that's investigated, it will seem like she was looking for over-the-top, amateurish, literary ways to sabotage the plane—one of which actually worked."

"How did Mixler supposedly manipulate her into doing that stuff?"

"The same way he enticed her to drop everything and hustle out of town: by telling her that he could get Aaron to option a script that she'd write the story for, and she needed this background to get going on a treatment to show him when he landed Sunday evening. So she's out there incommunicado in Pomona while a hostile takeover of her father's company is under way. No one has been able to reach her since Friday afternoon. As soon as the B-24 crash is confirmed publicly, the plan is to kill her and make it look like a suicide following up on Aaron's murder."

"Without a note?" Selding asked skeptically.

"I bet there will be a note. Typed with her own fingers on her own keyboard as part of the story she's supposedly working on."

"And why is it supposedly in my interest to implicate myself in this mess?"

"Because they're going to kill Charlotte Buchanan as soon as word gets out that the plan hasn't worked, that's why," Rep said, with a pedantic little hiss of impatience.

"But if you're right they're going to kill her while I'm in custody, denying this silly story. I'll be one person in the country who couldn't possibly have committed the murder."

"Ah, yes," Rep said, brightening as he saw where the pedagogic problem lay. "That brings us to the Pinkerton Rule. I'm probably the only copyright lawyer in the country who's an expert on that doctrine. We won't go into why."

"What's the Pinkerton Rule?" Selding asked wearily.

"The Pinkerton Rule is that every member of a criminal conspiracy is guilty of every crime committed in furtherance of the conspiracy—including conspirators who personally had nothing to do with particular crimes. In other words, because you helped Mixler out with the laptop switch— never mind the helicopter explosion and the other stuff— you'd be as guilty of Charlotte Buchanan's murder as the guy who actually pulls the trigger."

"Oh," Selding said.

"And as you may know, there's sort of a reverse affirmative action push on capital punishment these days," Rep said, in the same kind of trying-to-be-helpful voice he used when telling clients they should consider an intellectual property audit. "As an affluent white guy, you'd be sort of the ideal candidate for a federal execution."

"Oh," Selding said.

"So what you need to do is tell this story quickly to someone with a badge so that Charlotte Buchanan's life can be saved."

Selding looked, understandably, a bit nauseated. Not nauseous, Rep reminded himself—although that too, now that he thought about it.

"You have about fifteen minutes to consider your options," Eastman said. "The nearest place with big airports at the moment is Chicago, and that's where I'm heading. If we can get clearance, it won't be too long before we're on the ground."

"They're not going to let you land this boat at O'Hare, are they?" Rep asked in astonishment.

"Wouldn't even try. Or at Midway. And I'm not going to count on Miegs Field even being open at this hour, assuming I could find it in the first place."

"I see," Rep said. "So what's the plan?"

"Well, ten years ago I made a neat little flick called *Water Rats* about the Coast Guard. Sort of *The Perfect Storm* with Miranda warnings. Made it with Galaxy, in fact. We used a post-production facility that Galaxy subleased from Tavistock. It was less than a mile from the Great Lakes Naval Training Center outside Chicago, and because we were hyping good guys and an anti-drug message they let us land there sometimes."

"Not to be a worrywart," Rep said, "but why should they let you land there now?"

"Because I'm going to radio in about an emergency. Something about someone on board reporting a malfunction in the oxygen tanks."

❦ ❦ ❦

Forty-five minutes later, Rep was sitting beside a functional, gray metal desk in a Spartan office, sipping coffee and thinking this was too good to be true. There actually was a United States Coast Guard office at the training center. The Coast Guard, as it happens, is the one branch of American armed services that routinely arrests civilians, and therefore has officers who are trained to act like cops. The first one they'd drawn here had acted like a bored and cranky cop, irritated at wasting his time preparing a routine report in triplicate on a bunch of amateurs who'd taken an antique airplane up without knowing how. Five minutes into Eastman's emphatically non-routine account, however, the officer had gotten real interested—interested enough to call in two colleagues to share the fun.

One was now in a closed room having a detailed chat with Eastman. The second was interviewing Selding. And the original—younger than Rep, earnest, polite, thorough— was in this room getting Rep's version on tape and in longhand.

"So what's the connection between all this movie stuff and Tempus-Caveator trying to buy out a chemical company?" he asked.

"You know something," Rep said, "I'm not sure. I haven't thought that through yet."

"I suppose they could be doing it to increase your client's motivation—you know, despair over the problem she has created for her father's company or something—but it seems like overkill."

"You're right," Rep said. "That's one of the answers I don't have."

"And here's another thing. This phony e-mail—that was really slick. But if your client, what's-her-name—"

"Charlotte Buchanan," Rep said.

"—right, Charlotte Buchanan. If this Mixler guy had actually conned her into flying to northern California, why did he have to do the runaround with the laptops? Seems like he could have talked her into sending you the e-mail message herself."

"Because if she'd done that there'd have been a risk that I'd e-mail her back."

"Or go charging after her, I guess," the young lieutenant said.

"Right," Rep said.

Suddenly Rep paused with the cup three inches from his lips. "Go charging after her" ran through his mind.

"What's the problem?" the Coast Guard officer asked.

"There's something else wrong here," Rep said. "Why would Mixler use a phony e-mail to tell me where Charlotte was actually going to be?"

"Well, if you're right, and we assume a plane crash and an apparent suicide by your client followed by an investigation, Mixler would want you to tell the police about the e-mail. Because it would show that Buchanan knew Eastman was going to be in the air Sunday afternoon, and would show she was planning on intersecting with him."

"Or was obsessing about him," Rep said. "But we're missing something. He absolutely would not want me to get in actual contact with her, so the one thing he wouldn't tell me is where she was really going to be. Plus, for the whole Buchanan-scapegoat thing to work, she had to be in position to sabotage the plane. So she couldn't be in northern California. She should be a lot closer to Oshkosh, Wisconsin. Like, say, Fond du Lac. Or Milwaukee."

"Or here," the Coast Guardsman said. "After all, we know from your wife that Mixler himself was in Chicago very late Friday night."

"Exactly!" Rep said. "I think you're exactly right."

"Of course, 'Chicago' doesn't narrow it down too much."

"Right, but I can think of one place we should check right away. Eastman said on the plane that there's what he called a post-production facility near here that Galaxy

Entertainment used to sublease from Tavistock. If Mixler really is holed up with her in this area, that would be a natural place. Can we send a couple of guys to take a look at it?"

"You have to be out of your ever-loving mind," the officer said politely. "With all respect, what exactly have you been smoking?"

"What do you mean?"

"We're the Coast Guard. We have jurisdiction over waters that are navigable in interstate and foreign commerce. If we didn't assume that that plane of yours was over Lake Michigan at some point, we'd be pushing the outside of the envelope just to take statements from you guys. We can't send uniformed members of the United States armed forces barging into that post-production facility unless someone diverts the Chicago River through it."

"Of course you can't," Rep said, deflated. "I should have known that. Can I talk to Eastman?"

"Not until my colleague opens that door you can't. We can't break into an official interview. This is a real interesting story you're telling, but what we start with is, an airplane deviated from its flight plan and made an emergency landing on a military base, which is a no-no. He was the pilot, and there are some procedures we're going to have to follow."

"Okay," Rep said. He drummed his fingers on the table in a rare show of frustrated petulance. "Right. But this woman's life is in danger. What can we do?"

"Well, *we* can't do much."

Rep's face brightened at the emphasis the Coast Guardsman put on the pronoun.

"Tell me this," Rep said. "How would a civilian—say, a civilian who wasn't the pilot and whose questioning has been completed—go about getting off of this United States military installation, without any officer here being responsible for it?"

"Now that's an interesting question," the officer said. "On *The X-Files* once I saw Mulder do it by hanging on the side of a truck that was conveniently on its way out the gate. Or maybe it was Scully and the truck was going in."

"That sounds pretty ambitious."

"Yeah, if I were you I wouldn't try that. What I'd do if I were you is, I'd take that telephone book off the shelf there and make sure of your address, and then I'd call a cab. After that I'd stroll out the front gate. Give the guard there a nod on your way out."

"So you're, ah, not opposed to my just going?" Rep asked.

"With all respect, sir," the young lieutenant said, "I am affirmatively in favor of your going. Affirmatively and strongly in favor."

Chapter 16

Oooh-kaayyy, Rep thought as the cab pulled away, leaving him on the edge of a gravel and mud parking lot. *What do I do now? Knock on the front door?*

The four-story building about eighty feet away seemed out of place in the down-market urban frontier where the cab had dropped him. Its charcoal-gray brick and white-faced concrete suggested an effort at shabby elegance that should have graced an industrial park in some antiseptic exurb. Here it seemed vaguely effete, like a tweedy school-master who had wandered into a salesmen's convention.

A light shone dimly through third-floor windows on the side nearest Rep, well above the glaring haloes that were splashed along the outside of the first story by ground-mounted security lights. He made out a pale, blue glow through the plate glass dominating the first floor's front wall. He crunched gingerly across the gravel until, about ten yards from the building, he could infer the source of the glow: small television monitors arrayed along the far arc of a large, C-shaped security desk. A guy with his feet propped inside the desk looked like he would have had to show i.d. to buy Marlboros, his blond hair lying in a surfer cut, his black muscle shirt displaying plenty of muscles. He was smoking something, handling whatever it was like a joint rather than a cigarette. If Rep had shown up yet on any of the monitors, the guy gave no sign of being concerned about it.

Of course, Rep thought, *I wouldn't be either if I were in his shoes. Or, in this case, sandals.*

Keeping his ten-yard distance, Rep made a hesitant and un-enthusiastic circuit of the building. The windows showing up in the haloes all looked like unopenable thermalpane. Around back he found a receiving dock with two heavy, steel, vertically opening doors at its rear. Rep would have bet heavily against forcing the lock on either with a credit card— or "'loiding" them, as Eastman had recently taught him to call the process. On the far side of the building he spotted the inevitable outdoor smokers' haven: a redwood picnic table amid three benches and a sand-filled bucket. A service door darker than the surrounding gray brick broke the face of the wall a few feet from the table. He could try the door, of course, but he knew it would turn out to be locked and that when he walked up to the well-lighted area he was sure to appear on one of the surveillance monitors.

Rep shrugged fecklessly. The devil-may-care, quick-witted private detectives he had watched on television while doing algebra and geometry homework as an adolescent wouldn't have been stumped by a situation like this. They would have called for a pizza delivery to this address, and then fast-talked their way into the delivery guy's uniform. Or rappelled up to the HVAC system on the roof, loosened a couple of screws with pocket change, and slipped in through the duct work. Or whistled the four-tone access code they'd somehow figured out, so that the security system would unlock the doors itself. But Rep wasn't going to do any of those things. He still didn't have any better idea than knocking on the front door.

He trudged toward the front corner, angling closer to the building with each stride. As he was about to turn he glanced up and, craning his neck, found himself staring directly into the lens of a surveillance camera. Startled, he smiled and waved in what he hoped the lens would translate as a friendly, non-threatening way. Then he hustled around to the massive front doors, peered in at the guard, and rapped on the thick glass.

No reaction.

Repeat performance, same result.

The guy at the desk looked stoned. Leaning back in his swivel chair, feet still on the desk, he kept his gaze intently on the ceiling, which seemed to fascinate him.

The fact that a third-shift security guard was smoking pot on the job didn't surprise Rep in the slightest. He often wondered at the mentality of the first genius who'd said, "Hey, let's find people who'll work for minimum wage and give them guns!"

The sandals and the muscle shirt, on the other hand, seemed more and more anomalous the longer he thought about them. This was Chicago, the upper Midwest. People in the Midwest like uniforms. Really, really like them. Boy scout leaders, American Legion Post officers, firemen, train conductors, bus drivers, meter readers, animal control officers—none of them ever show up in mufti for anything remotely official if they can help it. They come with all the blue and gold and khaki and forest green and chenille patches and gold braid they can justify. Rep had seen rent-a-cops who could have taken command of the Coldstream Guards without changing a collar button. He had never before seen one in the Midwest who didn't boast at least navy blue shirt and slacks with sleeve patches and an equipment belt. If this building had a regular night watchman, Rep figured, this guy wasn't it.

Which was all very interesting, but left unsolved the problem of attracting the guard's attention.

Walking back around the corner, Rep found the surveillance camera he'd smiled at and stood once again in front of its unblinking eye. He jabbed toward the building several times with his index finger in the hope that the guard would see this and interpret it as a plea to come to the door. Three solid minutes of this, interspersed with impatient glances around the corner, accomplished nothing but to make Rep feel silly.

Frustrated, he reached up in an effort to thread his fingers through the protective cage around the camera and knock crankily on the lens, hoping that a screen-sized knuckle might attract more attention than rapping on the window had. By itself, it didn't. What it did do, as he irritably jostled the thin metal bars that enclosed the camera, was set off an intermittent, high-pitched alarm at the security desk. The alarm apparently took its job more seriously than the guard took his, for the piercing *BEEPS!* it produced were loud enough for Rep to hear outside.

He scurried back to the front door, waving energetically, just in time to see the guard start to react. The guy at first sat rigidly erect as he seemed to concentrate very, very hard. Then realization apparently burst through and he bolted to a standing position, bent over the beeping monitor, hands on either side of it, focusing on it with willed intensity, as if the slowly penetrating shock of the alarm had brought him a millisecond of stone cold sobriety.

The interval of lucidity, alas, wasn't enough for Rep's frantic gesticulations and renewed window-knocking to attract the guard's attention. The gent did work his way out from behind the security desk, although he made that modest task look quite challenging, but he didn't pay the slightest attention to Rep. He began running—or, at least, doing something that in his present condition he apparently took for running—not toward the front door but toward the far side of the building where the service door was.

Cursing in exasperation, Rep reversed course yet again and ran back around the corner.

Ran.

At full speed.

In the dark.

This was more concentrated physical exertion than he'd committed with his clothes on in five years. Still ten feet from the picnic table, he saw the service door start to swing open. Gut stitched, muscles burning, and lungs aching, Rep strained to pick up his pace. He managed it, but only for a second or so. Then a searing pain lanced through both shins and he suddenly found himself airborne as a stumble over one of the picnic benches sent him flying.

The sound of Rep's own startled yelp reached his ears at the same moment as the strangled "HUHHH!" produced by the guard when Rep's head and shoulders collided with him and slammed him into the inside of the outward-swinging door. Rep and the guy hit the ground at the same time, both stunned but Rep at least not baked on top of it.

The guy flailed confusedly with a left fist and a right elbow, which connected respectively with Rep's ribs and his cheekbone. Rep had devoted great energy and ingenuity through much of his life to assiduous avoidance of fists swung in anger, and this experience confirmed the wisdom of that course. He found the ad-libbed blows excruciating.

Rep, fortunately, didn't have time at the moment to reflect further on the situation, which was that the door was now swinging inward on its powerful springs, trying to shut and in the process pressing insistently against his body and the guard's; and that the guard was writhing, trying to get up. What Rep had to do was get up before the guard did, get through the door, and close it with the guard on the outside. Had Rep taken even a moment to think, a lifetime of bitter experience would have told him that he had just about as much chance of accomplishing this as he did of making the Olympic decathlon team.

Modest though it was, however, the guard's low-rent pummeling proved highly motivational. Instead of thinking, Rep acted on pure reflex. He rolled toward the building, away from the guard's blunt, punishing knuckles and sharp elbow.

He scrambled awkwardly to his knees and then to his feet. Then he darted inside the building.

The guard displayed none of Rep's clumsiness. He rolled quickly and adroitly away from the building. He bounced nimbly to the balls of his feet in one fluid motion. At that point, however, he spoiled the effect by putting his hands on his knees and retching for awhile as the door closed behind Rep.

Third floor, Rep thought breathlessly, as thrilled as he was astounded at having actually bested someone else, however fortuitously, in a physical contest. His urban survival skills had been honed by years of work in a downtown office building, so he knew better than to try the elevator at this hour without an access card. He bolted instead up a broad staircase leading from the lobby. It's true that this staircase took him only to the second floor, which was completely dark, and that he didn't have the faintest idea of what to do next. But at least it was a start.

A few moments of reflection, stimulated by the certainty that before too much longer the chap outside would finish throwing up and begin giving consideration to reentry, led Rep to a constructive thought: Ordinances of the City of Chicago and statutes of the State of Illinois undoubtedly required that, somewhere on this floor, there be an illuminated EXIT sign near a fire door leading to a stairway. He went in search of it and presently, after only a few bumps and scrapes and the overturn of a floral display that he told himself probably hadn't been all that pretty to start with, he found the sign near the back of the building's far side.

He paused at the fire door for five deep breaths. Getting past the guard and into the building was like swishing a twenty-foot jump shot: it happens once in awhile and it feels good, but if you're a guy like Rep you really don't count on doing it again any time soon. The only argument in favor of going on was that there wasn't any alternative. He opened the door and hurried up the unadorned concrete stairs before he had a chance to talk himself out of it.

He cracked the door at the top a sliver, and then a bit wider as he saw nothing but slightly varying shades of dark. He slipped out of the stairwell, crept across perhaps eight feet of hallway, and began feeling his way down a long wall that turned out to be unbroken all the way to the end, where he met the intersecting wall at the front of the building.

Hm. Not the most obvious choice for office building interior design. But then, of course, this wasn't primarily an office building. What had Eastman called it? A post-production facility.

Rep felt his way back along the wall toward the opposite end. His gropings in this direction eventually brought him to a corner, which he rounded. He was now moving parallel to the back of the building, going toward the side he'd first seen when he got out of the cab—the side where he'd noticed light glowing from the inside.

Rep's plan was simple. He had no thought of a chivalric rescue, like Lancelot slicing Guinevere away from the stake just as the faggots began to crackle, or Han Solo snatching Princess Leia from under the noses of Darth Vader's stormtroopers. What he wanted was to see something—say, Charlotte Buchanan in gag and handcuffs—that would provoke a useful reaction from whoever handled 911 calls in Chicago. Therefore, he had to get to the light. He proceeded.

He hadn't gone more than ten feet before he heard something. He couldn't identify the sound exactly, although it vaguely suggested machinery laboring. He crept toward the sound and, because he was moving slowly, hurt his knee only a little when he banged it against something dark and hard protruding at an angle from the inside wall. Five seconds of tactile investigation sufficed to tell Rep that it was a door, left miraculously (or suspiciously, depending on how you looked at it) ajar. He slipped through the doorway.

As soon as he was through he ducked—understandably, because an F4F Wildcat was coming at him, its whirling propeller bracketed by flame that spat from its machine guns. Or, rather, he realized, the mirror image of a World War II fighter was coming at him, for he was looking at the back of a flat, rear projection screen. (Technically, what he was looking at was a very old-fashioned version of something called a traveling mat, but he didn't know that.) Mounted at the rear of a large stage, the screen/mat undulated slightly as red, blue, and white lights beamed at it from the panting projector in an otherwise inky room.

Rep skirted around the stage and moved about thirty feet deeper into what he now thought must be a very large, internal room taking up most of the building's third floor. On the screen, the fighter planes gave way to crashing surf. What commanded Rep's attention, though, was a rectangle of light in the middle of the wall now opposite him. Dropping to his hands and knees so as to keep his shadow off the screen—though if anyone else were in the room, they must certainly have some idea by now that they had company—he scuttled with efficiency if not dignity toward the rectangle. During his transit the Manhattan skyline replaced crashing surf on the screen.

The light was coming through frosted glass in the upper half of a door. Rep managed to reach the door with only one more minor glitch, stubbing his knee—that's right, his *knee*—on a pile of bulging mailbags that cluttered the floor on the stage side of the portal. Without pausing to wonder what mailbags were doing in a screening room, he pulled himself up to the window, where he found only an inch or so of clear glass at the margin. Sneaking an eye over the lower right-hand corner of this border and bracing himself for something gruesome, he looked into the building's only lighted room.

It was fifteen feet wide with three outside windows and a closed door at the end to his left. Six non-descript Masonite work tables sat perpendicular to the outside wall, paired on either side of each window. Two held what Rep might have recognized as Movieola film editors if he'd been thirty years older. Another held binders, writing pads, cheap pens, and similar miscellaneous office supplies. The other three supported word processors and printers.

At the nearest of these, surrounded on floor and table by layers of discarded Evian bottles, Diet Coca-Cola cans, cardboard coffee cups, empty pizza and Chinese food boxes, and a vast quantity of paper defaced with the printed word, sat Charlotte Buchanan. Bernie Mixler paced in her vicinity, reading from a sheaf of pages that he clutched.

Golly, Rep thought, *the pizza delivery guy scam might actually have worked.*

During the thirty seconds or so that Rep spent examining the scene, Buchanan alternately frowned in the apparent throes of creative agony and typed in furious bursts. Nothing in the scene suggested much in the way of criminal activity. After Selding's confession and Rep's adventures in just getting into the building, in fact, the whole thing struck him as a tad anticlimactic.

A key on a ring rested in a lock immediately below the doorknob. Rep stood up, took a pass at brushing himself off, turned the key decisively and opened the door. Buchanan looked up with distracted interest as he strode in. Mixler glared at him in unalloyed and unpleasant surprise.

"Oh, it's you," Buchanan said, smiling the way well brought-up people do when they're trying to be polite and having to work at it. "Hi, Rep. You look a little scuffed up and shopworn, like you're maybe a month past your sell-by date."

"What are you doing here?" Mixler demanded—which, to be honest, was a pretty fair question. If Rep wasn't here to call the cops, what was he going to do?

"I'm here to take Charlotte somewhere else," Rep said.

"Where?" Buchanan asked. "And more important, why?"

"Where doesn't matter much," Rep said. "Why is that you're in danger here. Some bad people have unpleasant plans for you. You're not supposed to leave this building alive."

This was the most dramatic thing Rep had ever said in his life. Buchanan reacted with the kind of half-exasperated, half-tolerant moue that had gotten Claudette Colbert sharply smacked when she tried it on Clark Gable in *It Happened One Night.*

"No, no, Rep," she said with exaggerated patience. "You're the logical, rational one. *I'm* the melodramatic fantasist."

"Did you send me an e-mail on Friday about meeting Aaron Eastman in Pomona, California this weekend?"

"Of course not. Bernie has set up a meeting with him Monday in L.A. And I wouldn't necessarily be e-mailing you about it anyway, would I? It's business, not legal." Buchanan noted this distinction with fastidious satisfaction, the way someone who had seen her first baseball game two days before might differentiate savvily between fastballs and sliders.

"Well, I got an e-mail from you Friday evening saying exactly that," Rep said. "If you didn't send it, somebody else did, and they used your laptop to do it."

"I don't see how that could be. I've had my laptop under my control since I left home Friday afternoon." Buchanan tapped a cased computer at her feet with her toe to emphasize the point. Mixler snorted derisively.

"It was out of your control for at least thirty seconds when you went through security at O'Hare," Rep said. "That's when your computer was switched for another one that looks just like it."

"You say that like you saw it happen," Buchanan commented. "Did you?"

"No. But I know it did happen, the same way I know your battery was out of power the first time you tried to boot up after getting through security Friday afternoon, wasn't it?"

"Yes, as a matter of fact, and I'll give you credit for a very lucky guess."

"Well, okay then," Rep said, not sure how to handle the concession—after all, he wasn't a litigator. "Let's see, maybe I can make some more lucky guesses. How about this? When Mixler called you and said he'd arranged this Eastman meeting, he told you to meet him at a particular gate in Chicago so you could fly out together Friday night and he could explain the project. But once you got through security, he met you, told you the meeting was postponed until Monday, and said he'd spend the weekend here in Chicago with you putting something serious on paper for Eastman."

Rep paused, hopefully checking Buchanan's face to see if any of this was penetrating. The evidence wasn't encouraging.

"Well, sure," Buchanan said. "I mean, right on, yes, absolutely. But you *should* know most of that, Rep. I mean, not the details, maybe, but the overall concept. It all started with your idea about a face-to-face meeting between me and Eastman."

"That's right," Mixler said. "No big mystery. He's telling you stuff that I told him."

"That's not true," Rep said, stamping his foot in impatience at the blatancy of the lie.

"No need to overplay your hand, counselor," Mixler said with complete composure. "Just take the credit."

"Really, Rep, it's going to work, I can feel it," Buchanan added, excitement swelling in her voice. "Bernie has been incredible. He came up with the premise for a story, an up-dated modus operandi that's tailor-made for a hip, self-knowing, ironic comedy-suspense flick. He's already got Eastman hooked on the basic idea, and he's convinced that I can produce a really powerful treatment that will close the deal. He had me do some research on it and track down an old movie that used a variation of it, and it was just dead on."

"The movie was *Green for Danger*, right?" Rep said.

"Exactly! And it's perfect. I've been writing for something like sixteen hours straight, and we've really got something. No penny-ante book publisher without publicists, offering some bush-league twenty-five hundred copy first printing. We'll go straight to the movies, and then use the movie deal to sell the book instead of the other way around. Bernie figured everything out and explained it all to me."

"And she has to get back to work," Mixler said. "We've made plenty of progress, but we're a long way from home."

Rep opened his mouth to start picking logical holes in the world according to Buchanan, but he checked himself. Mixler knew Buchanan's dream, and that was all the leverage he'd needed. That dream was more powerful than any logical argument Rep Pennyworth was likely to produce. Logic in this situation was about as useful as a slingshot in a tank battle.

He couldn't even mention Selding's confession, not that it would have made much difference. The plan Selding had confirmed required Buchanan to be alive at least until the first news reports about Eastman's plane being missing on its way to northern California Sunday afternoon, because in the script Mixler was writing for the cops that dramatic event would be what caused Buchanan's final meltdown. If Rep started spouting off about how he and Eastman had cleverly thwarted that whole scenario, the obvious decision for Mixler and company would be to kill her right away.

Me too, come to think of it, Rep reflected uncomfortably.

"Let me ask you one other thing," Rep said, his voice racing with desperation. "In this neat little story Bernie is helping you with, does someone by any wild chance write a suicide note?"

"Yessss," Buchanan admitted in a get-on-with-it tone.

"Not exactly unprecedented in dramatic suspense films," Mixler interjected. Rep ignored him.

"And this suicide note has gone through several drafts, all of which are lying on the floor here somewhere?"

"Yes," Buchanan said.

"Which I couldn't possibly have seen and Mixler couldn't possibly have told me about, right?"

"Right. And so—what?"

"Do me a favor. Pull up the latest version—the one that shows Bernie's full input. Read it, and try to remember the changes he suggested. Ask yourself what people would think if those words were attached to an e-mail sent from your laptop to, say, me and your father about thirty minutes after Aaron Eastman's plane crashes because everyone on board passed out from lack of oxygen."

"You're making this sound like a really lame made-for-TV movie," Buchanan said. "Maybe not even. Maybe direct-to-video."

"This is getting us nowhere fast," Mixler snapped, stepping toward Rep. "Look, I'm sure you're a very good lawyer, but the longer you talk about writing the crazier you sound. You may not know it, but this young lady sitting here is a MAJOR writing talent. MAJOR. All caps, italics. If Eastman goes for what we're working on here, she could be the hottest thing in Hollywood since whosis, that guy who wrote *A Few Good Men* and *West Wing*. We've got a major project here with major prospects, and we have to get it done."

Mixler had by this point gotten to within nosehair-counting range of Rep, but Rep scarcely noticed. He was focusing on Buchanan. Her face as she listened to Mixler was glowing. She'd spent her life hearing opportunists tell her how great she was and in that department she ought to be able to tell dog food from steak. At the moment, though, she apparently didn't have a single critical faculty functioning.

Impulsively, Rep snatched the sheaf of papers Mixler was holding. Mixler's protesting shriek, though impressively shrill, was lost in the next words they all heard. Those words came from the projection room, just beyond the open door where Rep was standing. They accompanied a man stumbling vigorously against Rep's back on the strength of a vigorous assist from their speaker.

The words were:

"Get in there, you worthless sack of burnt-out weed."

Startled by the impact, Rep staggered forward, jostling Mixler off his feet and onto a pile of all-nighter snack detritus in the process. He turned around to find himself the sole support of the guard from downstairs, looking now like a poster boy for this year's JUST SAY NO campaign.

The shover-speaker stood in the doorway with his hands on his hips. He was about six-two, with light-brown hair in a no-kidding buzz-cut that could have gotten him an extra's role as a jock frat-rat in whatever this summer's *Animal House*-ripoff was. He was wearing a short-sleeved shirt of royal blue mesh that left his midriff exposed, and a matching pair of spandex biker's shorts. He looked like he played a lot of beach volleyball, and that when he did he could spike his serves if he wanted to.

Rep now understood—just a tad too late for his understanding to do any good. The guy had been staying in the projection room, unobtrusive as long as Mixler had Buchanan under control, but available if needed. He had left in a hurry to check things out when the monitor alarm went off and his accomplice at the first-floor desk didn't respond promptly. That was why the screening room door had been open for Rep. This guy had probably been going down in the elevator at the same time Rep was coming up the stairs.

"What did you do that for?" Mixler squeaked indignantly from his pizza box mattress. "I'm in charge here, and things were going just fine."

"Skip it," the guy at the door said. "You're not in charge anymore. This has just become an operational situation." He tapped a tiny cell-phone clipped to the waistband of his breeches.

"What do you mean?" Mixler demanded, shaking congealed mozzarella disgustedly from his little finger as he clambered back to his feet.

"The whole thing is blown," the new guy said. "I got the word while I was downstairs, rescuing the moron here after he managed to get himself locked out of the building he was supposed to be watching. Eastman flew his B-24 into Great Lakes Naval Training Center late tonight. I don't know how he did it, but he got onto the plan. Cops are involved. Selding finally called a lawyer and thank God he called the right one. There's a chopper on the way to pick us up from the roof. Time to abort."

Rep shuddered a bit at the verb. The suggestion of termination attached to it struck him as not at all metaphorical and uncomfortably apropos.

Chapter 17

The six-tenths of a second that Rep had to think things over was ample for him to conclude that the situation was hopeless. He had gotten past the pothead downstairs on a providential fluke, but the guy facing him now hadn't OD'd on anything but testosterone. His vigilant eyes darted alertly from Rep to Buchanan. No way Rep was getting by this gent, much less taking Buchanan with him.

The reason he had only six-tenths of a second for this reasoning process was that that was all the time it took Charlotte Buchanan to grab an empty Evian bottle and hurl it at Mixler, nailing him across a generous portion of his face.

"You SCUM!" she screamed, loudly enough to be heard distinctly over Mixler's feral howl. "It was all LIES—ALL THE TIME!" While making these observations, and supplementing them with bitterly tearful commentary on the nature of Mixler's ancestry and the marital status of his parents at the time of his birth, she was busy scuttling around Rep to set on Mixler with pounding fists and snap-kicking feet.

The reflexes of the guy at the door as he jumped to intercept Buchanan were remarkably fast—but they were nothing compared to the speed Mixler displayed in retreating from her. Desperate to get something solid between himself and Buchanan, Mixler leaped toward the guy in the doorway.

He banged into him just as the guy was taking his first step toward Buchanan. Mixler was the one person in the room the guy hadn't been looking at, so the collision blindsided him. For a split second he rocked backward, slightly off-balance.

It was during that split second that Rep acted. Not that he had the first clue about how to fight properly. He just ducked his head and, fists swinging wildly, flung himself at the guy.

If Rep had been five-nine his artless gesture would have failed. By pure good luck, however, Rep's sixty-seven inches of height was exactly the right altitude to bring the crown of his head smashing into the guy's solar plexus—the thinly covered hollow spot just below the breastbone and in painful proximity to the lungs. Being hit there not only hurts—a lot—it is momentarily disorienting. It causes an explosion of breath from the chest and a scary blackness starred by electric red and white flashes in front of the eyes. Get caught doing it to a well-padded player in the NFL, where it is called "spearing," and you will be penalized ten yards and fined several thousand dollars. Having it happen is known as "getting the wind knocked out of you," and most people who have experienced it will tell you that if they had to choose between doing it again and being hit full force in the groin with a baseball bat, they'd have to think about it.

The guy in the doorway didn't collapse in a heap, but he did stagger backward two steps into the screening room, blinking and shaking his head. He dragged Rep with him because he had reflexively grabbed Rep's arms to keep himself from falling as he felt his balance giving way. After the two backward strides he let go of Rep and slapped the air behind him with his hands as if he were trying to break a fall.

This gave Rep time to do one constructive thing, and he did it. He slammed the door behind him and pulled the key out of its lock, leaving himself and the thug in biker's shorts by themselves in the screening room. Among other benefits, this had the virtue of shielding Rep's ears from further exposure to Mixler's blood-curdling screams and Buchanan's savage yells, for the screening room was insulated against intrusive sounds from outside.

Hands on his hips and shoulders bowed, the guy shook his head as he recovered his breath. After two or three seconds he looked up at Rep, a sobered, good-sport smile playing at his lips.

"Great shot, dude," he panted. "That one got me where I live."

"Sometimes it's better to be lucky than good," Rep said with a nervous shrug.

"Right. What they say. So. Whew." The game smile now turned into an engaging grin. "I'll be needing that key now." The guy held out his right hand.

Rep thought for a moment about the enormity of what he was about to do. Then, pretending to stretch his right hand out in surrender, he suddenly swung his arm back and flung the key as hard as he could into the far front corner of the room. The guy looked in unpleasant surprise over his shoulder as the key and its ring clapped on the floor in the darkness. Then he looked back at Rep, with a rueful head shake.

"I didn't need that," he said. "Now, if I go looking for that key, you can make a run for the other door. And if you actually made it out, that would complicate my life. So I guess I'm going to have to get back into the editing room without the key."

This comment called for the second most dramatic thing Rep had ever said in his life. He said it.

"You'll have to get by me first."

"Yeah, like that'll be a big problem," the guy said, snorting and rolling his eyes in disgust. Then his expression softened. "Look, my bad, I apologize. That was uncalled for. I have no reason to diss you. But looky here, dude, what do you think this is? The back lot at MGM? *Red River*? Montgomery

Clift beats up John Wayne because a scriptwriter says so? No way, my friend. This is the real world. Unless you have a gun in that Men's Wearhouse suit you're wearing, you are *not* gonna stop me."

The guy said this in a half-placatory, half-frustrated let's-be-reasonable tone, as if he were explaining to a stubborn six-year-old why he couldn't stay up past midnight. And Rep saw that he was perfectly right. The guy was going to be able to do just about anything he wanted to, and Rep didn't see how he could stop him for longer than it would take to throw two or three punches. Whatever pathetic little sacrificial gesture Rep chose to make wasn't going to change the outcome. Rep was about to get himself seriously hurt, and it would be an exercise in pure futility.

Still, he stood there.

"Have it your way," the guy said. Raising blade-like hands in a martial-arts posture, he took one menacing, unhurried stride forward.

Rep's cerebellum chose this moment to remind him of one thing he actually did know about fighting. He had heard it years before from Bill Cosby, on the *Tonight Show*. Cosby had opined, based on his experience growing up in the tough streets of Philadelphia, that you should punch not for the nose but the throat, because no one can take a good punch in the throat and not go down.

Rep rocked his right fist back and then snapped it forward with all the strength he could muster. Not just the physical strength in his underused bicep, but something deeper. Rippling through his right arm and down to the four unblemished knuckles on his curled right hand was the rage and fury born from thirty years of bullying and casual, demeaning, thoughtless dismissals of his physique; ashen memories of being not just the last player picked but the player captains fought furiously not to have on their teams. His punch flew with power Rep didn't dream he had. It landed solidly, and when it landed it really hurt.

That is, it really hurt Rep.

Bill Cosby had apparently never fought the thug in biker shorts. As the gentleman closed in, he clamped his jaw firmly on his collar bone, guarding his throat. Rep's punch thus struck not the vulnerable soft tissue around the guy's carotid artery but his brick-solid chin. Rep's knuckles screamed in agony. Even more interesting, a shock-like sting burned the back of his right shoulder. He didn't feel any tingle travel from his fist, up his arm, to his shoulder. He just felt the solid, slamming pain in his right hand and then, instantly, the stinging buzz in his shoulder.

Rep thought this was probably a bad sign.

He was right.

Rep expected to crumple under a volley of blows in the next three seconds. Instead of pressing his assault, however, the guy stepped back and gave Rep a baffled look.

"No kidding, was that your best shot? I mean, no offense, but that's the lamest excuse for a roundhouse right I've ever seen—and I grew up in the 'burbs, man."

Though he had yet to take a single punch, Rep very much wanted to throw up. He had thought the situation was incredibly bad, and it was worse than he had imagined.

Still, he stood where he was.

"Oh, I get it," the guy said, snapping his fingers and grinning in epiphanic delight, then gesturing toward an imaginary light bulb coming on over his head. "It's like this honor thing, right, like in *Pat Garrett and Billy the Kid?* Like Pat Garrett is asking this whore where Billy is, and she knows but she won't tell. So James Coburn, who's playing Pat Garrett, right, anyway, James Coburn slaps her across the face. Nothing really mean, just a little clop across the chops. And so she says, the whore says, 'You'll have to do me one more time before I tell you, I owe Billy that much.' So Coburn slaps her again, and she spills her guts, but it's okay 'cause she held out for two slaps, right?"

Rep didn't say anything. He was afraid that if he opened his mouth he'd start sobbing. The temptation to bow to the inevitable rose like bile in his throat. Not giving in to it was the last thing he could do, so that's what he did. In feckless terror, he stood his ground.

"Just for the record," the guy said as he moved in again, "I'm not Pat Garrett."

It seemed to Rep that, given the overwhelming mismatch, some crafty kind of brains-over-brawn maneuver was called for. For a long, terrible second, nothing occurred to him. Then he remembered the canvas mailbags he'd stumbled over earlier.

Ducking quickly, he grabbed one, ignored the searing pain that lanced through his right shoulder long enough to lift it, and swung it at the thug's head. Unfortunately, he hit the thug's left hip. This did less damage to the thug than it did to the mailbag, as the sudden pressure on its bulging middle burst the bag's mouth and sent envelopes cascading over Rep's shoes.

Pretty much out of ideas now, Rep dropped the bag and started punching as hard and fast as he could. The guy blocked the first couple with his forearms, then didn't even bother, concentrating instead on his own offensive efforts. He put a quick, snapping left into Rep's short rib, followed by a driving right into Rep's gut. As Rep doubled over, the guy slap-punched him over the right ear with the blade of his left hand, then caught Rep's nose and mouth with a shattering right uppercut.

Rep's knees buckled and his head snapped up and back as he felt both dental work and cartilage loosening. He sagged, held up by the door behind him and the close-quarters pummeling he was absorbing in front. He couldn't see anything because his eyes had reflexively shut. As his assailant's club-like fists landed repeatedly on Rep's ears and temples he thought that not seeing anything was probably a pretty good idea. He felt blood oozing both inside his mouth and from his right ear. The pain in his ribs, his stomach, and his head transcended anything he had ever imagined. The most astonishing thing, though, was how tired he suddenly was. He had been fighting (if you could call it that) for, what?—ten seconds? If that. Feeble though they were, however, his martial efforts had already drained every ounce of endurance from him. His shoulders heaved as he panted in his desperate search for breath, and he could scarcely even lift his arms for the third-rate punches that he tried to throw.

Rep dimly noticed a two-second respite in the punishment he was receiving. This was due to the bad guy stepping back and winding up for a *coup de grâce*, which he delivered to the left side of Rep's face. The punch sent him staggering sideways and then plummeting down onto spilled envelopes and mailbags on the floor. He lay there, one of the envelopes pasted to his face by viscous blood that seeped from a laceration above his right eyebrow. He remembered hoping, in the moment of consciousness that remained to him, that Melissa wouldn't have to identify his body.

He was only out for about thirty seconds. He woke up to a dully thudding sound. This turned out, upon a moment's cautious investigation, to be caused by the bad guy slamming the mailbag Rep had used against the window in the door that was now perhaps six feet from Rep. The thug didn't seem to be getting anywhere. Which, Rep thought, would figure. Insulating the screening room against outside sound meant thick glass for the window—thick enough, apparently, to withstand this kind of muscle power.

As Rep gingerly craned his neck for a better look, he noticed the envelope stuck to his forehead and in a spasm of irritation pulled it off. He started to hurl it away, but before he could do so the light coming through the frosted glass in the editing room door picked up the boldface address preprinted on it: ACADEMY OF MOTION PICTURE ARTS AND SCIENCES. In care of an accounting firm.

Rep wasn't up to a physical shrug, but he managed a mental one. *It'd figure. Galaxy Entertainment had subleased the place from Tavistock, according to Eastman. Then Tavistock hadn't used it for a few years because it had outsourced its audiovisual work. There were probably all kinds of movie leftovers lying here and there around the building.*

Rep found this logical exercise unsatisfying, somehow. He couldn't say why, really, aside from the physical agony he was going through, which did tend to take an edge off of mental pleasures. The mailbag's dull, rhythmic slams against frosted glass distracted him from further analysis.

"Know what?" the bad guy said after three or four more thuds. "This is a lot like work, and I'm not getting anywhere. Everyone in that editing room will be staying put, because the other door is locked from the outside with the same key as this one, but the chopper is going to be here in twenty minutes and they'll be wondering what happened to me. So I'm going to try a different approach. You stay where you are, now, or I might get cranky. I'm mad enough about having to restuff this mailbag before we load it."

The guy went away then. Rep thought that was very nice of him, given Rep's lack of enthusiasm for further interaction with the gentleman. With a wary glance through a swollen and blood-encrusted right eye, he saw the guy disappear into the darkness-shrouded far corner of the room—where Rep had thrown the key. Suddenly Rep had another unbidden thought.

What's this stuff about refilling and loading mailbags? Is the guy a neat-freak on top of everything else? For no reason he could have named at the time, the unanswered question asked by both the Coast Guardsman and Eastman came back to him. *What was the connection between Tempus-Caveator staging a hostile takeover of an old-economy dinosaur like Tavistock and the conflict with Eastman that was causing all this trouble?*

Rep opened the envelope he was still gripping. It held a single sheet. A title at the top identified it as a NOMINATING BALLOT ONLY. A subhead instructed the reader to, "Identify by title only NO MORE THAN five films first commercially exhibited in the United States during calendar year 1996 to be considered for nomination for the Academy's BEST PICTURE Award. *This nominating category is open to all members of the Academy.*" Whoever submitted this one understood the concept of the bullet ballot, for he or she had named only one movie: *Red Guard!*

Except that apparently no one had submitted this ballot. It was still sitting here in this obscure Midwestern post-production facility with thousands of other unsubmitted ballots, years after *Red Guard!* had not received a best picture award nomination—or any other major nomination. And this had happened because—

Well, of course, Rep couldn't know for sure why it had happened. But suppose Galaxy Entertainment had accumulated nominating ballots from everyone in any guild who depended on Galaxy's good opinion, ostensibly so that they could be submitted in bulk. *Send them all to us; we'll make sure they get in*, just like ward-heelers sweeping through nursing homes to collect absentee ballots two weeks before an election. The nominations sent to Galaxy would overwhelmingly favor a Galaxy production—like *Red Guard!* A good percentage of the voters who liked that movie, in fact, might send their ballots to Galaxy, in an effort to curry favor.

Then suppose that instead of submitting those nominating ballots Galaxy Entertainment had buried them. Ballot-box stuffing in reverse. What did the politicians call it? Vote suppression. *Red Guard!*'s chances had died in a Chicago post-production facility.

If Rep's teeth hadn't been chipped he would have whistled. Who would have thought that a major Hollywood studio and its corporate master had no more integrity than the average politician? Well, anyone who read either *Variety* or

Joan Didion, okay, but even so. Eastman wasn't only right, he had no idea how right he was. If he replaced fantasy computer hacking with these mailbags full of Oscar nominations in his treatment for *Screenscam*, he'd be pitching a documentary.

That was why these mailbags were here. And why the mailbags had to be refilled and loaded onto something. Not to mention why Tempus-Caveator wanted to acquire Tavistock for the mega-corporation equivalent of pocket change before Eastman generated too much buzz about *Screenscam*. These ballots weren't just a bitter producer's ranting or speculation or pointed questions about changing release dates and other odd behavior. They were documentary evidence, something tangible, red meat on the bones of Eastman's theory. They were the smoking gun that could turn *Screenscam* from a pesky nuisance into the kind of threat they use mushroom clouds to symbolize.

Would Tempus-Caveator actually buy a whole company just to get the suppressed ballots that some idiot had left in one building years before? Couldn't they just send someone in to steal them? That was probably what the tactical geniuses on the Committee to Re-Elect the President had said in 1972 before they sent James McCord and his buddies into the Watergate: *What's the big deal, we'll just burgle the place and take the bugs back out.* Not a happy precedent, considering the ultimate consequences of that little adventure. And anyway, the ballots weren't the only things Tempus-Caveator needed here. There might be e-mails stored in the back-up files of computers, hard copies of memos stuck in file cabinets and in-boxes and mail-room pigeon-holes. Sure, most of it had probably been taken out or tossed out. But Tempus-Caveator couldn't take a chance on a single scrap of paper or a single pixel being left.

A highly publicized congressional investigation had crashed and burned because Tempus-Caveator's obliging shaft of its own studio's movie had silenced a critical source of leaks and hard data. Now there'd be congressional committee chairmen drawing straws to jump on this thing with both feet. *This week's scandal of the century! The missing link in the China connection! Who cares if they stole our missile technology—THEY FIDDLED THE OSCAR COUNT!* Tempus-Caveator couldn't take a chance. Once that corporate behemoth realized that it hadn't completely covered its tracks, it had to go back in and make apodictally certain that it had gotten absolutely everything—and that meant total control, for an unlimited period of time.

The thug was still hunting the key Rep had thrown, but Rep couldn't forget his warning about staying where he was. Still, at least theoretically, the game wasn't over yet. If, without being noticed by the guy, Rep could somehow get out the rear door of the screening room; and then get to the other door of the editing room and break through it; and do all of those things before the guy found the key and opened the door between the screening room and the editing room—then Rep could, in concept, get Buchanan out of the editing room and escape.

This possibility would be more viable if Rep could stand up, but he didn't think he could manage it. He wasn't sure he could even move. And he was quite sure that, if he did somehow move, the bad guy would spot him long before he reached the rear door, and would do some more unpleasant things to him.

Rep did not want this to happen. He wanted it not to happen more than he had ever wanted anything not to happen in his life.

And yet Rep did move. He pulled himself minutely along the floor, toward the back hallway door by which he had first entered the room a couple of thousand years or so ago. As Melissa had said, Rep drew lines—and somewhere between the gut punch and the uppercut he had drawn one. He was useless in a fight. Without mentally articulating it in so many words, however, he felt that as long as he could find inside himself whatever it took to do something, however hopeless and Quixotic, that could somehow redeem the uselessness. Not compensate for it or make it okay. Just keep it from being the thing that defined who he was.

He had actually managed to crawl ten feet or so when the still keyless thug noticed him. With a disgusted expletive, he hustled toward Rep.

Rep had thought he couldn't stand up, but that was before the thug started coming at him again. Finding himself highly motivated, Rep struggled to his feet and commenced a shambling dash for the door to the back hallway. Within four strides he saw that he wasn't going to make it. The thug had an angle to the far corner of the stage, which he used to cut off Rep's line to the door while he closed in on Rep.

Rep already knew how Rep versus Thug would come out, so he thought it best to avoid the intersection that the thug had in mind. Close enough to smell the anchovies on the thug's breath, Rep half vaulted and half fell up to and onto the stage. The thug followed suit. Rep's memory bank apparently included a malicious synapse with a particularly mordant sense of humor, for it now reminded him of a classic cartoon line from his very early youth: "Exit, stage left." Rep retreated from the thug across the breadth of the stage, scampering past the image of an elegantly appointed English country house library from the stock footage loop that the projector was still throwing onto the traveling mat. All too soon, he ran out of room.

Rep spun around and feinted with his head and shoulders toward the screen. That was the shortest route to the hallway door, so the thug checked his own onslaught and darted in the direction of Rep's feint.

Rep essayed a panicky leap back off the stage onto the floor. He staggered, then fell, and sheet lightning bolts of white-hot pain shot through his torso from right shoulder to left hip. He felt as if he didn't have a breath left in him as he tried to rise. Moving as much on his hands as his feet, he stumbled a few yards in front of the stage, back toward the hallway door. He knew that this time it really was over.

He was right. The stock footage now featured an office building interior at night, so the thug was racing past a long row of desks next to black windows as he got a running start and then launched himself into a headlong dive off the stage at Rep. Rep instantly collapsed under the force of the flying tackle that climaxed the dive. The thug pulled Rep to his feet, whipped him around so that the thug was at Rep's back, and elbowed him twice in the kidneys. Rep braced himself for further blows, but they didn't come.

"Would you mind telling me something?" the thug asked instead of hitting him again. Rep correctly took this as a rhetorical question. "Why am I whaling on you after you went to all the trouble to hand me the answer to this little head-scratcher we have on our hands here? You've been trying your level best to get it through my head that I oughta be thinking about that other door like you were, and instead of being grateful I crease you up some more. Boy, there's just no pleasing some people, is there?"

Dispensing with further commentary, the thug spun Rep around to face him, grabbed him under the arms, and with one quick squat and heave unceremoniously slung Rep over his left shoulder. When the guy stood up, Rep found his legs pinned firmly under the chap's left arm while his torso hung over the thug's back. The guy had reached behind him with his right hand to grab Rep's right wrist, in the process holding Rep's left arm against the guy's back.

"See, way I see it," the guy said affably, "the other door to the editing room isn't soundproofed, so it shouldn't be any big trick to bang through it. You bleed on my spandex, by the way, and I might use you as a battering ram."

Without any strain that Rep could detect, the guy carried him out of the screening room and into a rear hallway that now seemed pitch dark. Forty more strides, maybe, and they'd turn the corner. Then some loud noises and other unpleasantness. Then, or sometime not too long after that, Rep and Charlotte Buchanan would die. And, slung over this ectomorph's shoulder like a rag doll, there wasn't a thing in the world Rep could do about it.

At about this time on a TV show they'd be due for a cleverly contrived *deus ex machina*, but Rep didn't see much prospect of one here. Big screen and small screen heroes would have done something elegantly smart ahead of time, set some trap, left a subtle signal for some cop so they could hope for a miracle—a last-second cavalry charge, the opportune arrival of the 82nd Airborne Division, something along those lines. But Rep hadn't done anything like that, and so he couldn't.

He was still wallowing in the sheer self-pity of this reflection when he smelled something. The odor was rich, metallic, a little sweet, like thick oil.

It was cosmolene.

People put cosmolene on guns.

Then Rep heard something that went with the smell. A voice, threatening and no-nonsense, but not growling. On the contrary, almost purring with confidence.

"Stop right there!" the voice said. "FBI! What you're feeling behind your right ear is a nine millimeter pistol, so just chill. Dead guys don't get their convictions reversed on appeal."

The thug didn't chill. He spun sharply to his right while letting go of Rep's arm, thereby slinging Rep's torso like a black-and-blue sandbag against the FBI agent. Rep's head hit some part of the agent. Rep wasn't sure which part, but it was quite hard.

Then Rep hit the floor. He heard about eight seconds' worth of grunts and punches, without any snappy patter from the thug in biker's shorts. Rep surmised that the thug was now somewhat more evenly matched than he had been in his fight against Rep.

Rep rolled a couple of turns away from the fight and started to crawl across the rear hallway. He didn't know where the hall lights were but he figured that turning on lights in a couple of rooms off the corridor couldn't hurt. That looked like about the most constructive contribution he was in a position to make at the moment.

He had almost reached the other side of the hall when he heard a loud, splintering crash from around the corner, followed very soon by labored breathing and floor scraping. He knew instantly what it meant and he crawled as fast as he could, but he wasn't fast enough. Before he could finish his journey across the corridor, something pounded bruisingly against his left hip and then—accompanied by a surprised yelp—against his spine. He concluded that someone running away from the editing room had rounded the corner and tripped over him. As if to remove any doubt, the same thing happened again a second or two later, with a yelp both higher pitched and angrier. Mixler followed by Buchanan, Rep surmised.

He scarcely even winced at the pain. After what he'd been through in the screening room, a couple of kicks in the hip and a knee or two to the spine were nothing. At the same time, he hadn't exactly acquired a taste for this kind of thing, so he scrambled with a bit more energy into one of the work stations on the far side of the corridor and began fumbling for light switches. It only took an eternity or so to get three lights on, bathing the corridor in a feeble, indirect glow.

Rep took some satisfaction in the scene the light disclosed. The thug in biker's shorts was prone with his hands cuffed behind him and the FBI agent's heel in the small of his back. Buchanan was towering over Mixler, who cringed on his fanny, cornered against the corridor wall. As Rep watched, Buchanan petulantly kicked Mixler's right shin.

"Knock it off," the agent ordered sharply.

"He *used* me," Buchanan said indignantly, as if no punishment short of the garrote could be too severe for such an offense.

"I don't care what he did," the agent said. "Once a guy's in custody you don't go kicking him in the shin."

"All right," Buchanan said grudgingly, and kicked Mixler in the testicles. She was winding up for a repeat performance when Rep hastily pulled her away.

"Do I need to call for backup or anything?" Rep asked.

"Already on the way," the agent said, tilting his head toward a microphone clipped to his jacket sleeve.

"Just out of curiosity," Rep asked then, hoping that anodyne conversation might deter Buchanan from further mayhem, "how did you happen to be here so miraculously at the precise moment you were needed, when all seemed lost?"

"I was following you," the agent said. "Or trying to."

"Really? Why?"

"You serious?" the agent snorted. "Residue of an explosive is found on your computer bag at an airport security check the same day a helicopter is blown up on the ground with that explosive one state and one Great Lake to the west. You refuse to cooperate with the investigating officers, who have to let you go. You ostentatiously book a flight for the following morning and check into an airport hotel for the night. Then, before you've been in the hotel room an hour, you sneak out of it, rent a car, and drive off—and it turns out you're driving to the very place where the helicopter blew up. Now what do you suppose someone who's been to detective school would do in a situation like that?"

"I suppose he'd be very suspicious and have me followed. And now that you mention it, I do recall seeing cop cars more than once in my rear-view mirror while I was driving to Oshkosh. But how did you know about my leaving the hotel and everything?"

"You may remember it was the local police who suggested the hotel. They didn't just pick one at random. The people at that hotel know the police and they do what they're told. You were tabbed for a tail from the moment you clammed up at the airport. The desk clerk tipped them when you hustled out. State police kept an eye on you until I could pick you up. I didn't have any trouble until you got on that antique airplane in Oshkosh that filed a flight plan about someplace in California and ended up landing in Illinois. I was a good two hours behind you by the time I pieced together enough radio messages to get to where you'd flown, but the Coast Guard officer who took your statement had a pretty good idea where you'd gone."

"Then you broke in here because you thought I might need help?" Rep asked, deeply grateful.

"No, I thought whoever was already in here might need help. You've been acting like a stone cold professional terrorist for at least thirty-six hours. I got here just in time to hear the tail-end of a nasty fight and then see someone coming out of that big room. In the dark I thought I was sticking my gun in your ear instead of this surfer-punk's. Now let's cut the chat and give me a chance to think. I know I'm going to be arresting people, but I haven't figured out what for yet."

"Gee," Rep said, "maybe I can help. How about conspiracy to interfere with interstate commerce, to-wit, the production of a motion picture and its distribution across state lines for purposes of commercial exhibition, by impairing the safe functioning of an aircraft, in violation of section twelve-thirty-eight of title eighteen of the United States Code?"

"Might do for a start," the agent said. "At least for the guys on the floor. But what am I going to arrest you for?"

"Arrest *Rep*?" Buchanan squeaked indignantly, stamping her foot. "He saved my life!"

"Yeah," the agent sighed, "but that's probably just a misdemeanor."

Chapter 18

As he rose euphorically from mellow dreams toward consciousness through a gauzy cocoon of pure feeling, Rep was pretty sure he wasn't in jail. He couldn't remember the dreams he'd just had, but they'd been a lot more fun than the jail dream. Odors finally tipped him off, just before he opened his eyes: a cloying fragrance of abundant cut flowers, and the sweet, distinctive smell of rubbing alcohol.

Hospital, he remembered. *That's right, I'm in the hospital.*

It was late Tuesday morning. He had been in the hospital since sometime on Sunday, first in Chicago and then—after the United States government decided that at the moment it couldn't think of anything to charge him with after all—in Indianapolis.

He vaguely remembered now, in fact, that he was supposed to leave the hospital today. The doctors had cleaned his wounds, doused them with antiseptic, stitched his lacerations, and bandaged him abundantly. They had rigged something to his right shoulder that was supposed to help the muscle reattach itself completely to the bone. They had swabbed out his mouth and mentioned that he might want to see a dentist soon. They had x-rayed him and scanned him and taped his ribs. They had checked his blood and his urine, verifying that the former was red and the latter wasn't. They had dosed him with painkillers. And they had explained that they couldn't come up with anything else to do even if the insurance company would have paid for it, which it wouldn't. When Melissa protested that someone as traumatized as Rep obviously had been should at least be kept under observation for a few more days, the chief of clinical staff had explained that a dozen beatings as bad as the one Rep had endured were meted out every weekend in Indianapolis bars, with the typical victim being shoved out of the emergency room after twenty minutes with an intern.

Not in custody, Rep thought. *That's nice. Leaving the hospital. That's nice too. I should really be feeling wonderful. Why does that nagging little ball of angst keep muscling its way through my brain?*

Oh, that's right. Because saving Aaron Eastman's life and then extracting himself and Buchanan from the clutches of the surfer-punk and the biker-thug hadn't exactly solved all of Rep's problems. There was still the little matter of a United States Attorney in Michigan who was very upset with him. And the fact that Charlotte Buchanan might never have been in danger in the first place if Rep hadn't messed up her case from roughly the second day he'd had it, which meant that Rep was now going to have to tell Steve Finneman a lot of things that he should have told him a long time ago. All of which would be bad enough in itself, but was even worse because Finneman would wonder whether one of the firm's biggest clients would be in danger of a hostile takeover at this moment if Rep had spoken up when he should have. Plus something hardly worth mentioning after all of those issues, but certainly not trivial from Rep's standpoint: Arundel had by now undoubtedly dug up all sorts of details about Rep's naughty little habit and his use of his firm computer to pursue it.

"Hi, honey," Melissa said shyly. "Are you awake?"

"Just now." He glanced over and warmed at the sight of her, even though her bravely pained expression told him that his battered face must still look hideous, bandages or not. "How long have you been waiting?"

"Not that long. They want to release you in about an hour, so I brought you some real breakfast."

She tendered a white paper bag and a jumbo take-out cup of rich coffee. The bag turned out to hold a cherry Danish dripping with white frosting, and a still warm scrambled-eggs-and-bacon sandwich between two pieces of toast.

"Bless you," he said fervently. "I knew I was the smartest guy in my class, and I proved it by marrying you."

"How are you feeling?"

"Not bad considering. I can probably run into the office today as soon as I get a shower and slip into a suit."

"No," Melissa said firmly. "Absolutely not. You're going to spend at least one more day in bed. I already told that to Steve Finneman."

"Steve called?" Rep demanded, antennae quivering.

"Yesterday afternoon. He was sort of hemming and hawing about how he hated to ask but could you possibly come in by three o'clock or so this afternoon."

A chilly little rush of anticipation raced through Rep's gut. He smiled with a touch of irony at Melissa. It looked like he'd have all the time in the world for bed rest before long. He took a stab at achieving a philosophical view of things: It might prove interesting to be released from the hospital and fired from his job on the same day.

"That's okay," he said. "Please dig my phone up so I can call Steve and let him know I'll be able to make it."

"You are so stubborn," Melissa said, her exasperation feigned only in part.

"Guilty as charged," Rep said, as the painkillers started to wear off.

❀ ❀ ❀

Rep had expected to ride home in Melissa's Taurus. The vehicle waiting for them in the bright sunlight outside

Hoffman-Glenn Memorial Hospital, however, was a wedding gown white stretch limousine. Aaron Eastman and Charlotte Buchanan, who had ended up splitting the rental charge, were waiting with it. They wanted to share the limo ride so they could tell Rep how grateful they were to him, and Rep didn't see how he could decently refuse. It occurred to him, in fact, to ask Eastman whether Point West Productions might be in the market for an in-house copyright lawyer, but then he remembered that he was still technically representing Buchanan in her claim against that company. Buchanan lasted almost a mile before she turned the conversation to herself.

"You were absolutely the only bright spot in this whole nightmare for me," she said to Rep. "It turned out I was conned and used the whole way. Even on *And Done to Others' Harm*. The only reason Julia Deltrediche took it in the first place was that Mixler promised her a movie deal with Tempus-Caveator for a book by one of her other authors."

"You don't say," Rep said. "I hate when people do things like that."

"They were thinking that far ahead?" Melissa asked politely.

"They didn't have to," Eastman said. "Mixler was trying to set me up for a plagiarism claim on his own, just because he hates my guts. Then when he heard rumors about the exposé I was thinking about and saw how his plot might fit in with Tempus-Caveator's situation, he took it to them and they bit."

"It was just like one more insurance policy for them, in case they ran into trouble over paying off politicians by burying *Red Guard!*," Buchanan said bitterly. "People dad's working with at Rep's firm say they may have had a dozen little contingency set-ups like that, ready to use if it turned out they needed them. From day-one they treated me like a pawn."

"'Unsavoury similes,...trouble me no more with vanity,' to quote Falstaff," Eastman muttered

"*Henry the Fifth*, right?" Rep asked. Melissa shook her head.

"*The Fourth*. Glorious mystery. Not his greatest play, but a glorious mystery."

"Oh, I *know* I sound self-absorbed and egocentric and everything," Buchanan said, sounding as if she were choking back tears with truly Spartan courage. "I mean, I know nobody actually beat *me* up or anything. But just because you're rich doesn't mean you can't be hurt. It just means you can't get any sympathy for it. Having doors slammed in your face hurts even if you fly first class when you go back home. Being used hurts even if you drown your sorrows with Pinch instead of bar scotch. Being lied to hurts. I don't expect anyone to feel sorry for me. No one ever has. But that doesn't mean I don't feel it."

She faced the other three people in the passenger compartment through several seconds of rather loud and astonished silence. It was Eastman who spoke next.

"You really believe that—that stuff you just said, don't you?" Although the words screamed sarcasm, his tone seemed genuinely intrigued.

"You bet I believe it," she said fiercely. "I have *lived* it—and I know I'll never be through living it."

"This is colossal," Eastman said suddenly, his voice rising with excitement. "I live and work in what is probably the twenty-five richest square miles on earth outside Saudi Arabia, and there's a liter of self-loathing there for every ounce of Starbucks coffee. You are the first person I've heard in my life express that kind of passion in defense of rich people. 'Do we wealthy not have eyes? If you prick us, do we not bleed?' That was *real*. That was *genuine*. You put that kind of passion on paper and by God I could make a movie out of it."

Buchanan's face lit up radiantly with hope.

"You mean you might do a film of *And Done to Others'*
Harm after all?"

"No, dear, I do *not* mean I might do a film version of
that story. In the first place, it's crap between covers. And I
mean that in the nicest possible way. In the second place,
your theory is that I've already made a movie out of it."

"Well, yes," Buchanan admitted. "Technically that's true."

"But I've had a RRIP/CHIP property at the back of
credenza for three years" Eastman said, pronouncing the
acronym as a two-syllable word and rolling the RR, "that I
could get financing for in fifteen minutes if I could lay my
hands on a script that didn't make me want to puke by page
three."

Buchanan looked quizzically at Rep.

"'RRIP' stands for 'randy rich people,'" he explained.
"'CHIP' means 'chick in peril.'"

"Right, of course," Eastman said impatiently. "Like if
Harold Robbins collaborated with Danielle Steel on an *Evita*-
ripoff without the songs and all the political stuff."

"And you think I could do the screenplay?"

"No, of course you couldn't do the screenplay. A screenplay isn't just good writing. It's a technical piece of work, a
product of craft. You have to know something about making movies to produce one. What you could write is the
novelization."

"But isn't the novelization based on the script, which is
what you say you don't have?"

"Sure, but thinking outside the box is my specialty. That's
why they call me Aaron Eastman. You write the novelization, then I hire some hack for Guild minimum to produce
a script based on the novelization, instead of the other way
around. This is a Go with a capital G. Have your shyster
here draw up the papers. Fifty thousand, half-and-half, one
percent of the net plus a most-favored-nations clause. I know
it's peanuts, but the mfn means no writer on the project
gets a better deal than you. Only don't have anybody smoke.

We can't do product placement deals since the tobacco settlement, and I'm not going to give actors lung cancer for free. I can't *believe* I thought of this! This is the greatest idea I've had in two days! God, it is so *wonderful* being me."

Buchanan almost hugged Rep. She checked herself at the last moment, deterred both by the sling on his shoulder and a little warning flicker in Melissa's eyes. She settled instead for a verbal embrace.

"You are the greatest lawyer on earth," she gushed.

"Thanks," Rep said. "I may be calling you soon for a recommendation."

⌗ ⌗ ⌗

"I'm really sorry to ask you to come in like this on your first day out of the hospital, Rep," Finneman said in his office at 2:30 sharp that afternoon. "But this Tavistock takeover attempt has raised the stakes on everything in the office."

"I understand," Rep said. He glanced sideways at Arundel, who occupied the other guest chair in Finneman's office. Rep supposed he was there to make sure Finneman didn't get too generous on the severance package.

"Tempus-Caveator is feeling some real heat now that Selding and Mixler are being seriously interrogated," Finneman continued. "They must have covered their tracks, but they don't want us sniffing up their trail along with the feds. They want to drop the takeover bid, and their lawyers are coming in at three to negotiate exit terms."

"Isn't that good for us?" Rep asked.

"Indeed," Finneman said.

"Problem is, though, we're not sure we can afford such good fortune," Arundel said. "They'll want us to buy back their block of stock at a healthy premium over the market price, and we're a little bit strapped for that kind of cash at the moment."

"Can't we say no?" Rep asked.

"Then they'll still hold the stock and be a continuing takeover threat," Finneman explained. "Or else they'll drop the stock on the market all at once, depress the price catastrophically, and drive our loyal shareholders to open revolt."

"That's extortion," Rep said indignantly.

"Yes," Arundel said. "Or M and A, as we sometimes call it."

"Anyway," Finneman said, "it's going to be a tough negotiation. We'd like you to sit in on it."

Arundel couldn't resist a minute head shake, and Rep for once had to agree with him. He realized that the questions he'd just asked had suggested a truly stunning naivete. Arundel's secretary probably had more business sitting in on the upcoming negotiation than Rep did.

"I'm at your disposal, naturally," he said. "But I'm not sure I really have anything to contribute."

"Well," Finneman said after an uncharacteristically nervous throat clearing, "Mr. Buchanan thinks you have a great deal to contribute. And as we say in the law business, the client is always right, except when he questions the bill."

On that incontestable note they rose to head for the conference room where they'd do battle with the powerful lawyers representing one of the most powerful corporations in the world. During the stroll, Arundel hung back a bit, and tugged at Rep's sleeve to beckon him back as well. Rep took the hint.

"Just a suggestion," Arundel whispered, "but after you show the flag for Buchanan's benefit you might want to take advantage of the first break to beg off and go home because of your injuries."

"And not worry my pretty little head about the negotiations?" Rep asked.

"Something like that. You see, I didn't want to bring this up, but I've felt it was my duty as an upper-tier partner with the firm to look into some rather disturbing rumors revolving around your misuse of the firm's internet connection for improper personal purposes."

"Did that liven things up for you a bit?" Rep asked.

"This is serious," Arundel hissed, reaching inside his coat and extracting three sheets of paper, folded lengthwise. "We're talking about a very important element of firm policy. I've seen a tape. And this is a list of the pornographic web sites you've visited from your office computer."

"You can keep that, if it excites you," Rep said.

"I haven't mentioned this to Steve yet," Arundel said. "I hope I won't have to. I hope you'll bow out at the first decent opportunity."

Rep experienced a moment of utter astonishment, as he recalled times his belly had flipped at one of Arundel's sneers or raised eyebrows. Arundel apparently didn't know—apparently had no clue whatever—that he simply wasn't in the same league as the average biker-thug. On top of that, Arundel's threat implicated a principle that Rep regarded as sacrosanct: You should never pass up a chance to quote a famous riposte.

"Publish and be damned," he said, in a tone that the Duke of Wellington himself would have approved.

After ninety-eight minutes in the firm's largest conference room, Rep still didn't think he had much to contribute to the negotiations, which as far as he could see had gotten roughly nowhere. Tempus-Caveator had sent seven lawyers from Amble, Speak & Nesty, its New York firm. Three of these lawyers were partners, who sat at the conference table. Four of them were associates, who sat behind the partners. Every now and then, one of the partners would refer to some piece of information and reach his right hand over his shoulder without turning his head, whereupon one of the associates would instantly put a document verifying the information in the partner's hand.

None of them acted like emissaries of the side that had, after all, lost and was suing for peace. On the contrary, all seven of the lawyers made it clear that they viewed the matter of extracting fourteen million dollars over market price from a company for its own stock as a trivial detail scarcely worthy of their time and effort, and that they were impatient to get it over with so they could return to civilization.

Rep, on the other hand, had spent the entire negotiation sitting sphinx-like next to Finneman. Stitched, bandaged, bruised, and arm-slung, with his mouth pulled into a snarling rictus by pain and broken teeth, he looked like he belonged not at a corporate law firm conference table but in a public defender's office—and on the wrong side of the desk.

He wished at the moment that he could pop a prescription painkiller. He didn't, though, because he was determined to avoid anything that could possibly impair the slim prospects of a deal. He dared to nourish a tiny, flickering hope that if Tavistock could somehow manage a settlement that left it with two quarters to rub together, Arundel might be so giddy that he'd forget about telling Finneman that Rep was what Finneman would undoubtedly regard as a pervert. If that happened, he might have a job for six more months.

The partner directly across the table from Rep was saying something about cutting to the chase when Rep heard a commotion outside the conference room door. Punctuating the commotion was a female voice saying desperately, "You can't go in there!" Suddenly, much too late, he remembered the final warning he'd gotten from the Assistant United States Attorney in Michigan. Just when Rep had begun to think that he might be able to salvage a shred or two of his dignity after all, that particular chicken was coming home to roost, bringing with it the risk of turning Tavistock's negotiating position into a shambles.

Rep jumped up to try to preempt the entrance, but he wasn't nearly fast enough. As everyone else—including Tyler Buchanan and Tavistock's other representatives—looked up in surprise, the doors burst open and two burly men strode in. They were wearing blazers, but you could tell they didn't really mean it. Lucite-encased gold shields hung prominently over the breast pockets of the blazers. They walked straight to Rep, and the one in front thrust a piece of paper into Rep's hand. The paper had CRIMINAL DIVISION stamped on it in prominent, 24-point boldface.

"This Friday," he said. "Nine on the dot. Grand jury room, federal courthouse, Grand Rapids, Michigan. Don't bother asking for an adjournment. And if you think you might be late, bring your toothbrush."

They turned around and walked out, serenely ignoring the hubbub their entrance had created. Pocketing his subpoena, Rep turned to Finneman stammering the beginnings of what he hoped would come out eventually as a coherent apology. The faces of Buchanan and the Tavistock minions with him were eloquent with consternation. Across the table, Tempus-Caveator and its partner-lawyers were hurriedly conferring, presumably about how much they were going to jack up the premium they'd been demanding. Finneman's voice immediately drowned out everything else in the room as it rolled in an unruffled rumble across the table.

"Please forgive that little intrusion," he roared. "Would you gents like a caucus?"

One of the partners on the other side nodded, and Finneman shooed everyone on Tavistock's side of the table out into the hallway.

"I'm really sorry about that, Steve," Rep murmured after they were outside.

"Oh, I wouldn't worry about it too much," Finneman said. "I think a little break might do us all good. I suspect they'll be a bit more reasonable when we go back in."

"While we're waiting," Arundel muttered, "we might take a few minutes to wander down to my office. There's something I think you might want to look at before we decide who walks back into the conference room after their caucus."

Well now, that was subtle, Rep thought, as his gut rose to his throat for the eighth or ninth time since he'd awakened that morning. If having a grand jury subpoena served in front of his senior partner and a major client hadn't sunk him, the trinkets Arundel had in his office surely would. It served him right. You swim with the sharks, you risk being lunch.

"You know what, Chip?" Finneman said. "I don't think this caucus is going to go much more than three minutes."

He was right. Buchanan and a couple of others barely had time to make it back from the men's room before the conference room door opened and the Tavistock delegation was summoned back in. The lead lawyer for Tempus-Caveator looked tough, and confident, and determined— just the way the thug in biker shorts had looked, now that Rep thought about it, the moment before Rep had put his head in the guy's solar plexus.

"That little performance was entirely unnecessary and I might even say bush league," he said. "We know whom we're dealing with. We never said we wanted any trouble. That's why we're here. Understand, though, we won't be bullied. If we're going to get something done, let's get it done. We're prepared to cut our premium to one percent—but we have to get the deal done tonight."

"Let me assure you that we view that as a responsible and constructive step in these negotiations," Finneman said complacently. "But I think this talk of premiums is not helpful or, I might say, not relevant any longer. Here's what I think we can do. We'll drop our lawsuit and along with it our request that the court authorize immediate depositions. You'll give Tavistock a five-year option at the lower of today's price or future market price on all the Tavistock securities you hold today."

"But we could get creamed if the price of the stock goes down in the future," one of the partner-lawyers protested.

"That would be a good reason for you to help the price of the stock stay up. You will also agree to sell all of your Tavistock holdings that we don't buy on the market, over five years, with no more than five thousand shares sold on any one day. And you'll pay the bill Tavistock's going to get from us. Tell you what, though. If we get the papers signed before dark, we'll cap the fees at six hundred twenty-five thousand dollars."

The lawyer across the table from Finneman looked a little green around the gills.

"We're going to have to discuss those terms very thoroughly," he said, in what even Rep could recognize as a stall.

"No you're not," Finneman said. "Nothing to discuss. Last, best, and final offer. Take it or leave it."

The excitement that Rep felt during the eight seconds of silence that passed then was downright sexual. There was no other word for it. This M and A stuff might be fun after all.

"All right," the partner-lawyer across from Finneman said. "Let's write it up. We have a plane to catch."

The write-up took almost two hours. Then the lawyers and the corporate predators from New York went away. Buchanan extracted promises from everyone still present, secretaries included, to meet in a private room at the Commerce Club at 8:00 p.m. for a celebratory dinner that he was now heading off to arrange personally.

"Gosh," Rep said to Finneman at that point. "How did that happen?"

"Oh, I'm just guessing," Finneman said. "But the way I see it, a company like Tempus-Caveator may think it's tough as nails and may play fast and loose with the campaign finance laws, and may even be able to line up a couple of stunt men with big muscles and long records to help a schmoo like Mixler with some rough stuff. But it doesn't have anyone on staff who can go around giving people the wherewithal to blow up helicopters and arrange oxygen tank switches. They'd have to go to, oh, an outside consultant for that. And that consultant, and its family, might be very upset if they thought someone associated with Tempus-Caveator had gotten it crosswise of the kind of people who get hauled in front of federal grand juries, because those people tend to be associates."

"You mean they thought I was, what, Sonny Corleone's wimpy younger brother or something and they were about to get in the middle of a family feud?"

"Or something, I'd say. I mean, *look* at you. And look at the way those U.S. marshals dealt with you. It's not the kind of treatment you'd expect for an upstanding taxpayer and model citizen, is it?"

"I guess not."

"Speaking of which," Arundel said with a sigh suggestive of vast patience nearly exhausted, "and before this celebratory dinner, I really do have to insist that we check out something in my office. This is serious. There's a lot at stake here."

"Well, Chip," Finneman said, "if it's that important to you, by all means let's go see what's on your mind."

Rep figured that anything he said could only make things worse, so he followed along in silence. They trooped up stairs, down halls, and around corners through the now largely empty law firm to Arundel's corner office, where this insanity had all begun. Arundel walked in first, left the lights off, and snapped on the VCR/television still sitting on the metal cart in front of his desk. Rep hung back to close the door. *Very* firmly. The oddly cheerful music that Rep recognized from *The Discipline Effectiveness Program* came on.

Rep studied the carpet while Finneman gazed with apparently unruffled dispassion at the screen. After about five minutes, highlighted by a hairbrush vigorously smacking a well-filled pair of jockey shorts, Finneman turned toward Arundel.

"Does it pretty much go on like this?" he asked.

"It gets worse, if you can believe it."

"Well, Chip, this is a side of you I frankly wouldn't have suspected."

"It's not *my* tape," Arundel bleated. "It belongs to Pennyworth."

"Then why is it in your office?"

"Because someone had to investigate this!" Arundel insisted, whipping out the list of web sites and tendering them to Finneman. "There's also these. This is not some trivial thing we can just sweep under the rug. Using firm resources to access pornography creates enormous potential liability for the firm."

"Well, I'm a little older than you are and I don't know about calling it pornography," Finneman said placidly as he scanned the list. "Seems to me it's a little like smoking. It might not be fashionable and you don't hear people bragging about it—but I don't see how it can be pornography if you could do it on network television in the nineteen fifties."

Finneman turned off the television. Rep and Arundel looked for a moment at each other, equally astonished at the old man's reaction. Then Arundel pivoted abruptly and stalked toward the door. Rep had just managed to set himself in motion when Arundel opened the door. He was, accordingly, quite surprised by the next words he heard:

"On your knees!"

Rep recognized Mary Jane Masterson's unmistakable contralto. Rep moved toward the door in hopes of finding out why she would be directing this unusual command at Arundel.

Masterson stood six feet from the door. She sported thigh-high, black leather, stiletto-heeled boots. She was wearing a black leather teddy. She was holding a leather-handled scourge with six long, black, leather tails.

"On your knees!" she repeated. "Now! Drop your trousers and present your worthless bottom for the lash!"

She started to say something else, but she stopped abruptly when she saw Rep and Finneman peering around Arundel's shoulders.

"You sure that tape was Rep's?" Finneman asked jovially.

"I-I-I-I-" Arundel said.

"Golly," Rep said.

"Am I fired?" Masterson said.

"If it were just this," Finneman said, "you most certainly would be fired. We can't have associates flogging partners, at least without management committee approval. But if you're through playing with that whip for the moment, there's something far more serious I've been meaning to discuss with you: theft of food from the employee lounges."

"How did you know about *that*?" Masterson squealed, snapping the whip ferociously in frustration against the carpet.

"After Rep told me about his little adventures," Finneman said, "I figured out everything except what had happened to the delicatessen death-threat that Mixler had sent to him, hoping he'd figure it came from our client. Then I remembered some complaints the secretaries had mentioned about food disappearing, often when you'd just been in the lounge, and I put two and two together. It's still four, even in the digital age."

"You mean that awful thing was a death threat?" she demanded. "It tasted terrible, even after I microwaved it."

"We are a profession that depends on honor," Finneman said, "so theft is beyond the pale. It calls for a sanction far more draconian than dismissal. You're being transferred to the firm's labor department. You'll be defending employment discrimination claims."

"You mean I'm *not* fired?" Masterson asked in astonishment.

"I can almost hear you now in your first negotiation," Finneman said, looking dreamily at the ceiling. "'How do I know your client's claim is a fraud? Because every employment discrimination claim is a fraud.'"

"I-I-I-I-I-" Arundel said.

"Don't thank me," Rep said. "The expression on your face is enough."

Chapter 19

Before sitting down on the quaint metal chair, Rep took an elegant little foam pillow from his flight bag and positioned it carefully on the seat. Melissa, who had already started sipping from the mocha latte he had fetched for her, lowered the cup and examined him with a mixture of sympathy and anxiety.

"Did I, er, do it all right, honey?" she whispered. "I mean, after Jennifer showed me how and everything?"

"You did it perfectly," Rep said. "After all, the proof is in the pudding, and I certainly didn't hear any complaints after the, ah, private time we had together."

"No, the private time was quite wonderful," Melissa said with dreamy contentment. "I won't pretend to understand it, but I guess that's like not understanding why one joke is funny and another one isn't."

"Right," Rep said.

"I mean, you don't really have to understand to laugh. In fact, it's generally better if you don't understand."

"I don't think even Professor Krieg would disagree with that."

"Don't disparage Louise, however slyly," Melissa said, wagging her finger. "She has officially accepted *The Irreducible Heterosexuality of Lord Peter Wimsey: An Objectivist Challenge to Sexual Orientation as an Inevitably Arbitrary Construct* as my dissertation topic."

"Isn't that terribly subversive?"

"Terribly."

"I mean, won't they march you out into the courtyard at the next PMLA convention so that Stanley Fish can rip off your epaulets and cut the buttons from your tunic and break your sword in two?"

"Oh, absolutely," Melissa said. "That's what appeals to Louise about it. It's so reactionary that it's the ultimate rebellion. Advising me on that dissertation will keep her on the cutting edge."

They were having this conversation a little over three weeks after the climactic confrontation between Tavistock and Tempus-Caveator. Rep's bandages were gone. He and Melissa were sitting—gingerly, in his case—at one of the abundant Starbucks dotting Orange County International—the L.A.-area airport with a larger than life-sized statue of John Wayne outside. They had just spent the weekend at Jennifer Payne's semi-annual Ensure Domestic Tranquility Conference, which billed itself as featuring Hands-On Marital Counseling and Spousal Attitude Adjustment. In less than an hour, if all went well—and for the last three weeks all had been going rather well—they'd be in the air, on their way home.

Their banter having run its course, Rep stared contemplatively into his own coffee cup. Then he looked back up at Melissa and gazed steadily at eyes he never tired of seeing.

"I had the strangest feeling about something back there at the, ah, at the conference," he said in a quiet voice. "And now that I've thought about it, I'm absolutely sure it was right. That was mom, wasn't it? Jennifer Payne is my mother."

"I'm certain of it," Melissa said. "I actually mistook her for you for an instant when I just got a glimpse of her face the first time I saw her. And it explains why she went to such incredible trouble to help you, once you'd revealed your name on the net, and why she was such a guardian angel for me at the scene party."

"She didn't say anything or give any sign," Rep said.

"No. She'll never be able to admit it openly, even to you. Even in private. She'll keep quiet to protect you as much as herself. But I think one of the reasons you're so sure is that she wanted you to be sure."

"I think you're right."

"And because she's a star in the scene, we have a perfect excuse to come out here regularly if we want to."

"That's true," Rep said.

Melissa then giggled mischievously as she reached with flirtatious coyness into her purse and extracted a brown envelope.

"I brought a souvenir for you," she said.

She slipped the envelope across the table to him. Finishing his coffee in a gulp, he set the cup out of the way and chanced a sly look at the envelope's contents. It was a computer-printed brochure. Its title read:

JENNIFER PAYNE ATTITUDE ADJUSTMENT CENTER
TOP 10 CHAT ROOMS
TOP 100 SPECIAL INTEREST WEB SITES

"This is extremely thoughtful," Rep said. "And 'souvenir' is exactly the right term for it. Thank you."

"What do you mean?" Melissa asked. "I actually thought of it as one of those useful, practical gifts."

"Coals to Newcastle," Rep said, shaking his head. "I have the most confident conviction that from now on I'm not going to require any stimulus except from the mischievous minx across the table from me."

"What a sweet thing to say," Melissa said. "I'll bet Harriet Vane never heard anything that romantic from Lord Peter."

"I think you can count on it," Rep said. "By the way, I have something for you."

He drew a small, gift-wrapped package from his inside coat pocket and handed it to her. The wrapping had been done a bit clumsily, according to a form-follows-function approach, the way a man would do it by himself. She opened it eagerly, fumbling with the ribbon a bit in her hurry.

"Oh, darling," she said when she had the box open. "A roach clip! How thoughtful. You shouldn't have."

"Well, I just wanted to let you know that, you know, I trust you to know what's right for you, and—you know."

"Yes," Melissa said, "I do know. I do truly appreciate this. And it will be kind of a souvenir too."

"Not practical and useful?" Rep asked, unable to conceal the relief in his voice.

"Well," Melissa said, "it's a bit hard to explain. When Louise and I had our little chat about how her theory that Lord Peter was gay was full of it, there was a lot of free associating going on in my head. One of the topics that sort of popped up was kids, which we're going to have someday. And that got me to thinking about what I'd do to someone who sold marijuana to our oldest when he or she got to be, say, thirteen. While I was sitting there in the hospital looking at you, banged up the way you were because you drew a line and wouldn't cross it, I realized what the answer was."

"Dare I ask?" Rep demanded.

"Only if you want to hear that I'd cut his testicles off," Melissa said, putting her own cup aside and briskly standing up.

Rep stood up, stuffed the pillow carefully back in his flight bag, and fell into step beside Melissa.

"Who would have thought?" he asked. "Life is endlessly surprising."

"Can't argue with that," Melissa said. "Who would have thought an old dinosaur like Steve Finneman would have such a liberal attitude toward alternative sexual practices?"

"Well, actually," Rep said, "what he has is a very traditional attitude toward money."

"What do you mean?"

"Charlotte Buchanan's father had told him that he wanted me to become the billing partner for Tavistock. That meant he had to work things out so that, whatever I did short of outright felony, I'd stay with the firm."

"What a nice surprise," Melissa said with the mildly polite interest of someone for whom money had become a secondary concern.

"This really is a charmingly ironic situation all around when you think about it, isn't it?" he commented.

"Truly," Melissa agreed. "There's nothing left to do, really, except stop to buy me a candy bar."

"Ah," Rep said, "the proverbial munchies. Fair enough. What would you like?"

"Well, naturally," Melissa said, "an Oh Henry."